L ord Herring pulled a key from his vest pocket. "Sir Mason was a member of this club for a very long time. He had the Green Room for his exclusive use. He said it was a tidy space away from his office—handy for his private papers and such. The staff tell me no one except Mason has been in here for five years. He even employed his own cleaner."

Herring placed the key in the lock and turned. A heavy deadbolt slid aside. The door swung in and seven heads peered into the dark room.

"Hold on," Herring said. "There should be a switch." He fumbled a hand around the wall. A bulb flickered on. Seven sets of eyes adjusted to the light.

After a moment of shocked silence, it was Ruby who spoke.

"Oh my," was all she could say.

Hi Charlie

The Archer Legacy ◆ Book Two

EMERALD CASKET

RICHARD NEWSOME

ILLUSTRATED BY
JONNY DUDDLE

WALDEN POND PRESS
An Imprint of HarperCollinsPublishers

Walden Pond Press is an imprint of HarperCollins Publishers.
Walden Pond Press and the skipping stone logo are trademarks and
registered trademarks of Walden Media, LLC.

The Emerald Casket

Library of Congress Cataloging-in-Publication Data
Newsome, Richard.
    The emerald casket / Richard Newsome ; illustrated by Jonny
Duddle. — 1st U.S. ed.
        p.   cm. — (The Archer legacy ; bk. 2)
    ISBN 978-0-06-194493-2
    [1. Mystery and detective stories. 2. Supernatural—Fiction.
3. Adventure and adventurers—Fiction. 4. Precious stones—
Fiction. 5. India—Fiction.] I. Duddle, Jonny, ill. II. Title.
PZ7.N486644Eme 2011   2010030772
[Fic]—dc22   CIP
                                                                 AC

Typography by Amy Ryan
12 13 14 15 16   CG/BR   10 9 8 7 6 5 4 3 2 1
❖
Originally published in Australia in 2010 by The Text Publishing
Company
First U.S. paperback edition, 2012

For Sandy Davey and the mighty kids of year 6/7D at Graceville State School—with much thanks

THE EMERA

GERALD'S JOURNEY AND VA

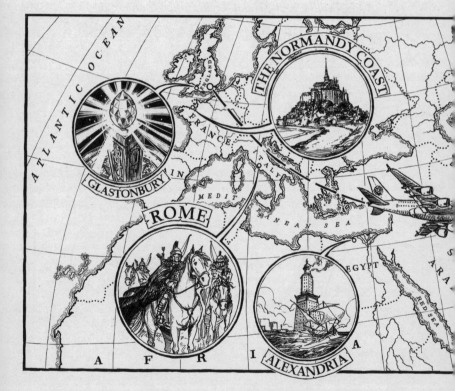

LD GASKET ❧

RIOUS POINTS OF INTEREST

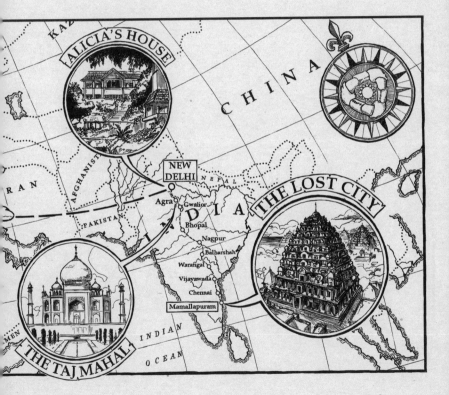

PROLOGUE

A meaty hand slapped down on top of the alarm clock. Of all the sounds that Constable Lethbridge of the London Metropolitan Police might want to hear on a Sunday, a buzzer at six o'clock in the morning was not high on the list.

He rolled onto his back. One hand patted his belly. The other set off in search of the itch on his left buttock.

Still, he wasn't too grumpy at the early start. After the last few weeks, any day out of uniform was bound to be a good one.

Lethbridge dressed and shambled down the stairs, whistling tunelessly, and yanked out the copy of the *Mail on Sunday* from the slot in the front door. He padded into the kitchen and a half dozen cockroaches scuttled under the fridge. The sink was stacked high with dishes.

He switched on the kettle, grabbed a packet of corn-flakes from the cupboard, and poured himself a bowl. The light inside the fridge cast a pitiful glow over its contents: a bottle of pickled onions, a packet of cheese slices, and an open tin of baked beans unfinished from dinner the night before. He lifted out a bottle of milk and nudged the door shut with his bottom.

Lethbridge settled in a chair and unfolded the paper. The front-page headline read: BOY BILLIONAIRE SOLVES GEM HEIST. He grunted and poured milk over his cereal. As he lifted a spoonful to his mouth there was a knock at the front door. The spoon splashed back into the bowl. Lethbridge tramped to the front room and opened the door.

There was nobody there. He looked left and right along the street of terraced houses. No one.

"Bleedin' school holidays," he grumbled.

He shut the door and trudged back to his breakfast.

He sat down, turned the page of his newspaper, and shoveled a spoonful of cereal into his mouth. Just as he was about to scoop up another he gagged and spat out the corn-flakes with a retch.

"Ewww!" He inspected the use-by date on the milk and screwed up his face. The bowl was added to the pile in the sink and he poured the rancid milk down the drain. He dangled an Archer-brand teabag into a mug, filled it from the kettle (not forgetting to add a generous spoonful of honey), then wandered out the back door into the garden.

Striking up his tuneless whistle he ambled down the path and opened the door to the back shed. He poked his head around the doorframe and trilled, "Is there anybody ho-ome?"

A chorus of coos answered back.

A smile broke out on Lethbridge's face. He closed the door behind him and placed his mug on a table in the middle of the room. He kicked an old milk crate across the floor, climbed up to a small loft, and retrieved two pigeons—one black and one gray.

"Who's a beautiful boy then?" Lethbridge clucked as he climbed down. "Has 'oo had a good trip?"

With a nudge of his elbow he knocked away a prop holding open the roof to the pigeon coop and it banged shut. He let the black bird fly up to perch on a rafter. The other he cradled on his lap as he flopped down onto the milk crate.

"Has 'oo brought me a little present?"

A tube was attached to the bird's leg, and from it Lethbridge removed a tiny roll of paper. The pigeon fluttered to the ceiling to join his mate. Lethbridge unrolled the message and snorted with derision. He lifted a cloth from the table to reveal a chess set, moved the white queen four spaces, and studied the outcome.

"What are you up to?"

Engrossed in his game of correspondence chess, he failed to notice the gray pigeon deliver its second message of the day when a large dollop dropped from the rafters and slopped into his tea.

Running a hand over his chin Lethbridge stretched out to pick up the mug. He stared at the swirling mixture for a second, shrugged, and took a sip. Then he smacked his lips, took a large gulp and let out a satisfied *aaah*.

He pulled a chewed pencil stub from his pocket and was about to write his next move on the back of the piece of paper when the two pigeons flew down from the rafters. The black one settled on the edge of the table and the gray landed on Lethbridge's shoulder, tugging at the hair sprouting from his left ear.

"All right, all right," Lethbridge chortled. "Hungry, are we?"

He wedged the pencil stub behind his ear and stuffed the paper into his shirt pocket. Then he bent down and levered off the lid of a cocoa tin by his feet. Lethbridge looked inside and sat up with a groan.

"Sorry, lads. Out of food. There's more in the house."

He scooped up the birds and shuffled back up the path, his tuneless whistle now accompanied by cooing.

With the pigeons deposited on the kitchen table, he scrabbled around in the cupboard under the sink and emerged with a packet of seed.

"Here we go, my lovelies. Oi! What are you up to?"

The two homing pigeons were attacking the open honey jar, pecking at the congealed breadcrumb scum around the rim. Lethbridge struggled to his feet, waving the packet at the birds.

"Go on. Get out of it." Seeds flew everywhere. Lethbridge let out a string of profanities before checking himself.

"Sorry, my beauties," he apologized to the pigeons, which had abandoned the honey for the smorgasbord of birdseed now on offer across the linoleum.

Lethbridge grabbed a dustpan and was scooping up the mess under the kitchen table when there was a bang on the front door. This time there was the sound of breaking glass.

Lethbridge stood up. His head and back smacked hard into the underside of the table, sending it bucking in the air. The honeypot catapulted over the edge and landed with a sticky splat on the small of his back, sending a lava flow of goo down his underpants. Lethbridge launched himself out the other side of the table and squelched down the corridor. He reached the front room to find the door ajar. Shards of glass lay across the entryway. Lethbridge halted—and heard the creak of floorboards above.

Someone was in the house.

He took a breath and steeled himself. Then he opened

the hall closet, leaned in, and pulled out his police baton, a two-foot-long tube of sleek black menace. Gripping it in two hands, he crept toward the stairs.

"The element of surprise is mine," he whispered.

Sadly for Lethbridge, the surprise factor lasted all of two seconds. He made it to the third step when a flash of black hurdled over the banister and landed on top of him. Lethbridge tumbled backward, his feet over his head. A lithe figure rolled over the top in a blur, leaping clear as the constable smacked onto his back with a crunching *oof.* The assailant landed catlike by the front door, tensed for action. The figure was clothed entirely in black, a scarf wrapped ninja-style around the head, leaving only a narrow slit to reveal a pair of dark eyes.

This was no pranking schoolkid on holidays.

Lethbridge struggled to regain his senses. He glared across at his attacker. "Right," he muttered. "You're for it."

The constable dragged himself to his feet. But before he could take a step, the intruder flashed a hand into a pouch at the back of his black costume. Within seconds a rock on a short rope was being swung in the air. It whipped across the room, splaying out to become three flat stones tied at a central point. Lethbridge was caught across the throat and stood in dumb shock as the sling wound around his neck. Two of the rocks smacked hard against his temples; the third finished the job with a sharp rap across the forehead.

Lethbridge went down like a felled oak.

When he woke, he was flat on his back on the kitchen floor. He blinked to clear the fog in his brain. A noise came from behind. He tipped his head and saw that the figure was ransacking the hall closet. His police helmet lay on the floor alongside his equipment belt. Lethbridge tried to stand but couldn't move. His ankles and wrists were tied, his arms bound across his chest. He was trussed up like a Christmas turkey. Lethbridge cast his eyes around the kitchen. The two homing pigeons were still pecking at the mess of birdseed on the floor.

With a grunt of determination, he rolled onto his stomach and edged up onto his elbows and knees. The pencil stub was somehow still behind his ear and he plucked it free. His other hand scrabbled inside his shirt pocket and pulled out the message from his chess game. He scribbled a rough SOS, then glanced across to the hallway. His attacker was still inside the closet. Lethbridge puckered up and made soft kissing noises until the black pigeon waddled across.

"That's my brave boy," he cooed. "Got a special mission for you."

Lethbridge gathered the bird into his hands and slipped the note into the tube on its leg. With an effort he twisted to face the open kitchen window and flung the bird into the air.

"Go, my proud beauty," he hissed. "Fly! Fly to freedom!"

Then he collapsed onto his stomach, exhausted but exultant.

The bird spread its wings and took a majestic circuit of the kitchen, a picture of perfection in flight. It then made a copybook landing square on Lethbridge's broad backside, where it set about feasting on the picnic of honey and birdseed that it found there.

Lethbridge closed his eyes and swore.

Out in the front corridor, the figure in black emerged from the hall closet. A gloved hand held a police notebook. A finger flicked open the cover and flipped through the pages. With a nod, the intruder slipped the notebook into the pouch in the folds of black fabric. When the hand reappeared, it held a small glass bottle. The contents were poured onto a cloth. With a few light steps the figure was by Lethbridge's side. A damp rag was clamped over the constable's mouth and nose.

The room began to melt and swirl. Lethbridge's eyes rolled back.

When he woke up several hours later, it was to find two bemused paramedics staring down at him.

And two pigeons pecking happily at his backside.

Chapter One

The canvas sack landed against the oak doors with such a judder it threatened to knock them off their hinges. Two more followed, each stuffed to bursting point. One of the doors opened inward and a tall, barrel-chested man, dressed in a dark suit, peered down at the pile of bags. They were stenciled with the words ROYAL MAIL. The man's nostrils flared a millimeter. His eyes narrowed. Then, with an exhalation that reeked of resentment, he bent down and dragged the first of the sacks into the house.

The volume of mail delivered to the mansion at Avonleigh had been growing steadily for a fortnight. The post office in the village High Street had tacked a HELP WANTED sign in the window. Three postal carriers had called in sick that week alone. Back strain. The local chiropractor was advertising for an assistant.

"It's jolly good for business, is all I can say," Mrs. Parsons from the post office told Mrs. Rutherford when she dropped in to mail a letter to her brother. "Better than Christmas."

Mrs. Rutherford nodded. "Yes, Avonleigh has come to life in the past few weeks. We couldn't be happier up at the house."

"So will he be coming to town soon?" Mrs. Parsons asked, her eyes wide. "You know, to meet a few of the locals? It would seem appropriate."

Mrs. Rutherford pursed her lips. "He's a little tied up at the moment. I don't think he'll be making any social calls for a while."

There was an uncomfortable silence.

"That is disappointing." Mrs. Parsons sniffed. "A new lord of the manor has obligations. Even if he is Australian. Mister Gerald should be reminded of that by those who ought to know better." She gave Mrs. Rutherford an icy glare.

"He prefers *Master* Gerald," Mrs. Rutherford said. "And I'm sure he'll meet everyone who is worth meeting in good time. A good day to you, Mrs. Parsons."

Mrs. Rutherford fixed an AIR MAIL sticker to the front of her envelope, marched from the shop, and dropped the letter in the post box out front. She consulted the list she'd written in the kitchen at Avonleigh that morning, checked the basket on the front of her bicycle to make sure everything was there, then settled onto the seat and trundled up the cobblestones. She'd only gone twenty yards or so when Mrs. Parsons stepped from the post office and onto the footpath.

"You can't keep him to yourself forever, Mrs. Rutherford!" she cried.

The woman on the bicycle smiled to herself and continued on her way, pedaling through the winding backstreets and onto a country lane, clicking and clacking over every bump and rut in the road.

It had been like this ever since the new master of Avonleigh had taken up residence. The first week or so had been quiet enough. Master Gerald had been able to wander in and out of town with his friends, still unrecognized. But after the events at Beaconsfield, and all the excitement in the newspapers and on television, it seemed the whole world wanted to know Gerald Wilkins.

The locals in Glastonbury were at Mrs. Rutherford every time she came to town.

"When will we get to see him, Mrs. Rutherford?"

"Is he as nice as they all say, Mrs. Rutherford?"

"Would he like to meet my daughter, Mrs. Rutherford?"

That last question in particular had become more frequent and more insistent. It coincided with the enormous increase in the volume of mail delivered to the mansion. As she was the housekeeper at Avonleigh, Mrs. Rutherford had also taken it upon herself to act as gatekeeper for the new master. He did have a few things on his mind. After all, it isn't every day a thirteen-year-old boy wakes to find he has inherited a colossal fortune from his great-aunt.

Well out into the countryside, the bike came to a halt outside a large set of iron gates. In the center of the gates was the image of an archer at full draw, his muscled torso set against a blazing sun. Mrs. Rutherford pressed a button on an intercom recessed into a mossy stone wall. The gates swung inward. She coasted through the opening and down a gravel drive lined with chestnut trees, the branches forming a canopy over her head.

Summer hung heavy in the air and Mrs. Rutherford took a deep sniff of the perfumes of the Somerset countryside—the loamy soil, the aroma of freshly cut grass, a blizzard of pollens. A team of gardeners tended to a hedge and flowerbeds as Mrs. Rutherford rattled past on her bicycle, sending them a cheery wave. She curved past the rose garden and the topiaries, beyond the croquet lawn and the turnoff to the old stables and the greenhouses, and was presented with the full Elizabethan splendor of the mansion at Avonleigh.

At the bottom of a gentle slope stood the main house, a four-story monument to the stonemasons' craft. Hewn from golden rock and assembled by artisans, the building stretched upward and outward, a palace fit for an emperor.

Manicured lawns, weed free and splendid, spread out on either side of the house.

Mrs. Rutherford wheeled her bicycle into a stone alcove and emerged with the wicker basket over her arm. She wandered around the end of the south wing. She reached an expanse of grass, took a look over her shoulder, then kicked off her shoes and took girlish delight in scrunching her toes into the velvet lawn. When she finally walked off the terrace and into the main drawing room, her cheeks were pink with life.

"Morning, Mrs. Rutherford." A girl of about thirteen sat cross-legged in the middle of the floor, surrounded by piles of envelopes and packages. "You're looking happy this morning."

Mrs. Rutherford placed her basket on a side table and brushed her hands down the front of her dress, a simple gray uniform that almost reached the oriental carpet at her feet.

"I am very happy this morning, Miss Ruby," Mrs. Rutherford said. "It is a beautiful day and one worth celebrating. I have plans for a particularly spectacular dinner this evening, if I do say so myself. Now, is there any sign of Master Gerald and your brother?"

The girl slit open an envelope with a silver letter opener. "They're mucking around outside," Ruby said. "I thought I better make a start here. Most of it's left over from yesterday."

A door banged open and the tall man in the dark suit entered. He dragged a mailbag across the carpet and added it to the stack in the corner.

"Are there any more, Mr. Fry?" Mrs. Rutherford asked. Fry was massaging his right shoulder.

"That's the last of them," he said, without a jot of enthusiasm.

"Excellent. You'll be happy to hear the post office is starting an afternoon delivery as well."

"Marvelous," he said, and trudged out of the room.

Ruby stifled a giggle. "He's not too happy today."

Mrs. Rutherford clicked her tongue. "He is never a bundle of joy at the best of times," she said. "But ever since Miss Archer's death—well, he's been even more unpleasant than usual."

"Has Mr. Fry worked here for a long time?" Ruby asked.

"Let me see. I'd been here twenty years when he started with Miss Archer, so that would make it some twenty-five years that we've had the pleasure of Mr. Fry's company."

"Wow. And did she leave him anything in her will?"

"A set of teaspoons, I believe. Quite nice ones. None of your tat."

"And she left the entire estate to Gerald?"

Mrs. Rutherford busied herself with a bowl of flowers on the mantelpiece. "That may explain why Mr. Fry hasn't been overjoyed since Master Gerald's arrival. Most inappropriate, I think, begging your pardon for saying so."

Ruby brushed aside a few strands of hair and retied her ponytail. "And Gerald is now the youngest billionaire in the world. It's all a bit fantastic, isn't it? One day he's at school in Sydney and the next he's flying to London to inherit twenty billion pounds."

"I understand there's a prince in Dubai who may be worth a touch more," Mrs. Rutherford said. "But Master Gerald's landed in it, that's for certain."

Ruby looked up at the housekeeper. "Do you mind if I ask what Gerald's great-aunt left you, Mrs. Rutherford?"

The woman smiled. "Not at all, Miss Ruby. Miss Archer left me the memory of a kind and generous soul, whom it was a pleasure and honor to know. And that is all any of us should ever hope to receive."

Ruby picked up another pile of envelopes. "So not quite like Gerald's mum and dad, then?"

Mrs. Rutherford sucked on her lips. "I'm sure I don't know what you mean, Miss Ruby. Master Gerald's parents are touring the Archer estate's global holdings of luxury properties to ensure that all is in order."

Ruby grinned. "So will they be back from that Caribbean island anytime soon?"

"Not while the gin holds out," Mrs. Rutherford said under her breath. "Begging your pardon for saying so."

At that moment two bodies rolled into the room, a

wrestling tangle of limbs across the carpet. Among the flurry of arms and legs it was possible to make out blond hair—Sam Valentine with his broad shoulders and summer tan. He slammed his opponent onto the floor, straddled his chest and pinned him to the rug.

"There!" he declared. "I win."

The other boy stopped struggling. His unruly mop of dark hair, plain T-shirt, and blue jeans gave no hint that this was the richest thirteen-year-old on the planet.

"Go easy," Gerald said. "Leg feeling better, is it?"

"That? Yeah, it's pretty much right."

"And how about the morbid fear of rats? How's that going?"

Sam flinched as if his worst nightmare had just walked through the door. In a blink Gerald flipped him over and sat on top of him, knees pressing his shoulders into the rug.

Sam howled, struggling to escape.

Gerald rolled off and the two of them got up from the carpet, laughing and breathing hard.

"Boys," Ruby said.

Mrs. Rutherford shook her head. "And they don't improve with age, believe me."

"Morning, Mrs. Rutherford," Gerald said. "Just showing Sam who's boss."

"Yes, I'm sure," Mrs. Rutherford said through lemon lips. "Now, you three are to deal with this correspondence today. I'm interviewing for a secretary to handle the mail, but for now it is your responsibility. Hop to it while I see how morning tea preparations are progressing." She bustled out of the room.

Gerald and Sam flopped down on either side of Ruby.

"Not fair using rats against me in a fight," Sam said to Gerald.

Ruby leaned across and patted her twin brother on the knee. "Then you should try being less of a wuss around them, shouldn't you?"

Sam muttered something about a medical condition and picked up the nearest pile of letters. Ruby slapped him on the wrist.

"Mitts off," she snapped. "I've already sorted those. Look, it's quite straightforward. Even for you. The colored envelopes go over here. That's the greeting cards and pathetic love letters from stupid girls. All the long white envelopes go here—that's the begging letters. The parcels go over by the fireplace and anything with a window in the front goes into this stack for Mr. Prisk to look at. Clear?"

Sam rubbed the back of his hand. "What's this pile then, Miss Frustrated Librarian?"

Ruby glanced at a mound of square buff-colored envelopes, constructed from expensive-looking parchment.

"That's invitations to opening nights, parties, and sporting events," she said.

Gerald scooped up an armful of envelopes. "This is ridiculous. Why are so many people writing to me?"

"Because you're richer than the queen," Ruby said. "They're all from people wanting something."

Sam held up a letter in one hand and a photograph in another. "This one wants locking up. Take a look at that." He handed the photo to Gerald, who inspected it with alarm.

"'Dearest Gerald,'" Sam read from the letter, "'I know you're the one for me. Ever since I heard about your brave escape from that awful Sir Mason Green at Beaconsfield I knew we were destined to be as one. Promise me your eternal love. Or I'll hunt you down and hurt you.'"

"What?" Ruby said. "You're making that up."

She snatched the photograph from her brother and took a look. Her eyebrows shot up.

"She just wants a new friend, that's all," Ruby said with a slight shudder. "She would have seen the news reports on TV—us recovering the stolen diamond, our run-in with Sir Mason Green—and she thinks we're worth knowing."

Sam laughed. "Not you and me, sister. No one wants to be friends with Sam and Ruby Valentine. All this is addressed to one person: Gerald Wilkins, care of Planet Gazillionaire. Population: one. It's about money, pure and simple."

They spent the rest of the morning going through the post.

Ruby upended another sack of mail across the rug and Sam groaned.

"Are you sure there's nothing in here for me?" he said. A handful of envelopes slipped through his fingers and onto the floor.

Ruby looked at him. "Who would write to you out here in rural Somerset?"

"Oh, I don't know. There might be a letter for me. From India, maybe. A little thank-you note. Or something."

Ruby laughed. "Sam, Alisha Gupta is not the least bit interested in you. She's not going to take time from her oh-so-busy social life to stick a stamp on an envelope for your sake."

Sam bristled. "Just because you two hate each other. Her dad was really happy we got his diamond back from Mason Green. And Alisha thought I was pretty brave."

"I seem to recall the word she used was *foolish*. Or maybe it was *grossly stupid*. Anyway, it was Gerald she was drooling over, not you."

Sam looked to Gerald for support, but he was sitting boggle-eyed on the floor, amid a mountain of love letters.

"They don't even know me," he said. "I could have fangs and drink blood for breakfast for all they know."

Sam flicked through a wad of photographs. "They'd probably find that attractive."

Gerald surveyed the piles that surrounded them. "I

didn't think being a billionaire would involve so much paperwork."

He plucked a letter from a bright pink envelope, releasing a perfumed shower of glitter. Then, out of nowhere, he asked, "Do you think Sir Mason Green will resurface?"

The once-respected businessman, philanthropist, and chairman of the British Museum Trust hadn't been far from Gerald's thoughts since the incident at Beaconsfield a fortnight earlier. Sir Mason Green was now an international fugitive, wanted for ordering the murder of Geraldine Archer—the very act that had paved the way for Gerald to inherit the Archer fortune.

"We won't see him again," Ruby said. "He found what he was looking for. Why would he come back?"

Gerald hoped that was true. He still found it difficult to sleep. And even when he did manage to drift off, there were the dreams.

The night in the cavern under Beaconsfield played over and over in his mind: Sir Mason Green using the stolen Noor Jehan diamond to unlock a legendary casket that had lain hidden in a burial chamber for seventeen hundred years; Green reaching into the casket and removing an ornate golden scepter and gazing upon it like he'd found some lost love. He'd grabbed Gerald by the hair and laid the rod across his forehead. That moment was now etched in high definition in Gerald's mind: the brain-collapsing vision that Gerald had experienced, the sensation of being shattered into an infinite number of particles and blown by a hot wind into every moment throughout the sands of time. He hadn't told anyone about this vision, not even the Valentine twins.

"Green's someplace overseas for sure," Sam said. "He's a billionaire—he could be anywhere."

"Don't let it hassle you, Gerald," Ruby said. "Inspector Parrott will take care of it. You don't need to worry about Sir Mason Green."

Gerald picked up another pile of envelopes. The top one had an elegant letter *R* embossed in red on the back. He tore through the stiff paper.

"Hey, look at this," he said. "A get-well card from Lord Herring at the Rattigan Club."

Sam laughed. "Didn't think you'd hear from him again."

"Unless he was threatening to sue you," Ruby said.

Gerald smiled to himself. The exclusive Rattigan Club—they'd got up to some mischief there trying to find the stolen diamond. All that old-world finery and stale cigar smoke. Those garishly decorated rooms. The Pink Room, the Blue Room, the—

"That's it!"

Ruby and Sam stared at Gerald with alarm.

"What's it?"

Gerald jumped to his feet. "I've got to call Inspector Parrott."

* * *

The next day, Gerald, Sam, and Ruby stood in a long corridor on the first floor of the Rattigan Club in London outside a door painted a lustrous bottle green. Mr. Fry had driven them up—three hours in the upholstered comfort of a customized Rolls-Royce limousine. Fry didn't utter a word the entire trip.

They were joined by Inspector Parrott and Constable Lethbridge of the Metropolitan Police, and the Rattigan Club chairman, Lord Herring.

"We've searched every inch of Sir Mason's office and his house and found nothing," the inspector said. "This investigation has reached a dead end. And a great deal of the interview evidence central to the case has gone missing." He cast a furious eye at Lethbridge. The constable glanced down at his shoes and absentmindedly slipped a hand around to scratch at his left buttock. "I hope this theory of yours leads to something, Gerald," the inspector said. "We need a breakthrough."

"It just struck me," Gerald explained. "I'd been in the Pink Room and the Blue Room and we'd run past a door to the Green Room."

Lord Herring pulled a key from his vest pocket. "Sir Mason was a member of this club for a very long time. He had the Green Room for his exclusive use. He said it was a tidy space away from his office—handy for his private papers and such. The staff tell me no one except Mason has been in here for five years. He even employed his own cleaner."

Herring placed the key in the lock and turned. A heavy deadbolt slid aside. The door swung in and seven heads peered into the dark room.

"Hold on," Herring said. "There should be a switch." He fumbled a hand around the wall. A bulb flickered on. Seven sets of eyes adjusted to the light.

After a moment of shocked silence, it was Ruby who spoke.

"Oh my," was all she could say.

Chapter Two

The Green Room gave up its secrets. On the right side, against the far wall, was a large wooden desk, neatly ordered with stacks of documents and magazines. The left side was lined with filing cabinets and bookshelves. In the middle of the room two armchairs sat on either side of a low table, on which sat a single cup of very stale coffee.

Gerald saw none of that. His eyes were fixed on the wall in front of him. It was a good thirty feet long and painted a light green. Its surface was covered in pen marks. At first glance, it could have been a work of modern art: an abstract wave of rectangles and lines sweeping inward from the extremities to collide in the center. But it was the image that sat in the hub of the converging arcs of ink that captured everyone's attention. There, at the heart of the bizarre mural, was a large color photograph of Gerald Wilkins. It was held in place with a silver letter opener stabbed through Gerald's throat.

"Are you serious?" Gerald yelped. He slumped back against the doorframe.

Everyone looked at Gerald, then back at the picture skewered to the wall.

"Does this count as a breakthrough, inspector?" Ruby asked.

Sam pushed through the jumble of people in the doorway and crossed the floor. He reached out to touch the silver dagger when Inspector Parrott barked, "Stop!"

Sam whipped his hand back as if a Doberman was about to latch on to it.

"This is a crime scene," the inspector declared. He took a pair of thin rubber gloves from his pocket and stretched them over his hands. "Only Constable Lethbridge and I are to handle anything. Clear?"

Sam nodded but stepped as close to the wall as he could without touching it. The others joined him. Except for Gerald. He remained rooted to the spot by the door.

"It's a family tree," Ruby said, studying the scrawls on the wall. "There are names in all these boxes. Hundreds and hundreds of them."

Everyone was drawn to the diagram of generation upon generation of Gerald's ancestors laid out with meticulous care.

Gerald still couldn't move. He stared unblinking at the wall opposite. What had he done to attract this attention? And what sort of man would go to this effort?

Gerald nearly hit the top of the doorframe at the sound of a gruff voice in his right ear: "Has the party started without me?"

He spun around to find a large redheaded man with an unkempt beard and a set of eyebrows like hairy awnings.

"Professor McElderry!" Gerald said, with some relief. "What are you doing here?"

The man stepped past Gerald and cast his eyes around the room. "Someone had to bring some intelligence to this event. And by the look of it, I'm not a moment too soon."

Inspector Parrott glanced up. "Ah, Professor. Thank you for coming on such short notice."

McElderry retrieved a pair of spectacles from his shirt pocket and joined the others by the wall. "The British Museum can spare me for a wee while," he said. He peered at the marks that covered the wall. "Or possibly quite a long while."

Gerald had last seen Professor McElderry over tea and scones at Avonleigh. It was shortly after the confrontation with Sir Mason Green. Since then the professor had been camped in the cavern under Beaconsfield, trying to decipher the riddles contained in the ancient burial chamber.

Inspector Parrott moved to the far right corner of the

room, following the pen lines as they branched out across the wall. "The first name over here looks like it's Clea," he said.

The professor had moved to the opposite corner. "Over here it's Quintus. Quintus Antonius, circa AD 350. Any of this sound familiar, Gerald?"

Gerald hadn't moved from the door, unwilling to get close to anything associated with Mason Green.

"Never heard of them," he said.

Professor McElderry grunted. He traced his way back along the web of lines until he reached their ultimate product: Gerald Wilkins. The full-page photograph was torn from one of the hundreds of magazine articles that had been published about him. The headline on this one was WHO'S A LUCKY BOY?

Sam piped up. "Gerald, did you see this?" He pointed to a hole in the picture. It was about the size of a quarter and was burned between Gerald's eyes. It looked like someone had twisted a hot poker into his forehead.

"What's all this mean, Professor?" Gerald asked in a soft voice. "Why would Mason Green want to know about my family?"

McElderry raked his fingers through his beard and took in the panorama before him. "There's a story from ancient Greece," he began, "about the god Zeus. He released two eagles: One flew east and the other went west." The professor spread his arms wide. "They flew clear round the globe and where they met"—McElderry brought his palms together with a sharp clap—"marked the center of the world."

"Looks like you're the center of someone's world, Gerald," Sam said.

Ruby's eyes scanned the length of the room. "Is this what they mean when they say the writing's on the wall?"

Gerald took a step inside. "I couldn't tell you who half my family was," he said. "How can Green know so much about me?" More important, Gerald thought, why would he care?

Gerald crossed to the photograph. He saw a boy with a bewildered expression on his face. He stared at the hole between his eyes, its edges burned brown and flaking. His fingers strayed to his head to the smooth gap flanked by his eyebrows. Had Sir Mason Green actually *branded* his face? He looked at the two names above his photograph: His mother, Vi, on the left, his father, Eddie, on the right.

Gerald hadn't seen his parents in weeks—not since he inherited his great-aunt Geraldine's fortune. The last he'd heard from his mother was when she telephoned from the Archer island in the Caribbean. She'd spent the previous week aboard the luxury Archer motor yacht with its helicopters, Jet Skis, and mini-submarine.

"Been keeping well, dear?" she'd said.

"You mean since the insane billionaire tried to kill me?"

"Try not to exaggerate, dear. It's irritating."

His thoughts were interrupted by a shout from Ruby.

"Come look at this, Gerald. These might be yours."

She was peering at some documents on Green's desk. Three opened envelopes rested on a pile of newspaper clippings.

"Seen these before?" she asked.

Gerald glanced over his shoulder. The inspector was going through the cabinets on the opposite side of the room. Sam was chatting to Lethbridge by the family tree, and the professor was busy flipping through the contents of the bookcases. Fry was looking at the photo of Gerald, a bemused smile on his face.

Gerald picked up the envelopes—one had the word FRATERNITY on the front and another had FAMILY TREE, both in his great-aunt's handwriting. The third had a line of doodles—the number 10, a circle with a line through it, a *Y*, an arrow, and a triangle. All three were empty, sliced open at the top with razor precision.

"These are the envelopes that my great-aunt left me," he said. "The ones that were stolen from her house." Gerald had thought he'd never see them again. Together with a letter from Geraldine, they were the only clues to what Sir Mason Green was up to. They'd been stolen by Green's enforcer, a cadaverous psychopath whom Gerald and the Valentines called the thin man. The last time they'd seen him he was screaming for his life from the middle of a flaming wheel as it rolled down a hill and into the night. Gerald tried to focus. It had been a busy couple of weeks.

Sam looked over Gerald's shoulder.

"That must be how Green got so much detail about your relatives," he said, pointing to the envelope marked FAMILY TREE. "What was in the other ones?"

"I never got the chance to look." Gerald glanced around again for the inspector, then slipped the envelopes into his backpack.

Sam lifted the stack of news clippings, revealing the surface of the desk. There was a large sheet of glass on the top and sandwiched underneath it was a map. Gerald took one look and called out, "I think you'd all better see this."

Professor McElderry let out a snort as he walked across from the bookcases. "That cheeky beggar has lifted half my library on Greek and Roman mythology," he grumbled. "Can't imagine how I didn't notice the books were missing."

Inspector Parrott joined them at the desk. "All right, what seems to be—" He stopped midsentence.

Colored lines sprawled across the glass, marking out a tangle of paths across the map. A box of marker pens sat at one end of the desk, and judging by the smudge marks, the lines had been drawn, wiped off, and redrawn a number of times.

Blue, red, and green paths spread across the map and

converged on a central point.

"Are you getting this down, Lethbridge?" The inspector glared at the constable. "I assume you've got a new note-book?"

Lethbridge fumbled in his back pocket, wincing as he removed a crisp new police-issue notebook.

"Still a bit sensitive back there, are we, Constable?" the inspector asked, with no hint of compassion. "Try to take better care of this one, if you can manage it."

Lethbridge grumbled to himself.

Ruby gave the policeman a curious look. "Is everything okay, Constable Lethbridge?" she asked. "Do you want to sit down?"

"I think the constable would prefer to stand," the inspec-tor said. "He seems to find it more comfortable that way." Lethbridge ran a hand across his left buttock and flipped open his notebook.

Inspector Parrott turned to McElderry. "This looks like your territory, Professor. What do you make of it?"

Professor McElderry leaned in low over the map.

"By those borders, I'd say Roman Empire—maybe around the end of the fourth century."

"What about these lines?" Ruby asked. "They all seem to end up in one spot."

"Rome," McElderry said. "Without a doubt."

"Well," Sam said, smirking. "You know what they say."

McElderry didn't look up from the chart. "If the next words to exit your mouth are 'All roads lead to Rome,' I will skin you, roll you in salt, and hurl you from the nearest window."

Sam opened his mouth, then shut it again.

"Ignore him, Professor," Ruby said. "He gets distracted easily. What do the lines mean?"

"They appear to mark three routes into the ancient capital. From the far reaches of the empire." McElderry traced his finger along the blue line. "See? This starts in the south of England, crosses the channel, then up along the coast to the River Elbe. Then it's inland, south over the Alps, and down to Rome."

"What about the red line?" Ruby said. "That's France."

"On the Normandy coast," McElderry said. "Then southeast to Marseille, across to Corsica, down through Sardinia, over to Sicily, and up the coast to Rome."

"And the green line heads up from the top of Africa," Gerald said.

"I think that's Egypt, actually," Sam piped up. "Probably Alexandria." Everyone in the room looked at him.

"What?" he said. "I like geography. See? It goes up to Crete, then across the Mediterranean."

The professor drummed his fingers on the desktop. "Fascinating," he said. "A map detailing three routes into the ancient capital."

Gerald scanned the chart, trying to read the mind of the man who had turned his life upside down. Then an idea popped into his head. It was no bigger than a mustard seed, but it landed in fertile ground.

"Maybe this isn't three paths into Rome," Gerald said. "Maybe it's three journeys out of the city."

"What do you mean?" the professor said.

Gerald pointed to the start of the blue line in southern England. "That looks very close to Glastonbury, doesn't it?"

McElderry adjusted his glasses. "Could be," he said.

"Maybe the blue line has something to do with the diamond casket," Gerald said. "Maybe it shows how it came to Glastonbury in the first place."

Inspector Parrott frowned. "What about the other two lines?"

Gerald felt his brain whirring. He turned to Sam. "Remember that page you found at Beaconsfield?" he said. "The one from that book of local myths?"

"Yeah?"

Ruby leaped in. "That's right! On the bottom it said the diamond casket was *l'une des trois*: one of three."

"So?"

"So maybe Green's looking for two other caskets as well," Gerald said.

There was a long pause around the desk while this possibility soaked in.

Then the inspector burst into action. "Right! Lethbridge! Get in touch with the police services in France and Egypt. Put them on high alert. If Green's looking for two more caskets, this is our chance to nab him."

Lethbridge grabbed his two-way radio and elbowed past Mr. Fry and Lord Herring as he left the room.

Gerald's fingers brushed across the red and green lines on the glass.

"What's he after?" Gerald said. "What's in the other two caskets?"

"I only know of the diamond one," McElderry said. "The others are news to me."

Gerald looked at the items on the desk. There was a small ceramic bowl containing some bits and pieces—a few keys on a gold ring, sunglasses, a dry-cleaning ticket. And a glossy black box, hinged at the back. He picked it up and opened the lid. Inside was a human skull.

Gerald stifled a cry. He turned to the professor and held up the box.

McElderry plucked out the skull and cradled it in one hand.

"Intriguing," he said, holding the relic up to the light. "Sir Mason Green may well have a fascination with Celtic lore."

"What makes you think that?" the inspector said.

"The cult of the skull—the ancient Celts used to boil

down their enemies' heads to capture the strength of their souls. Wonderful stuff."

Gerald swallowed. He looked at the skull, then at the photograph stabbed to the wall. There was a hole in the picture, drilled into the brow like a third eye.

He turned to the butler. "Mr. Fry," he said through a dry throat. "I think I'd like to go home now."

CHAPTER THREE

The view over the Somerset countryside from the Archer corporate helicopter was breathtaking. The landscape spread out in a patchwork of fields alive with summer color. Inside the cabin of the luxury Sikorsky S-76 chopper, Gerald, Sam, and Ruby sat in leather comfort, their noses pressed against the glass.

"This billionaire thing just keeps getting better," Sam said. He gazed out across the meadows and villages below. "This beats driving."

Ruby flopped back into her seat opposite Gerald, barely able to contain her excitement. "This is awesome, Gerald. I've always wanted to fly in a helicopter."

Gerald was no less excited. It was his first time in a helicopter as well. The fact that he also owned it only added to the bizarreness.

After leaving the Rattigan Club they had arrived at the London heliport on the Thames to find a selection of Archer Corporation helicopters on hand. All were decked out in the dark blue livery of the company, each with a golden archer painted across its belly. It was fortunate Gerald was momentarily struck dumb by the realization that he owned an air wing, because there were no words to describe his thoughts when Mr. Fry appeared wearing a brown leather bomber jacket and aviation sunglasses.

"You?" Gerald had finally said. "You're the pilot?"

Fry had flipped up the collar of his jacket and pulled an Archer Corporation cap onto his head. "Roger that," he said.

Less than an hour later they were sweeping across the countryside toward Gerald's house at Avonleigh.

"You know the best thing about taking a helicopter instead of the Rolls?" Gerald called to his friends over the whirring rotor blades.

"What's that?"

"You don't have to look at the back of Fry's head for three hours."

Ruby laughed and flicked off her belt to take a seat between Sam and Gerald. "What do you make of all that in the Green Room?" she said.

Gerald stared out the window at the fields below. "In the cavern under Beaconsfield, Green said he was surprised I didn't know about some great family secret," he said.

"There's obviously something in your family history that's got him excited," Ruby said.

"And the hole in the head?" Sam said. "That's just sick."

"Well, Green's gone now, off looking for whatever," Ruby said, "so we don't need to worry about that." Gerald saw Ruby give Sam a look that said *stick a sock in it*. "Anyway, what were you and Constable Lethbridge chatting about?" She was clearly trying to change the subject.

"He's funny," Sam said. "There was a break-in at his house and someone stole his notebook. He made it sound like he was jumped by a gang of ninjas."

"His notebook?" Gerald said.

"It had stuff about the diamond theft and everything that happened at Beaconsfield. Parrott's not happy."

Ruby chuckled. "He's a walking disaster area, that Lethbridge."

The helicopter swooped in over Avonleigh, made a low arc over the tennis court and pavilion, hovered a second over the orchard, then sent a flock of sheep scattering as it landed on a helipad in a field about a hundred yards from the house.

Gerald, Sam, and Ruby jumped from the cabin as the rotor wound down, still buzzing from the excitement of the ride. They were greeted by Mrs. Rutherford, who ushered them up to the house.

"I wish Mr. Fry wouldn't use that thing," she said. "Puts

the chickens off for a week. He goes all silly when he gets in that thing."

Gerald peered over his shoulder. Mr. Fry was walking around the helicopter, pausing to wipe a bug spot from the glass with his handkerchief.

"At least he seems happy now," Gerald said.

"Oh, yes," Mrs. Rutherford muttered. "Mr. Fry considers himself to be quite the top pistol."

Ruby giggled. "I think you mean top gun."

"Whatever it is, Mr. Fry seems to think it's appropriate to frighten my chickens with no thought to the consequences. Very selfish, I would say." Mrs. Rutherford mumbled something about boys and their toys as she led them up to the terrace.

"Perhaps it's just as well Mr. Fry brought you home quickly," she said. "Mr. Prisk has arrived and he has a number of things to discuss with you, Master Gerald. He's in the library, in the north wing."

Gerald and the Valentine twins walked through the imposing sandstone doorway and under a carving of the Archer family crest—three forearms, hands clutching elbows to form a triangle around a blazing sun. They veered down a broad corridor that was lined in walnut and hung with paintings of rural landscapes. They hadn't spent much time in that end of the mansion, preferring to enjoy the summer days outside.

Ruby nudged Gerald. "You okay?" she asked as they walked.

"I'm fine. Like you said, Green's a million miles away. And now the police have a clue where to find him. What's not to be okay about?" Gerald knew he didn't sound very convincing.

They reached the end of the passage and Gerald opened a wooden door to reveal an enormous room. It was lined with bookcases that climbed to the second floor creating a soaring sense of space. Halfway up the wall was a mezzanine walkway. And halfway around the walkway stood Mr. Prisk, leafing through a leather-bound volume. He stopped reading and gave a wave, tucked the book under his arm, and climbed down a spiral staircase.

Gerald was surprised to see Mr. Prisk looking so cheerful. His great-aunt's lawyer had exuded anxiety ever since Gerald had inherited her estate. It had been left to Mr. Prisk to appease the relatives who had missed out on any share of the fortune. It was the first time that Gerald had seen the little man looking pleased to be alive.

"Beautiful day, isn't it?" Mr. Prisk said as he settled in a wing-backed chair in front of a fireplace. "Just right for what I've got planned."

Gerald gave Sam and Ruby a curious look. They sat on a couch opposite Mr. Prisk, who pulled some documents from a briefcase.

"I have some news," Mr. Prisk said. "Some good news,

and some even better news. Would you like the good news first?"

Gerald leaned forward. "Yes please."

"I have been in touch with your school in Sydney. I spoke to the acting deputy principal." Mr. Prisk consulted a sheet of paper. "Mr. Atkinson. I have advised him of your change in circumstances and that you may not be back in Australia for some time yet. I must say, he was delighted. He said you should stay as long as you like."

Gerald's eyes narrowed. "That sounds like Mr. Atkinson."

"Which brings me to the even better news."

"What?" Sam said, joining Gerald on the edge of the couch. "Even better than not having to go back to school?"

"Quite. Your not having to return to Australia means you will have more time to work on this." Mr. Prisk handed across a pile of bound documents. Gerald took them onto his lap. The cover on the top one was emblazoned with the blue and gold Archer Corporation logo. He opened it.

"What is all this?" Gerald flicked through pages crammed with pie charts and tables of numbers.

"That's the June financial outcome for Archer Corporation," Mr. Prisk said. "The executive summary. The details are in here." He tapped a large document box with the toe of his carefully shined shoe. "Now I estimate that we can work our way through the first five divisions by the end of this week, then concentrate on the other five next week. I've drawn up an agenda and you'll note I've left a fair amount of time for discussing general business. Your great-aunt was most keen for you to understand the day-to-day running of the corporation. I'd say a few solid weeks of hitting the books will get you started."

Gerald recoiled. "A few weeks!"

"Five or six at most. Now the second-quarter trading for the year is traditionally fairly quiet in the northern hemisphere as we head into the summer months, but you'll be pleased to hear the new operations in Argentina and Peru are providing an excellent hedge in the current economic climate. If you turn to page one hundred thirty-seven in the green booklet, you'll find a detailed breakdown of the trading for—"

"Mr. Prisk?"

It was Sam, still balancing on the edge of the couch.

The lawyer looked mildly annoyed by the interruption. "Yes, Mr. Valentine?"

"If Gerald's going to be stuck doing all this work, what are we going to do?"

Mr. Prisk pulled a wedge of folders from the document box. "I expect you can go home."

A shocked silence hit the room.

"Go home?" Ruby said at last.

"Yes. I think that would be best," Mr. Prisk said. "There's really no further point in your being here. Gerald will be occupied for the rest of the summer. I'll make arrangements with Mrs. Rutherford to have you driven back to London."

Sam looked stricken. "I thought we'd be together till the end of the holidays."

"Then you thought wrong. Perhaps you and your sister might go pack your bags. Now would be a good time."

Sam looked to Ruby, then to Gerald, unable to put his thoughts into words. "But . . . but . . . but the food here is fantastic."

Mr. Prisk peered at Sam over the rim of his glasses. "Your dietary requirements are hardly sufficient reason to interfere with the daily workings of one of the world's great business enterprises. Gerald will one day take on the mantle of executive chairman of Archer Corporation. He has work to do."

"Silly me," Ruby said. "I thought he was supposed to be having a holiday."

Mr. Prisk took a sharp breath. "If I recall my own childhood, Miss Valentine, children were to be seen and not heard. And preferably not seen, either." Mr. Prisk's voice rose. "Gerald has greatness before him. The reports he will draft, oh, the planning sessions he will attend. He—"

Gerald interrupted. "Do I get any say in this?"

Mr. Prisk looked shocked. "Gerald. Your future is mapped. Nothing will be left to chance. Your days will be diarized. A schedule will be adhered to. Your life path is set in stone. Look, I've drawn up a calendar for the next eighteen months, it's all planned. Each and every day."

Gerald took the leather-bound diary that Mr. Prisk held out and flipped through the pages.

"What are these?" Gerald asked. Every day had at least six entries.

"Meetings," Mr. Prisk said. "Lots and lots of meetings. You will learn from the very best in the business. Think of it as school, only starting at seven in the morning and going till six or seven at night."

Gerald flipped through the pages in a panic. "What? Seven days a week?"

"I know," Mr. Prisk said, squeezing his hands together. "I can't wait to get started either. It's a good life."

Ruby snorted. "That's not living," she said. "That's barely existing."

Mr. Prisk looked up. "Are you still here? I thought you were packing."

They were interrupted by Mrs. Rutherford, who had appeared at the library door carrying a silver tray.

"Mrs. Rutherford," said Mr. Prisk. "Your timing is impeccable; it's as if you're reading my mind. Can you please supervise these children with their bags? They are returning to London. As soon as possible."

Gerald stepped over the pile of documents on the floor and appealed to the housekeeper. "Mrs. Rutherford, can't Sam and Ruby stay? I don't want to spend the rest of my holidays in meetings."

Mrs. Rutherford looked at the three stricken faces. She shook her head. "I am but a humble servant in this house," she said. "It is most certainly not my place to instruct the young master on how he should be filling his days."

Mr. Prisk nodded. "Quite right," he said.

Sam frowned. "You were doing plenty of instructing about sorting the mail yesterday," he grumbled. "Didn't seem to slow you down then."

Mrs. Rutherford cast a pointed stare at Sam. "I'm sure I don't know what you're referring to," she said. "Master Gerald is the master of the house. He is entitled to do as he pleases, regardless of what a lowly housekeeper such as myself has to say." Mrs. Rutherford allowed her eyes to stray across to Mr. Prisk. "Or anyone else, for that matter. Master Gerald is, after all, his great-aunt's successor. I don't recall Miss Archer taking kindly to being told what to do."

A spark went off in Gerald's eyes. He turned to the lawyer.

"I don't have to do any of this," he said.

Mr. Prisk moved between Gerald and the Valentine twins. "Yes, thank you, Mrs. Rutherford," he said, ushering her, Sam, and Ruby toward the door. "You have been most helpful."

Mrs. Rutherford gave Mr. Prisk her sweetest smile. "Always happy to be of service, Mr. Prisk. Come along,

Ruby. Sam." She turned to leave, then stopped. "I almost forgot." She held out the silver platter to Gerald. "The reason I came in here. This arrived for you, Master Gerald. Special delivery."

Gerald was still staring at Mr. Prisk. "I can say no to all of this work. I can do what I like, when I like."

"Now, Gerald. Let's not be hasty," the lawyer said. "There are important business considerations—"

"I could call up the Archer jet and go surfing in Hawaii. I could go anywhere." The realization washed across Gerald's face like an incoming tide. "I'm a billionaire. I can do *anything*."

Mr. Prisk shook his head. "You have obligations to the company, to oversee the budgets."

Mrs. Rutherford broke into Gerald's dawning self-awareness.

"Master Gerald? The letter."

Gerald snapped out of his trance and looked down at the envelope on the tray. He picked it up and studied the front.

"It's from India," he said.

Sam's face lit up. "Alisha?" he said, a little too eagerly.

Ruby raised her eyes. "Pathetic," she muttered.

Mr. Prisk continued to talk, his voice growing ever more anxious—"There are important capital works projects that need assessing, reports to review"—but Gerald had no ears for him. He tore open the envelope and pulled out a sheet of ivory-colored paper.

"It's from Mr. Gupta," he said.

Sam opened his mouth to speak but a glare from Ruby shut him down.

"He's thanking us again for finding his diamond."

"I've drawn up a spreadsheet that summarizes all the major issues," said Mr. Prisk, holding up a document that Gerald pointedly ignored.

"He's apologizing for not thanking us properly at the time."

"This chart shows the timeline we'll need to follow if we're to keep pace with the run rate—"

"And he's inviting us for a holiday. To India!"

Sam and Ruby leaped across the room and grabbed Gerald by the elbows. "India! We're going to India?"

Mr. Prisk's voice petered out. "No one's listening to me, are they? I'll just arrange for passports and visas then, shall I?" He collected his briefcase and trudged out of the room in a deep funk.

Gerald, Sam, and Ruby hardly noticed.

Mrs. Rutherford picked up the envelope that Gerald had dropped, placed it on the silver tray, and swept out of the library, the merest hint of a smile on her lips.

Chapter Four

For the next two days, Avonleigh buzzed with preparations for the trip. Lists were drawn up and checked off. There was a shopping expedition to nearby Bristol to purchase extra light clothes for the Indian summer. Bags were packed, unpacked, and repacked. Ruby and Sam talked their parents into letting them go with promises of behaving themselves, not getting into trouble, and keeping their rooms tidy for the rest of the year. Gerald guessed that two of the promises were fragile at best.

Mr. Prisk seemed resigned to Gerald not taking any interest in the family business for the foreseeable future. He consoled himself by setting some ground rules for the holiday. He revealed the details over breakfast.

"Mr. Fry's coming with us?" Gerald sputtered in a spray

of scrambled eggs and parsley. "Why does he have to come?"

Mr. Prisk removed a green sprig from his tie with a flick of an index finger. "Because, whether you like it or not, you are the executive chairman-in-waiting of Archer Corporation. I intend to ensure you survive long enough to take your place at the board table."

Gerald prodded his fork at the remainder of his breakfast. His appetite had deserted him. Over by the sideboard the butler fussed with a variety of trays, muttering to himself.

"I know you and Mr. Fry haven't hit it off, but this is a necessary security measure. I'm sure the two of you will overcome your differences soon enough," Mr. Prisk said.

Fry appeared at Gerald's elbow like an apparition. "Rubbish," he said.

"Pardon me?" Gerald said.

"Are you finished with your breakfast, sir, or should I take it to the rubbish?" Fry said, his face as immovable as porcelain.

"The corporate jet is being prepared and our in-country agent will meet you at the airport in Delhi," Mr. Prisk said. "I have advised him that discretion is paramount. It is vital that you not stand out."

"Why's that, Mr. Prisk?" Ruby asked.

"Because, young lady, Gerald is a prime target for kidnappers and extortionists. It will do us no favors if he is seen flouncing about in limousines and the like."

Sam looked up from his bowl of cereal. "I never took you for a flouncer, Gerald."

Gerald tried to suppress a grin. "Oh, I used to flounce something shocking," he said. "But don't worry, Mr. Prisk, my flouncing days are behind me now."

Mr. Prisk took a deep breath and gazed at the ceiling until the giggling stopped.

"And *that* is why Mr. Fry will be accompanying you," he said. "He is well skilled in martial arts and he'll keep a lid on any childish antics."

"Terrific," Gerald said. "Should be quite the holiday then." He screwed up his face, but he wasn't too concerned about the butler. They'd find a way around Mr. Fry.

The trip and the prospect of seeing Alisha Gupta again—in fact, anything that removed the memory of a silver dagger through the throat and a hole in the head— was appealing to Gerald at that moment.

Ruby's voice broke into his thoughts. "I didn't know you could do martial arts, Mr. Fry."

There was a sudden crash by the sideboard. They all swung around to find Mr. Fry looking down at the shattered remains of a pile of breakfast dishes that he had dropped onto the floor.

"Oh yes," Sam said. "We're in safe hands."

* * *

That night, after another belly stretcher of a meal from Mrs. Rutherford's kitchen, Gerald lay in cushioned comfort in his bed and stared at the ceiling. The act of digestion was occupying all his energy. His mind drifted to India and what adventures lay there. They were due to leave the next day and a feeling of blissful anticipation tickled at his senses. But soon, he found himself thinking about the Rattigan Club and the contents of the Green Room.

Sir Mason was clearly insane—he'd fallen over the edge of reason, pursuing Gerald's family back through the ages. Well, Gerald thought, Sir Mason was welcome to it. Gerald had survived thirteen years knowing nothing about his family history and he was happy to keep it that way. A holiday with Alisha and her father would take him well clear of whatever Sir Mason Green was up to and erase visions of skulls and daggers and branded foreheads. Gerald reached across and switched off the lamp by his bed.

He let the night wash over him. It was still the height of summer and the sun was not long below the horizon. A last hint of twilight peeked through the windows. Gerald closed his eyes.

The evening was mild and a slight breeze billowed the drapes, jangling the brass rings against the curtain rod. Gerald rolled over and tried to ignore the sound. The rattling continued. He sighed, then swung out of bed and padded across to the window to tie back the curtains. He tried to keep his eyes half closed so he could tumble easily back to sleep. But as he turned to go back to his bed, he froze. His heart lurched in his chest. Standing next to the bed, a long, slender blade in his hand, was the unmistakable figure of Sir Mason Green.

Words choked in Gerald's throat. He tried to call out but no sound would come. He stood paralyzed.

Sir Mason put a finger to his lips. He traversed the distance between them without making a sound and raised the tip of his sword to Gerald's throat. Gerald felt the steel against his skin.

Green motioned for Gerald to sit on the bed. Gerald was in a daze. He half stumbled to the mattress, the cool sheets registering against the backs of his legs. The man crossed to the door, opened it an inch, and peered through the gap, then bolted it shut.

The neatly clipped silver hair and the military bearing were the same as Gerald remembered. But as Green turned and crossed the room, his eyes seemed to bore right into Gerald's brain, right between his eyebrows.

"You know about the other caskets," Green declared.

Gerald struggled to reply. "You can have them."

"Oh, I intend to, Gerald," he said, his voice light and at ease. "But you should be looking for them as well."

"Why? Why should I care about them?"

Green laughed. "I would have thought your experience

with the first casket might have piqued your curiosity."

Gerald thought back to the diamond casket and the vision he'd endured when Green placed the golden rod across his forehead. That ancient relic obviously had some tremendous power behind it.

"Don't you want to know?" Green's voice taunted him. "Don't you want to know everything?"

Gerald's eyes shifted to the sword in Sir Mason's hand. It was identical to the one that had so nearly taken Sam's life at Beaconsfield. Gerald's heart was pounding. Breathing was becoming difficult.

"I am here, Mr. Wilkins," Green said, "to warn you."

"Warn me about what?"

"About the other caskets, of course. If you thought the contents of the diamond casket were bad for your health, imagine what might be in the other two."

"But—"

"And imagine if those caskets got into the wrong hands. Why, there could be a terrible tragedy." Green's eyes narrowed. "Or three."

Without warning, the man leaped at Gerald and grabbed him by the throat. He jabbed the tip of the sword into Gerald's chest.

"It's time you got some skin in the game, son." With a grunt, Green thrust the sword home, deep into Gerald's ribcage.

Gerald gagged; saliva blocked his throat. He felt like he was about to drown. He launched himself upright, finally waking. His T-shirt was soaked in sweat. He ran his hands down his chest. There was no sword, no wound. He stared at the curtains that were billowing freely in the breeze. He crossed to them, closed the window, and collapsed back onto the bed.

What had just happened?

A dream?

Or something else?

In his mind's eye he could still see the apparition of Sir Mason Green, gloating.

The interior of the Archer Airbus A380 Flying Palace had been featured in design magazines from Milan to New York. But the lavish descriptions in those publications didn't come close to Sam's response when he climbed on board.

"This. Is. Fan. *Tastic!*"

Gerald led a tour of the aircraft. Sam and Ruby's jaws dropped lower and lower the farther they ventured.

"There's a bedroom suite at the back, and once you're past the dining room and the bar area there's this great cinema setup. There's something like ten thousand movies and a stack of video games," Gerald rattled off. "Then upstairs there's an office with satellite access, a gym with a hot tub, and a library. It's pretty cool, actually."

"Pretty cool?" Sam said. "It's amazing. And all this is yours?"

"I guess so," Gerald said, slightly embarrassed. "I'm not really used to it yet."

"Keep it that way," Sam said. "You don't ever want to take this for granted."

Mr. Fry appeared behind them, carrying a clipboard and checking items off a list.

"Careful," Sam said. "Here comes the karate kid."

Fry marched past them. "Monthly meeting of Mensa, is it?" he said, without looking up.

"What's he on about?" Sam asked. Gerald shrugged.

"The captain wants a word with you before takeoff," Fry said over his shoulder.

Gerald watched the butler as he headed toward the galley at the rear of the aircraft. "At least he's not flying the plane," he said.

A tall woman in a blue pilot's uniform stepped from the cockpit.

"Hello, Mr. Wilkins," she said, shaking Gerald's hand. "I'm Captain Baulch. But please call me Laura. We're waiting on a final clearance from the tower, then we can get underway. I expect you and your friends are aware of the usual safety warnings."

They all nodded.

"Good," the captain said. "So you don't have to hear

any of that rubbish from me. I think all you really need are these." She opened a cupboard and pulled out three large plastic trays and three bicycle helmets.

Gerald took a helmet in one hand and a tray in the other. "What are these for?"

Captain Baulch looked surprised. "You've never been plane sledding?"

Fifteen minutes later, the Airbus was at the start of the runway, engines thrumming. The captain called back from the flight deck. "Ready?"

"Yep!" Gerald, Sam, and Ruby chorused. They each sat on a plastic tray on the floor at the front of the jet, helmets on.

"Righto. Hold on!" Captain Baulch pushed forward on the flight controller, and the jet accelerated down the runway.

Gerald gripped the sides of his tray and he glanced at his friends. Ruby gave him a quick thumbs-up. Sam was grinning insanely. The plane gathered speed and they started sliding. With a final surge of acceleration, the nose lifted from the ground and the three of them shot along the floor.

Gerald gave a whoop as his tray skidded past clusters of armchairs. He clung to the tray as he hurtled down the length of the plane. He was heading straight toward a couch in the bar area and he leaned hard to his left. He flashed past, buffeting against the leather cushions and

56

bouncing back into the middle of the cabin. The jet was now banking to the right. Gerald found himself veering wildly. He looked up in time to see he was on a collision course with a long dining table. He desperately hauled over to his right but his momentum was too strong. The jet's trajectory was pulling him straight toward the heavy metal and glass furniture. At the last second Gerald ducked like a startled tortoise, and the top of his helmet skimmed the underside of the table as he shot down its length and out the other end. He passed a startled Mr. Fry, who was still strapped into his seat near the galley, flicking through a copy of *Oi!* magazine. Gerald was heading at speed toward the closed doors of the bedroom suite. It was time to abandon ship. He dropped heavily onto his side and tumbled off the tray moments before it clattered into the wall at the end of the main cabin. Gerald came to a stop on his backside, facing the way he'd come, a dazed expression on his face. He was still buzzing from the ride when, with a high-pitched squeal, Ruby ploughed right into him. Her tray skimmed off the top of his helmet as she spun out of control and landed in his lap.

"That was awesome!"

Gerald untangled himself from a knot of arms and legs then looked around. "Where's Sam?"

"Dunno. I heard him crash."

They found Sam flat on his back halfway up the stairs

to the upper deck. His head was on the bottom step, his feet above him.

"Well, that was interesting," he mumbled.

Ruby grabbed her brother by the shoulders and pulled him upright. "How good was that!" she said. She turned to Gerald. "Can we do it again?"

"I don't think the captain's going to go around again just for us," Sam said.

A look of confidence spread across Gerald's face. "Why not?" he said. "It's my plane." He strode to the cockpit.

Fifteen minutes later Gerald, Sam, and Ruby were lined up on the trays, ready for another takeoff.

This time the three of them made it to the end of the main cabin in a jumble of giggles and laughter. Mr. Fry appeared and Gerald, Sam, and Ruby sheepishly handed over their trays and helmets.

"Lunch will be served in two hours," he said, as if announcing a death in the family. "Unless you decide to take a detour via Disneyland, in which case it will be much later." He trudged back to the galley.

"Is Mr. Fry married?" Ruby asked.

"Don't think so," Gerald said. "Can't imagine anyone volunteering to spend any time with him."

"I think we should find him a girlfriend," she said. "To cheer him up."

Sam smirked. "And who's going to cheer her up?"

They wandered into the cinema room, piling their arms with chips and soft drinks from the bar.

They each dived into a leather lounge.

"How long's it take to get to Delhi anyway?" Sam asked, clicking a remote at the enormous flat-screen television. A program guide flashed up.

"About nine hours, I think," Ruby said.

"Time to catch a couple of movies, then," Sam said. "What do you feel like? Action? Comedy?" Images filled the screen as he scrolled through the offerings from the plane's library of films. "Look. Here's that new war film, *Grunt Once Then Die*. What do you think?"

Ruby tore open a chip packet and stuffed a few into her mouth. "Yuck! Too violent. Isn't there something where people's heads don't get blown off? How about that new vampire movie?"

Sam reached over and took some chips from his sister. "Oh sure, killing soldiers in a war zone is offensive. But sink your teeth into someone's jugular and suck out their entire blood supply? That's the height of romance and sophistication."

Gerald sipped on his drink and grinned. He loved it when Sam and Ruby got going.

"What do you think, Gerald?" Sam said. "Gritty war movie or soppy love story? Gore-fest or bore-fest? Your choice."

"How about a horror movie," Gerald said. "That way you get a bit of both."

Ruby snatched the remote from her brother. "You're always compromising, Gerald. You need to be more asser-tive." She stabbed at the buttons, and the screen flashed with a rapid series of movie images. "How did you get to be so indecisive anyway?"

Ruby stopped flicking at an extreme close-up of a woman's face. Every pore, pimple, and facial hair stood out in massive high definition.

"Yow!" Sam cried. "That's hideous. What slasher movie is this?"

Gerald's eyes popped. "That's my mother."

The face on the screen pulled back and Gerald's mother, Vi Wilkins, settled into an armchair in a fashionably deco-rated lounge.

"Your mother?" Sam said. "Why's she starring in a horror film?"

Ruby leaned across and clipped her brother over the back of his head. "It's a videophone, moron," she hissed.

"Hello, Gerald? Gerald? Can you hear me?" Vi's voice filled the cabin. "I can see you but I can't hear you. Can you see me, my darling boy?"

Gerald sat open-mouthed but mute. He'd spoken a few times to his parents on the phone since they'd abandoned him at the start of the summer. But he hadn't seen them. The weeks spent cruising the Caribbean on the Archer yacht had turned his mother's skin a glossy brown, and her helmet of blond hair had been coiffed into a creation from a fashion magazine. But there was something else. Gerald couldn't pick it. Then it dawned on him.

"Mum. Have you had Botox?"

Vi lifted her chin and pulled back the corners of her mouth in an attempt at a smile. Her face barely moved.

"It makes me look twenty years younger, don't you think?"

Gerald thought it made her head look like a waxed apple.

"Um, yeah. It looks . . . really natural," Gerald said, mortified. "Where are you?"

"We're at the Archer compound on Martha's Vineyard, darling. The heat in the Caribbean was a little too much for your father, even with the outdoor air-conditioning. I thought he might be more comfortable here."

Sam leaned across and whispered in Gerald's ear, "You wouldn't want to risk melting." Gerald tried not to giggle.

"What's at this Martha's place?" he asked.

"This Martha's place?" His mother rocked back and laughed. "Gerald, you are too, *too* gauche, my darling. Martha's Vineyard—all the right people come here. To be anywhere else in the summer would be terribly infra dig. There's the Lodges and the Cabots, of course. And the Rockefellers and the Carnegies. Geraldine has a simply enormous place here, right on the water—but of course it's your place now, sweetie. Everyone's dying to meet you. We'll come back next summer and stay a few months, I think. The weather here is much kinder to your father."

Vi took an almighty breath and beamed into the videophone. "Who are your friends, dear?" she asked. "Introduce me."

Gerald was glad for the break in his mother's monologue. "This is Sam and Ruby Valentine. They're coming to India with me."

"So glad you're making friends and keeping busy. Hello there," Vi said, again attempting a smile.

Ruby and Sam waved at the screen. "Hi," they chorused.

"You take good care of my Gerald, won't you," Vi said. "He's my little soldier."

Sam bit his bottom lip. "He's a very brave little soldier, Mrs. Wilkins. Don't worry. He'll be fine with us."

Gerald glanced sideways at Sam, who had wisely leaned out of striking range.

"Anyway, Gerald. I was just calling to say hello," Vi said. "We're off to the Cabots' for brunch in a few hours, and I have to put my face on."

Sam opened his mouth to say something, but a death stare from Ruby shut him down.

Before his mother could end the call, Gerald spoke up. "Mum, did you hear about Sir Mason Green? And our family tree?"

Vi sucked on her lips. "Mr. Prisk told me about it. What a frightful chap Sir Mason turned out to be. A Knight Grand Cross of the Order of Saint Michael and Saint George! There was a time when that stood for something. Why he'd be interested in us is beyond me. Very disappointing. And speaking of disappointing, I'm none too impressed with our Mr. Prisk at the moment either."

Gerald blinked. His mother was being particularly random. "What's wrong with Mr. Prisk?"

Vi sniffed. "The enormous pile of correspondence and paperwork he expects me to go through. It eats right into my day."

Gerald couldn't hide the smile spreading across his face. "That sounds terrible."

"And here's a surprise for you. All this talk about family and I almost forgot. Have a look at this." Vi hauled herself out of the armchair and bent down to poke through a document box on the floor. Sam had to hold back a laugh as the videophone's automatic camera adjusted to give a close-up of Vi's backside.

She sat down with an envelope in her hand.

"What's that?" Gerald asked.

"It's a letter from Great-Aunt Geraldine."

There was a hollow silence in the aircraft as this announcement bounced off the walls.

"But," Gerald began, "she's dead."

Vi emitted a shrill laugh. "Of course she's dead, Gerald. I'd hardly be kicking back in magnificent luxury on Martha's Vineyard if the old bat was still alive!"

Gerald's mother had embraced the billionaire lifestyle with more gusto than he had. She pulled a sheet of paper from the envelope. Gerald noticed a splodge of red wax on the back.

"It's dated a week before she died," Vi said. "Written but not mailed. There's the usual blather about how you are and whether you're growing into a trustworthy young man. I swear, she was obsessed about your honesty. She seemed to think we hadn't brought you up right."

"I can imagine," Gerald mumbled.

Vi plowed on. "Here it is. There's some fluff about how important family is—blah, blah, love, respect, blither, blather—and then she says: 'If Gerald ever has any questions about any of his family history, then he should seek out the seven sisters.'"

"Seven sisters?"

Vi nodded. "No idea what she's on about. No one in the family has seven sisters. Maybe on your father's side? But then his lot didn't provide us with our little windfall, did they? So they're hardly worth worrying about."

Gerald sat back into the lounge. Seven sisters? What did Geraldine mean? His thoughts were interrupted by the sight of his mother blowing him a kiss.

"Lovely chatting with you, my darling, but must away. So much to do. Ta ta for now."

Vi's face dissolved into static, then *The Bride of Frankenstein* started playing.

Ruby plopped down on the couch next to Gerald.

"So, how did you get to be so indecisive?"

Gerald shook his head. "She casts a big shadow, doesn't she?" He took a deep breath and sighed. "I thought she might be more concerned about Green and our family tree, though."

"Gerald, you've got to stop worrying about Mason Green," Ruby said, giving his knee a pat. "None of those paths on the map in Green's room went anywhere near India. There's nothing to worry about."

Gerald picked up the remote and switched to a music video.

"You're right," he said. "There's more than a billion people in India. What are the odds of running into Mason Green there?"

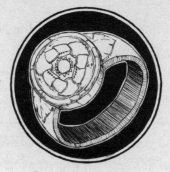

CHAPTER FIVE

An old black-and-white detective movie flickered on the big screen. Sam and Ruby were sprawled across the lounge, only half watching it. Gerald sat on the floor, putting the finishing touches to a sketch of Mr. Fry dressed as a French maid, complete with frilly apron and a long-handled feather duster.

"You're very good, you know," Ruby laughed. "You should frame that one."

Gerald studied the drawing. "Don't think Mr. Fry is going to make an offer for it, somehow." He flipped the page and started a sketch of the Valentine twins. "So," he said, his pencil darting across the paper, "I wonder what's in the other caskets."

Ruby glanced at him. "I thought we weren't going to

worry about Mason Green anymore."

"I'm not, I'm not," Gerald said. "I was just thinking about the Green Room and that stuff on his desk. That's all."

"Hmm." She didn't sound convinced.

Gerald glanced up at the screen. "These old detective movies are hilarious," he said. "Everyone talks a million miles an hour."

A man in a trench coat stood in an office, barking orders at a secretary.

"Maybe I should start treating Ruby like that," Sam said.

"Only if you enjoy major blood loss," she said. "What's he doing now?"

The man on the screen had picked up a notepad from a desk and was shading a blank page with a pencil. After a few strokes, a telephone number appeared.

"That's clever," Sam said. "The guy they're chasing must have written the number down and torn off the top page—there's the impression on the one underneath."

Gerald stopped drawing.

"What's the matter?" Ruby asked.

He dropped his sketchpad and dragged his backpack from under the couch. He fished inside and found the three envelopes he'd taken from Green's desk.

He laid them flat on the cabin floor.

"Surely you don't think . . ." Ruby said.

Gerald shrugged. "Worth a try. Green could have written something on top of these."

He took his pencil case and found a piece of drawing charcoal. He laid it flat on the envelope marked FAMILY TREE and rubbed across the surface—leaving a plain black smear.

"Nope," he muttered, then picked up the envelope marked FRATERNITY. He repeated the shading and this time the faint outline of some letters appeared.

"Hello," Gerald said. "Look at this."

Sam leaned in. "'Mama la ram,'" he read.

"French, maybe?" Ruby suggested.

"For what?" Sam said. "A confused male sheep?"

Ruby screwed up her face at him.

Gerald shaded across the final envelope with the random string of symbols on it but nothing showed up.

"What do those symbols mean?" Ruby said.

"No idea," Gerald said. "So we've got some gibberish and a ram called Mama."

Ruby picked up the remote and changed channels. "Can't believe everything you see in the movies."

Mr. Fry announced that they would land in forty minutes, then disappeared back to the galley.

"I'm looking forward to this," Gerald said, tucking his pad and pencils into his backpack.

"The whole country's meant to be amazing," Ruby said. She thumbed through a travel guide, full of photographs of ancient cities and temples. "The south was hit by the tsunami a few years ago but it looks like everything's back to normal. Can you believe it? A *billion* people."

"Do you think Alisha will be at the airport?" Sam asked.

"And from today, a billion people plus one moron," Ruby said, shaking her head. "Sam, get over it, will you? Alisha Gupta won't even remember your name. You are but roadkill on her motorway through life. You are a pimple on the bottom of—"

"Go easy," Gerald interrupted. "Let a man have his dream." Sam gazed out a window into the midnight blackness somewhere over the Himalayas.

"Pfft," said Ruby. She leafed through the travel guide. "Hey, here's something that could be handy," she said to Gerald.

"What's that?"

"It says here that ancient mystics used to recite a secret mantra to bring the dead back to life." She looked across to Sam as he gazed love-struck through the window. "Wonder if it works on the brain-dead as well?"

The jet made a rattling landing and taxied to a terminal building, taking a space by an air bridge.

They were greeted by an airport official who led them into a sparsely furnished VIP lounge. At one end of the room a customs officer in an ill-fitting shirt sat behind a bare wooden table. The officer inspected their passports and stamped each in turn. Mr. Fry had everyone's luggage on a cart and they followed him to the doorway.

"Keep close," he said to Gerald, Sam, and Ruby. "I'd hate to lose you in the crowd."

Sam glanced at his watch. "It's past midnight," he yawned. "Who's going to be out this late?"

The doors slid apart and a wave of hot air rolled through the gap. It curled up and over the air-conditioned coolness and dumped on top of them, squeezing gasps of surprise from their lungs. They stepped into chaos. There were people everywhere—a jostling mass of bodies at the doorstep to a new world.

The temperature was incredible. Even beyond midnight, it must have been ninety-five degrees or more. Heat radiated up from the ground, chewing through the soles of their shoes. It was impossible to tell where the warmth of the night ended and the heat of the crowd began.

Gerald stood in awe. Hundreds of people filled the area outside the airport building. There were people arriving and leaving, taxis and cars delivering and collecting, bags being dumped and carted. The queue at the taxi rank snaked across the concourse.

"What do we do now?" Ruby asked.

"We're supposed to be met by Archer Corporation's

in-country agent," Mr. Fry said, a little testily. "He ought to be here to take us to the Gupta compound."

In the crush of activity that surrounded them there was no sign of any waiting driver.

"Do you know what the agent looks like?" Gerald asked.

"I do," Mr. Fry said. "I believe you've met him."

"We've met him?" Sam said.

"Yes. It's Mr. Hoskins. From the bookstore in Glastonbury."

Gerald was stunned. They hadn't seen Mr. Hoskins since before the clash with Mason Green in the chamber under Beaconsfield. He'd been very helpful in their quest to find the diamond casket but left town before they'd had a chance to thank him. The news that Mr. Hoskins was Archer Corporation's agent in India was almost as surprising as the discovery that he was Mrs. Rutherford's brother. For while Mrs. Rutherford was gentle, kind, and thoughtful, Mr. Hoskins was—

"What's that grumpy old fart doing here?" Sam asked, neatly filling in Gerald's thoughts.

"He said he was an old friend of the family," Gerald said. "But I had no idea he worked for the company."

"If he's spending time out here, that'd explain his tan," Ruby said. "Can you get sunburned at night? This heat!"

They waited. But there was no sign of Mr. Hoskins.

Gerald scanned the crowd. He spotted a lone figure

standing by a light pole, maybe twenty yards away. He noticed that with all the coming and going this person hadn't moved, a constant in the changing tide of faces. In spite of the heat, the person was dressed entirely in black: trousers, long-sleeved shirt untucked, and a loosely wrapped headscarf. For a split second Gerald imagined it was the thin man back from the dead to torment them. He shuddered. The memory of that vile creature still haunted him: the sneer, the remorseless brutality, the rank odor of bleach that hung over him like his own personal nuclear cloud. Sir Mason Green had said his hired thug was obsessive about germs and thought humanity was infested with bacteria. This made him a poor dinner companion but a very effective killer.

But the figure beneath the lamppost couldn't be the thin man. The thin man was painfully pale. A narrow gap in the headscarf revealed a flash of nut-brown skin and piercing dark eyes.

Eyes that were locked on Gerald.

Gerald nudged Ruby. "Do you see that guy over there?" he said, not shifting his gaze from those hypnotic eyes.

Ruby looked up. "Yeah. What about him?"

"What did Mr. Prisk say? About kidnappers?"

Ruby moved her head to get a better view of the figure in the lamplight. "Whoever it is, there's a lot of interest in you."

Gerald shuffled to his feet and stood behind Sam. The eyes traced every movement.

"Not being paranoid, are you?" Sam asked.

"No. But I wish Mr. Hoskins would hurry up."

The black-clad figure remained motionless, staring. Gerald could feel the eyes drilling into him.

"This is starting to creep me out," he muttered.

A piercing blast split the air: a car horn's shrill rendition of "*La Cucaracha*." They spun around. An iridescent yellow armored vehicle bore down on them like a runaway tractor. It mounted the curb with a howl of brakes and rocked on its springs. A second later a head emerged through the sunroof.

"What took you lot so long? I've been waiting for ages."

"Mr. Hoskins!" Gerald said, with some relief.

"So much for being discreet," Ruby said as the rotund body of Mr. Hoskins climbed down from the enormous vehicle.

Gerald glanced toward the lamppost. The figure in black had disappeared.

Gerald, Sam, and Ruby piled into the back of the car and soaked in the cool air inside. It took Sam two hands and all his strength to pull shut the armor-plated door, which closed with a resounding clunk. Mr. Hoskins and another man loaded the luggage into a second vehicle. The driver's door opened and Mr. Hoskins clambered in.

"Where's Mr. Fry?" Ruby asked.

"He's going to follow in the other car," Mr. Hoskins said. "I thought you lot could use a break—misery guts that he is."

They pulled out into the traffic like an ocean liner leaving port and joined a line of vehicles heading toward the city. Mr. Hoskins leaned on the horn and unleashed a musical tirade as he changed lanes.

"Mr. Hoskins," Gerald said.

"Yeah?"

"What type of car is this?"

"This, young Gerald, is a Conquest Knight XV—the foremost urban assault vehicle on the market."

"I see." Gerald paused. "Are there many bright yellow Conquest Knight XVs in Delhi?"

"Reckon this'd be the only one."

"I see."

There was an uncomfortable silence.

"Got a problem with the transport, sunshine?"

Gerald shook his head. "No. No. It's fine. Really comfy. But Mr. Prisk said we should be careful and, um . . . discreet."

Mr. Hoskins snorted. "That uptight pencil pusher needs to get into the real world." Another burst of "*La Cucaracha*" blared into the night. "You can be discreet or you can get things done. Take your pick."

The Knight ploughed through the traffic, a tangle of cars, scooters, trucks, motorcycles, and autorickshaws. Even though it was close to one o'clock in the morning, the streets were crawling with people.

"Is it always this busy?" Ruby asked, her nose pressed against the tinted window. A motorbike with a family of five on the back zipped past them.

"One thing you'll find here," Mr. Hoskins said, lurching into the next lane, "is you're never too far from the next person."

Gerald leaned between the front seats and gazed through the windshield. "How come you never told me you worked for Archer Corporation?"

"You never asked," Hoskins replied. "Don't find out stuff unless you ask."

Gerald wondered what he had to do to get a straight answer from some people. Mr. Hoskins in particular was about as opaque as they came.

Then Gerald had a sudden flash of inspiration. "All right," he said. "Do you remember at Great-Aunt Geraldine's funeral? You said she never came to visit me in Australia because she had to protect something. I'm asking you now: What was it that she was protecting?"

Mr. Hoskins popped a peppermint into his mouth and chewed.

"I can't tell you that," he said.

"But you just said you don't find out things unless you ask!"

Hoskins continued chewing on his mint. "Well, you

can't believe everything you're told, neither. And that's advice you can take to the bank."

Gerald flopped back between Sam and Ruby. Why did Hoskins insist on speaking in riddles?

Then Gerald had a thought. If Mr. Hoskins wasn't going to be any help, maybe someone else might. "Do you know if any of my relatives have seven daughters?" he asked.

Hoskins adjusted the rearview mirror and gazed into the backseat.

"Seven daughters?"

"That's right. Geraldine mentioned them in a letter to my mum."

Hoskins stared unblinking into the mirror.

"No," he said at last. "Never heard of them."

Gerald held Hoskins's gaze for a few seconds, then turned his head to look out the window. For some reason, Gerald thought, Mr. Hoskins didn't seem to trust him.

The fatigue from the long flight kicked in and Gerald, cocooned in the plush comfort of the Knight XV's leather seats, drifted off to sleep. At one stage he had a vague sense of the vehicle slowing and of voices outside, but he was so shrouded in weariness that it all just washed over him. Then there was a blur of movement as he floated out into the heat of the night. Was he walking? Or dreaming? He could feel his feet plopping down onto the ground, one sluggishly following the other. Was there a whisper in his ear? Then it was cool again. And he was lying on smooth sheets. Head on a pillow of impossible softness. Horizontal bliss. He slept.

Sir Mason Green said nothing when he visited that night. He stood by the bed, silent.

This time, Gerald was ready. He knew it was a dream.

He opened one eye and saw that his imaginary Sir Mason was staring at a piece of paper in his hands. After a minute, he let it slip from his fingers. As it wafted to the floor, Gerald saw it was a photograph of himself, Sam, and Ruby. They were on a picnic blanket under a tree at Avonleigh, laughing. Their faces reflected the joys of summer. All looked serene. Apart from the hole burned between Gerald's eyebrows, and the slash marks across Sam and Ruby's hearts.

Gerald flipped his pillow and welcomed the cool side to his cheek, then settled to his slumber.

He woke to the sound of water. He propped onto his elbows and found that he was in a vast four-poster bed, complete with a canopy trimmed with maroon and gold brocade. If Aladdin's cave had an adjoining bedroom suite, he seemed to have woken up in it. Silk sheets swept across his waist. He leaned back on an elaborately carved headboard festooned with pillows of all shapes. The walls were hung with tapestries, and block-printed fabrics ballooned like parachutes across the ceiling. Cushions were stacked in the corners of the room and the stone floor was covered with an enormous red, gold, and white woven rug.

"Far out," Gerald breathed. Even after living in a billionaire's mansion for the past month, he was stunned by this step up in luxury and style. He looked down and discovered he was still dressed in his clothes. He swung his feet onto the rug and enjoyed the sensation of silk beneath his toes. The sound of running water again attracted his attention. He crossed to a set of windows, pulled back the shutters and gasped. Outside, a stream of crystal-clear water bubbled past the window, tumbling over boulders and winding through an expanse of lawn down to a pond beneath a copse of trees. Butterflies danced in the morning sunlight. If he was still in the middle of a bustling city, this must be some sort of oasis.

"It's all fake, of course."

Gerald turned around. Ruby was leaning against the door. She was wearing oversize cotton pajamas and her arms were folded across her chest. "The water's chlorinated from a pump house," she said. "The rocks are polished concrete. The pond's tiled, for pity's sake. I think the trees are real but that's about it."

"What's got you in such a good mood?"

Gerald changed his clothes and followed Ruby into

a spacious lounge. Two other bedrooms opened onto the space, which appeared to be the centerpiece of a large colonial villa. Glass walls on two sides overlooked the enormous water feature and the gardens that seemed to go on forever. A covered walkway led across the lawn to a much larger building. Sam lay slumped in a pile of cushions, eating a croissant.

"Grab one," he said in a spray of pastry flakes. "They're delicious."

Gerald took a pastry and a glass of lime juice from the sideboard and fell back onto a sofa.

"What've you found to be grumpy about?" Gerald asked Ruby.

"She's just looking forward to seeing Alisha again," Sam said with a smirk.

"You can go jump," Ruby said to her brother. She took a bite from an apple and turned to Gerald. "You saw how she treated me last time. She was a complete princess, making out she was so much better than me. And now look at this place."

"What about it?"

"Don't you see? It's all so fake. Like some theme park for the rich and tasteless. I wish we hadn't come."

"Do you remember how Alisha made fun of Ruby's shoes?" Sam laughed. "And ignored her after we got the diamond back? That was hilar—"

Ruby cut her brother short. "I thought you were in the process of jumping, melon head. Look, Alisha Gupta represents everything I hate. She's conceited, she's spoiled, and she'll bat her pretty eyelids at you boys all day long to get her way."

"Um, Ruby—" Gerald said.

"No, let me finish. She's the type who uses her looks to compensate for yawning holes in her personality. And it's something boys never see through—"

"Ruby."

She counted on her fingers. "She's bland, she's boring, she's opinionated—"

"Ruby!" Gerald hissed.

"What?"

"She's . . . behind you."

A stillness hit the villa. Ruby's eyes closed and stayed that way. Alisha Gupta stood in the doorway, and for a moment the only noise was the air conditioning kicking up a notch to cope with the inflow of warm air from outside. Alisha stepped into the room as if she was walking onstage. She was dressed in a traditional robe of golden silk, her long dark hair draped loose across her shoulders. She crossed to Gerald, leaned down, and pecked him lightly on the cheek.

"Gerald," she said with delight. "It's so good to see you." Her voice rang like morning birdsong. "And Sam." She skipped over and grabbed Sam by the hands and squeezed, pulling him to his feet. "You're looking so well after your adventure. It's lovely to have you here." Sam stood there with a look of dumb rapture on his face. Then Alisha's eyes fell on Ruby, who was still dressed in her rumpled pajamas, her hair piled on the top of her head like a collapsed haystack. "And it's nice to have you here too, Rosie."

Ruby ran her hands through her hair, trying to straighten out the mess. "Um . . . it's Ruby, actually."

"Oh, that's right. *Terribly* sorry."

"Look, about what I just said—"

Alisha arched an eyebrow. "I'm sorry? Were you speaking? I hope I didn't interrupt. Because that would be unforgivably rude." She looked Ruby square in the eye. "Perhaps you might say it again."

Before Ruby could mumble a response Alisha swept an arm into Sam's and led him to the door. "Come along to the main house," she said, casting a glance back over her shoulder at Gerald. "Father wants to say hello." Sam padded along happily, but Gerald hung back.

"I'll wait till Ruby's ready," he said. "We'll be there in a minute."

Alisha gave him a curious look, then left the room with Sam on her arm like a handbag. The moment the door closed behind them Ruby was at Gerald. "See how she treats me? Like I'm some lower form of life."

Gerald tried to smother a snigger. "You've got to admit,

you said some nasty things. She's bound to bite back."

Ruby stamped off to her bedroom. "Why did she invite me if she hates me so much?" she called back through the door.

"Beats me," Gerald said. "The invitation came from her dad, anyway."

Ruby emerged wearing a T-shirt, shorts, and sneakers, her hair pulled back in a ponytail. "Maybe when she's done pulling the wings off all these butterflies we might get to know each other better."

Gerald shook his head. "You love a grudge, don't you?"

"Grudges," Ruby said flatly, "have made the world what it is today."

They found Sam and Alisha inside the main building, in a wood-paneled library overlooking a patio and an enormous swimming pool. Sam was inspecting the contents of a display case. He looked up as they entered the room.

"Gerald, come see this," he said.

The wooden cabinet held a collection of coins and carvings, illuminated by display lamps. On the middle shelf was an array of gemstones: glittering rocks in almost every color imaginable. In the middle of them all sat an enormous diamond. Gerald gasped at seeing the Noor Jehan again. The last time he'd seen it was when they'd returned it to Mr. Gupta at Beaconsfield. It sparkled brilliantly under the lamps—*Noor Jehan*: the light of the world.

"You can hold it if you want." Alisha stood up from a silk-draped couch and walked across. She unlatched the glass door to the cabinet and tossed the diamond to Gerald.

He gasped at the sight of the priceless gem sailing through the air toward him. He juggled the catch, wrapping his fingers around the stone, and stared down at the most valuable diamond in the world.

"Are you sure we should be playing with this thing?" Gerald said, not taking his eyes off the gem in his hands.

Alisha let out a trilling laugh. "There's more security around this compound than at the White House. That diamond isn't going anywhere."

Gerald felt a tingling in his fingers. A dull glow seemed to come from the heart of the gem. And then Gerald yelped in surprise as the Noor Jehan popped out of his grasp like a wet cake of soap. Alisha caught it neatly with one hand and placed it back in its stand in the display cabinet.

"What's the matter?" Ruby asked Gerald. He was wriggling his fingers in the air.

"That thing just gave me a jolt," he said. "Like it was electric."

A jovial voice boomed across the room.

"It does seem to come to life sometimes, doesn't it?"

Gerald looked up to see Mr. Gupta walking toward them with hands outstretched and a smile on his round face. "Greetings, Gerald. I'm so glad you and your friends have come for a visit. I trust Alisha has made you welcome."

Gerald's eyes darted to Ruby. She was gnawing on her bottom lip. "Just like home, Mr. Gupta," he said.

The man clamped an arm around Gerald's shoulders and squeezed. "Your timing is perfect. Now I can thank you properly for recovering my diamond. It's been in the family for more than fifteen hundred years—it's the center-piece of my collection. It would be very poor form for me to lose it."

"It was very kind of you to invite us, Mr. Gupta," Ruby said in her politest voice. She avoided Alisha's eyes.

Mr. Gupta let out a raucous laugh. "The least I could do—seeing as you were in the neighborhood."

He tapped a fingernail on the glass of the display case. "All these bits and pieces are from the Gupta empire. At that time, our ancestors controlled almost all of India. Sadly, those days are long gone. But a few trinkets have been handed down through the centuries."

Gerald looked around at the opulent furnishings and the palatial scale of the house. He guessed that more than a few trinkets had found their way into Mr. Gupta's care.

A servant dressed in a long white robe appeared bearing a tray of iced drinks. Mr. Gupta ushered Gerald and the twins to a suite of armchairs. Alisha made a point of sitting very close to Sam. But she didn't take her eyes off Gerald.

"It's very hot in Delhi this time of year," Mr. Gupta

said, taking a sip from a frosted glass. "The monsoon rains that usually cool us down are late. So, if it fits in with your plans, I suggest you spend only a few days here before escaping the heat. My company sponsors a tiger reserve in Kerala, and if you like, you can have a week on a houseboat there, cruising the rivers. I think you'll find it fascinating."

"That sounds great," Ruby said. "I've always wanted to see a tiger in the wild."

Alisha leaned forward and rested a hand on Ruby's knee. "Let's hope they're not very good swimmers. We'd hate to have an accident."

There was an awkward silence. Ruby pressed her lips together, restraining herself. Then Alisha turned back to Sam and unleashed a smile that would light a small village, revealing dimpled cheeks and two rows of orthodontically perfected teeth. "First, I want to give you a taste of Delhi. A traditional market. Let's go this evening."

Sam slipped back into his stupor and nodded readily. Gerald wasn't sure, but he thought he could hear Ruby's teeth grinding.

"I've told you, Alisha, I'm not happy with this market idea," Mr. Gupta said. "There are too many dangers."

Gerald sensed some tension. "If it's a problem," he said, "we can do something else."

Alisha stood up. "There is no problem, Gerald. Other than my father wanting to keep me behind glass like the rest of his precious collection." She glared at Mr. Gupta, then sailed out of the room.

Mr. Gupta's face darkened. He excused himself and went after his daughter.

Ruby grinned to herself. "Trouble in paradise?" she murmured.

The servant returned with a fresh tray of drinks. Ruby selected a tall glass filled with sweet lime juice.

"Will there be anything else, miss?"

"Not for me, thank you. But my brother could use some smelling salts." The servant gave her a startled look and hurried off.

"Do you see what I mean?" Ruby said to Gerald. "Alisha bats her eyelids and Sam rolls over and wants his tummy tickled. It's pathetic."

Gerald looked at the expression that lingered on Sam's face. "He would make a good puppy."

"One that needs fixing," Ruby said. "Where do you think Mr. Fry is? Or Mr. Hoskins?"

Before Gerald could answer, Mr. Gupta's servant reappeared and told them they had a phone call. He pointed a remote control at a screen mounted on a wall. After a second of static, Professor McElderry from the British Museum morphed into focus.

Gerald slapped Sam on the shoulder. "Come on," he said. "Wake-up time."

McElderry's red beard almost filled the screen. He cleared his throat with a moist hack and beamed at the three of them over his reading glasses.

"Hello, you lot," he said. "Not melted into a puddle yet?"

"Morning, Professor," Gerald said. "Early start for you, isn't it?"

"Birds and worms, Gerald. Birds and worms. Look, we've had a bit of a breakthrough. Naturally, when I say 'we,' I mean 'I,' but that's for the history books to record."

Ruby snickered and whispered to Gerald out of the side of her mouth, "Bit full of himself."

"Miss Valentine," the professor rumbled. "This is a video call. If you can manage to control yourself, I'll continue."

Ruby mouthed a silent "Sorry," and retreated to a chair by the desk.

"I've done some research on your family tree, Gerald—on your mother's side. Do you remember the name Quintus Antonius? He was on the far side of the wall in the Green Room. It appears he was a consul in the court of the Roman emperor at the end of the fourth century. Seems he and the emperor, Theodosius, were very close."

"I'm related to the best mate of a Roman emperor?" Gerald said.

"Looks that way. Following Sir Mason's record of your heritage, I've managed to find some mention of your ancestors in our archive at the museum."

"Really?" Gerald said. "What?"

"Not much, I'm afraid. Quintus had three sons. Around AD 390, when the boys were all young men, they were summoned with their father before the emperor. He sent them on a mission. But I can't find any information about what it was. They left Rome one night and then . . . pffft."

"*Pffft?*" Sam said.

"They disappeared. Fell off the map. No record of them again," the professor said.

Gerald sighed. "So that's a dead end, then."

"That is," McElderry said, "no record until now."

"Pardon?"

McElderry exuded smugness. He picked up a notebook from his desk. "I managed to translate a section of the script that was carved into the rotunda under Beaconsfield. A quick call to a colleague at the Vatican Library confirmed it. Gerald, the person who built that Roman burial chamber was none other than Gaius Antonius."

There was a silence.

"Who's he?"

"The eldest son of Quintus Antonius, that's who," McElderry said.

Gerald went blank, but Ruby spoke. "So the person who built that chamber is directly related to Gerald?"

McElderry leaned back, beaming with triumph. "Precisely. But there's more to it. Think back to the map in

Green's study. Remember the blue line that traced the route of the diamond casket to Glastonbury? I wager that Gaius Antonius was the courier who brought it to Britain."

Gerald finally found the wit to speak. "What difference does all this make? That was sixteen hundred years ago."

McElderry pulled back a corner of his mouth. "Gerald, what do all good burial chambers need?"

"Um . . ."

"A body, of course!" the professor said. "And we . . . *I* . . . have found one. Right under the plinth that held up the diamond casket. Gaius is not too pretty after all these years but it's amazing what a box of bones can tell you, especially when they offer up something like this."

The professor dug in his waistcoat pocket, pulled out a tiny object, and held it up. It took a second for the auto-focus to adjust but when it did it drew gasps from everyone in Mr. Gupta's library. McElderry held a gold ring that bore the clear insignia of three forearms clasped at the elbows to form a triangle around a blazing sun.

"Your family seal goes all the way back to ancient Rome, Gerald," Professor McElderry said. "The Vatican Library was able to confirm that this emblem is from the Antonius family . . . your family, Gerald."

Gerald sat heavily on the arm of Ruby's chair. "I don't get it, Professor."

McElderry banged the table with his fist. "Think, boy! Three caskets. Three lines on the map. Three sons!"

Sam piped up. "Three bears. Three musketeers. Three blind mice."

The professor's brow furled into a knot. "You truly are the stupidest boy in the world," he growled. "I believe the three caskets were smuggled out of Rome by Gerald's ancestors and taken to the ends of the empire."

Ruby straightened in her chair. "The three arms must represent the bond of the three brothers."

"So what's the sun?" Gerald asked.

"Illumination, maybe?" Ruby said. "Or power?"

"Or a common purpose," the professor said. "Whatever it is, Sir Mason Green wants the contents of these caskets. He's got one and he sees Gerald as a key part to securing the others. You are the center of his plan."

An image filled Gerald's mind of a photograph pinned to a wall, a silver letter opener stuck into the throat and a hole between the eyes. He shivered.

"Okay, Green followed that blue line to Glastonbury," Gerald said. "And he found that golden rod. But the other two lines go to France and Egypt. That's nowhere near us in India. We're miles away from wherever Green might be, right?"

McElderry glanced across to his left. "Do you want to make an appearance now?" he said. Another head slid into frame.

"Inspector Parrott!" Ruby said in surprise.

The police inspector did not look pleased.

"I thought I better let you know the latest on the investigation," he said. "Unfortunately, we've had no success in finding Sir Mason Green."

"Now there's a surprise," Ruby mumbled.

"There have been unconfirmed sightings in Egypt but nothing concrete. However, we do have some news on another aspect of the case. Your report about Green's associate. This so-called thin man—"

Gerald and Sam sat bolt upright.

"Forensics have finished their investigation of a burned-out cable drum that was discovered in an orchard on the outskirts of Glastonbury—the one you said this thin man was caught up in."

"Yes?"

Parrott hesitated a second. "There were no human remains."

Gerald looked at Sam in disbelief. "You mean he survived and walked away? Impossible."

"Possible or not, I've taken the precaution of contacting the Interpol office in Delhi," Parrott said. "One of their criminal intelligence officers will be in touch, just to keep you in the loop. And to see that you're . . ." He paused, fumbling for the right word.

"That we're what?" Gerald asked.

"That you're . . . enjoying your holiday," the inspector said.

Ruby stared hard at the video screen. "Surely you don't

think he's going to hunt us down?"

The inspector glanced down. "Err, of course not. But there's no harm in being cautious. I understand you have your own security arrangements?"

Gerald blinked. "We do?"

"I think he's referring to Mr. Fry," Ruby said.

"Oh," Gerald said. "Him."

"We'll keep looking for this thin man," the inspector said, "but in the meantime, mind how you go."

"Mind how we go?" Sam spluttered. "The guy's a psycho."

The inspector fiddled with his cufflinks. "Then *really* mind how you go."

Gerald suddenly had a thought. "Professor, you've been looking at my family tree. Did you come across any of my relatives who had seven daughters?"

McElderry scratched his bristly chin. "There were a hell of a lot of people on that wall, Gerald, but no, I don't think so."

Before the professor could go on, the lights in the room cut out and the screen fizzled to a white spot in the middle, then went blank. A few seconds later the hum of generators came from outside and the lights blinked back on, but the videophone was dead. Mr. Gupta's butler rushed into the room, full of apologies for the blackout. "So frequent this time of year," he said.

Gerald stared at the blank screen. "I can't believe the thin man lived through that fire. He was right in the middle of it."

"Even if he did live, he'd be horribly injured," Ruby said. "There's no way he'd be able to find us."

Gerald shuddered at the memory. "What do you reckon, Sam?"

Gerald and Ruby both turned to Sam. He was gazing toward the library door.

"Has anyone seen Alisha?" he asked.

Ruby clenched her jaw. She tossed a small brown bottle to Gerald. He caught it in one hand.

"What's this?" he asked.

"The butler gave it to me," Ruby said. "Smelling salts. Feel free to pour it down his stupid throat." She stormed past Sam and back toward their villa.

Chapter Six

Gerald was starting to think Ruby was right about Alisha in one respect: She had an uncanny knack for getting her own way.

He was amazed how easily Alisha manipulated her father. She worked on him throughout the day, finally convincing him that a trip to the market was a good idea: a chance to show off the city's color and diversity. She also persuaded him to stay at home. But Mr. Gupta did win one concession.

"You must have supervision," he said. "Kidnappings for ransom still occur."

And that is how Gerald, Sam, Ruby, and Alisha wound up in the back of a large black Mercedes limousine at dusk, cruising down the long driveway out of the Gupta compound, with Mr. Fry in the front passenger seat and a tall, slender woman behind the wheel.

"Who is she?" Gerald whispered to Alisha, indicating the woman in the driver's seat.

"My worst nightmare," Alisha replied. "Miss Turner, my governess. She brings me home from boarding school at Cheltenham in the holidays. Then she sticks around to act as the fun police. You have no idea."

Gerald glanced at the back of Fry's head. "I think I can imagine."

Miss Turner struck Gerald as someone who liked to be in charge. She had pointedly directed Mr. Fry to the passenger seat. Aged somewhere in her thirties, she wore her hair in a precise bun that pinned her as a ballet-school graduate. She was dressed in a pair of tight gray pants with matching sleeveless top and sculpted biceps. The almost flawless pearl of her cheeks stood in stark contrast to the polished tungsten of her sunglasses. If Gerald had to pick one word to sum up Miss Turner, he'd have a hard time choosing between *intimidating* and *terrifying*.

The car slowed as it approached the street, and two security guards appeared from inside a squat hut to haul open the front gates. They saluted and the Mercedes eased onto a broad avenue. They passed colonial-era mansions surrounded by manicured gardens. The peaceful drive lasted until they reached the corner. Then they swung into the melee of vehicles heading toward old Delhi.

"Is it always like this?" Sam asked as the limousine swept along in a torrent of scooters, autorickshaws, cars, and motorcycles. Horns blared around them as vehicles tried to navigate through the surge of traffic. Gerald's eyes bulged as an oncoming bus pulled into their lane and hurtled straight at them. But like pedestrians on a busy city crossing, the drivers swerved, missed each other by centimeters, and continued on their way.

"No one's hit me yet," Miss Turner said, hauling the steering wheel over to the left as an overloaded scooter zipped by.

"They wouldn't dare," Ruby whispered to Gerald.

"Good driving is like anything else," Miss Turner said. "It's all about control. As long as you're the one in control, you can be master of the situation. No different from looking after you four."

Mr. Fry gave an approving nod.

"I can see you two are going to get on well," Gerald said.

The closer they got to the old city, the more choked the traffic became. There were people everywhere. Along the roadsides sweating couriers pushed handcarts stacked high with bales of goods. Laneways, too narrow for motorized vehicles, were crammed with shops and stalls. They snaked away from the main road into the depths of the marketplace.

Gerald was mesmerized. "There's just so much . . . *life*," he said.

Sam gawked out the window. "Did I just see a cow down that street?"

"Of course," Ruby said. "Cows are sacred here. Didn't you know that, geography boy?"

Alisha elbowed Gerald in the ribs and winked. "Miss Turner," she said. "It might be a good idea to park and walk from here. The traffic's getting worse."

The governess grunted a response and pulled over to the side of the road. Before Miss Turner could switch off the engine, Alisha had pushed open the back door. She heaved Gerald to get out. The backseat emptied.

"Okay," Alisha called into the car. "We'll see you back here in a couple of hours." She grabbed Sam and Gerald by the hand and dragged them toward a laneway seething with people. Ruby glanced back at Mr. Fry and Miss Turner sitting in the limo staring open-mouthed at their disappearing charges. She shrugged and dived into the crowd after the others.

"Come on!" Alisha squealed. "Let's have some fun." She skipped deeper into the throng, pulling Sam and Gerald with her. Ruby gave chase, dodging and weaving, and grasped Gerald's free hand.

Like a whirlpool, the crowd swallowed them whole.

* * *

The smell and the heat. That's what struck Gerald the most—like an overlong Christmas hug from your least favorite uncle. They were pressed in on all sides by the heaving mass, and the temperature rose ever higher. A heady mix of aromas assaulted Gerald's nose: clouds of burning incense, body odors, spices, frying foods, open drains, animals . . . it was a pungent perfume unique to the marketplace.

After the initial crush at the entryway, the crowd thinned from oppressive to almost tolerable. Gerald, Sam, Alisha, and Ruby found themselves at the start of a maze of alleyways. Weathered buildings stretched along either side of them, some two stories, others three and four. Sections of mismatched corrugated iron and plywood jutted out at all angles from above the shop fronts. A tangle of home-strung electricity cables stretched overhead. Most of the shops were smaller than Gerald's modest-sized bedroom at home in Sydney; they stood side by side like an endless row of caves worn in a cliff face. The bazaar was bursting with activity.

Gerald found himself falling into step behind a boy maybe nine years old. He was barefoot and stripped to the waist, and on his head, balanced on a folded tea towel, he carried a block of ice the size of four house bricks. In the stifling heat of the marketplace, cut off from any cooling breeze, the ice melted freely down his face and over his shoulders. The boy tottered through the crowd of shoppers, one hand steadying the ice and the other slicing between the people in front of him like a butter knife, until he skipped out of view.

"You have no idea how good it is to be here with you." Alisha beamed at Gerald. She still clutched his hand and only let it go when her mobile phone chirped in her handbag. She fished it out and looked at the screen. A grin flashed across her face.

"It's Miss Turner," she said. "Shame about the phone reception in these markets." She dropped the phone back into her bag. "Who's hungry?"

Alisha fronted up to a food stall. A stocky man with a checked cloth knotted around his head to catch the sweat was nevertheless sweating over two large pans of bubbling oil.

She returned with a plate piled with golden brown pyramids of pastry glistening under a sheen of oil.

Gerald picked one up in his fingertips and took a bite. His eyes sprung wide.

"Hot!" he gasped. "Hot, but yum."

"Potato samosas," Alisha said.

The Indian takeaway around the corner from Gerald's house in Sydney had samosas on the menu. But they were bags of soggy flour compared to the flavor bomb that had just exploded in his mouth. Alisha held the plate out for Sam and Ruby.

"So, what's with your dad?" Sam said through a mouthful. "How come he won't let you out without a babysitter?"

Alisha snorted. "He's afraid someone's going to throw a bag over my head and hold me for ransom," she said. "As if anyone here knows who I am."

"But your dad's really rich," Ruby said. "That makes you a target."

Alisha glared at Ruby. "I think I can look after myself. Five years at boarding school has taught me a few things. I don't need to be rolled in bubble wrap."

The last of the day's sunlight fell behind the surrounding buildings. Lamps flickered on around the stalls, baking the market in a yellow glaze. Gerald's nose tingled. Alisha pointed down a dog-legged laneway to a crowd of people stepping past large cane baskets brimming with brightly colored powders of yellow, orange, and red.

"The spice market," she said. "The smell might be a bit strong for you. Can't have you crying."

As the girls paused to inspect a rack of clothes, a movement in the shadows caught Gerald's eye. He glanced up in time to see something move past the end of the alley. He was astonished.

It was an elephant.

Gerald grabbed Sam by the elbow and pointed in disbelief. "Did you see that?"

Sam jumped in alarm. "What? A rat?"

"An elephant, you idiot," Gerald said. "Come on, let's check it out."

Glad for an excuse to leave the girls to their shopping, they elbowed through the crowd and tumbled out onto a broad walkway. Gerald looked to his right—an endless sea of heads—then to his left. And there it was: the back end of a great gray elephant swaying through the crush of people. Gerald and Sam weaved up to the animal, which was making its steady way down the road. Strings of bells were tied around its feet and neck, jangling in time to its ambling gait, and its face was decorated with white paint. A man leaning on a long bamboo pole and walking next to the beast appeared to be its handler, not that he was doing much handling. The elephant seemed to know where to go.

Gerald bounded along, trying to get in front. "Can you believe this?" he called to Sam over the heads of the crowd. Sam caught up and they both managed to get a few paces ahead.

The elephant came to a halt in the middle of the path, its bells falling silent. People gathered around and paid the handler some money. The elephant raised its trunk and tapped each of them on the head.

"He's blessing them," a voice by Gerald's elbow said. Gerald startled and looked around to find a man standing beside him. He could have been aged anywhere between thirty and seventy. The man was dressed in a white tunic and his hair was dyed a dull orange. He had an enormous black mustache that occupied half his face, which wore an expression of benign happiness.

"It's a temple elephant," the man said. "People seek good fortune with his blessings."

"He must be tame," Gerald said. "With all this going on."

The man smiled a knowing smile. "The elephant is patient."

Gerald nodded and turned back to watch the string of blessings.

"Do you know," the man spoke again, "that all Hindu gods have an animal to carry them in this mortal world?"

Gerald nodded again. He wasn't in the mood for a conversation with a complete stranger.

"They're called vahanas," the man said.

"What?"

"The gods' vehicles—they're called vahanas."

"Oh."

"My word, yes. The elephant is the vahana of Indra."

"Indra?"

"The storm god. The monsoons are almost upon us."

Gerald grunted and looked around for Sam. The man suddenly grabbed Gerald's right hand.

"Hey!"

"I can tell your fortune," the man said.

Gerald tried to pull away but he was clamped tight around the wrist.

"You are an interesting one," the man muttered, running his fingertips across the open palm. "You will face great challenges, great temptations. . . ."

Gerald yanked back on his arm, but the man was insistent.

"Do you mind?" Gerald said.

"You are on a quest, yes? To find something long hidden?"

Gerald shook his head. "No. I'm not looking for anything."

"Not yet, perhaps. But soon enough. There are those who will do all they can to stop you. You must resist them. For what you seek is quite near."

"I'm sorry, but I'm not searching for—"

The man lifted his head and looked into Gerald's eyes. In an instant, the man's expression of happiness vanished. He stared at Gerald in dismay.

Gerald stared back at him. The clamor of the market fell away. All Gerald could hear was the man's voice.

"The tenth gate is about to open," he said in a hoarse whisper. He released his grip and held trembling fingers up close to Gerald's eyes. "But you are not yet ready."

The man spun around and went to flee. But Gerald grabbed him by the arm. It was his turn to hold on tight.

"Are you talking about the casket?" Gerald asked. "Do you know where the casket is hidden? Is it behind some gate?"

The fortune-teller struggled to free himself. "I will tell," he beseeched. "But you must let go." Gerald pressed his lips together then relaxed his grip.

The man rubbed his arm. "Much is set down in your future that you cannot change," he said, gasping. "You will face a decision, a choice that you must make." He looked at Gerald with stricken eyes. "When the time comes, you must remember this: Nothing is certain."

Gerald recoiled. "What did you just say?" he demanded.

The man ran his hands down the front of Gerald's shirt, straightening his clothing. "It is nothing," he babbled, stumbling backward. His eyes darted in all directions, as if afraid of being watched. His face was smeared with dread.

"Did you say 'nothing is certain'?" Gerald asked again, advancing on the man. "Is that what you said?"

The man backed across the laneway, bumping against people in his haste. "I was wrong," the man said. "A mistake." Before Gerald could get any closer the man squeezed between two stalls and vanished into the rust-colored night.

"What's the matter?" Sam asked as he caught up. "What was he on about?"

Gerald stared at the narrow gap where the man had escaped.

"Nothing is certain," Gerald said through tight lips.

Sam shrugged. "What's the big deal?"

Gerald turned and stared into his friend's face. "I've never told anyone this," he said. "On the last day of school term, the day before I left for England with my parents, I was daydreaming in history class."

"So?" Sam said. "I've been known to snore."

"I was being chased by a monster."

Sam let out a snort.

"Yeah, I know," Gerald said. "It sounds lame."

"Only *sounds* lame?"

"Shut up. This monster was yelling at me. And he only yelled one thing."

"'Nothing is certain'?" Sam said.

Gerald nodded. "It must be a coincidence. But my day-dreams have a habit of coming true."

Sam looked at Gerald with a puzzled expression.

"You remember," Gerald said. "First in the British Museum and then in Mr. Hoskins's bookshop. I went off into some trance, saw a vision, and then thirty seconds later it came true."

"What did that guy say to you?"

"I don't know. I was too busy trying to get my hand back. Something about some challenges. And what I seek is hidden behind the tenth gate."

"Are we seeking something?"

They were interrupted by the arrival of Ruby and Alisha.

"It would be nice if you tried not to vandalize the stalls," Alisha was saying. "I'm sure the shop owners would appreciate it."

Ruby turned to Gerald in exasperation. "I bumped into a stack of tablecloths and they fell into a puddle," she said. "It was an accident. These alleyways are so tight. I offered to pay for the dirty ones."

"Don't worry," Alisha said. "I sorted it. I explained you were English and couldn't possibly help it. The shopkeeper more than understood."

Ruby's lips showed white. Gerald thought she was about to explode. "Excuse us a second, will you?" he said to Alisha and Sam. He pulled Ruby across to a stall piled high with cotton shirts.

"That's okay." Sam beamed after them. "Take your time."

Gerald tried to mollify Ruby. He failed dismally.

"Tell me," she ranted. "What have I done? What have I done to make her treat me like this?"

"Let's see. There was the bit about her being bland, boring, and opinionated . . . ," Gerald started.

"Okay—"

"And then you said she had massive flaws in her personality . . ."

"Well, I think I actually said 'holes,' not 'flaws,' but—"

Gerald counted off on his fingers, "Conceited, spoiled—"

Ruby held up her hands. "All right. I admit I was a bit harsh," she said.

"A bit?"

"All I'm saying is I knew she was going to be awful to me."

"So you got a few shots in first? You two need to sort it out or this holiday is going to be a nightmare for all of us. Okay?"

Ruby mumbled something under her breath and scrunched the toe of her shoe in the dirt.

"You thirsty?" Gerald asked.

Ruby gave a sullen nod. They found a stand selling bottles of water and soft drinks. Gerald reached into his shirt pocket for some money, and a quizzical look appeared on his face. He pulled out a piece of cardboard—dog-eared and worn—about the size of a credit card.

"What's that?" Ruby asked.

"The fortune-teller must have slipped it into my pocket." He waved off Ruby's questions and held the card under a lantern.

"It's a picture of some tower," Gerald said. He flipped the card over. And let out a loud gasp. "Holy cow!"

On the back of the card, scratched in black ink, was a rough drawing of the familiar three forearms, forming a triangle around a blazing sun. Ruby snatched the card.

"Your family seal. What's some fortune-teller doing with that?"

Gerald took the card and stared at it. "Can I talk to you about something?"

Ruby was still in a deep sulk about Alisha. "I guess so. What is it?"

Gerald took a deep breath. "I've been having dreams— Sir Mason Green dreams."

"I thought you were going to stop worrying about him."

"I know. But the dreams keep coming back. He spoke about the other two caskets. About how he's going to get them. And if he finds them first, there's going to be three tragedies."

"Gerald, listen to me."

"And the thin man has somehow survived and now this fortune-teller guy says something about someone trying to stop my quest—"

Ruby took hold of Gerald by the shoulders and shook hard. "Gerald! Sir Mason Green is half a continent away. You don't have to keep on about him."

Gerald stood silent. He blinked at Ruby.

"It's all just coincidence, okay?" she said. "You've got to stop obsessing."

Sam sauntered over. He looked like he'd been rolling in catnip.

"What's going on?" he asked. "Alisha's bored."

Ruby switched her frustration. "And as for you," she said. "Come back to the land of reality. She doesn't even like you!"

The sky was now dark and the market flickered with lanterns and shadows. Gerald was buffeted as a surge of people elbowed past them—a man in dark clothes bumped hard into his shoulder—but his mind was on the card from the fortune-teller. Surely that couldn't have been a chance meeting. He was dragged from his thoughts by Sam.

"Has anyone seen Alisha?"

Gerald looked up but all he could see was a mass of bodies squeezing and rolling through the tight confines of the market. Then, about twenty meters away on his right, he spotted her. Alisha was chatting to a storekeeper and stuffing something she'd bought into her bag. She lifted her head and turned toward Gerald. A broad smile burst across her face and she waved.

Gerald grinned back. He could understand Sam's infatuation.

Then a figure clothed entirely in black emerged from the sea of people. In a second, Alisha was grabbed by the upper arm. There was a brief struggle. Then she disappeared.

Chapter Seven

"She's gone!"

Gerald pushed through the crowd to where Alisha had been standing. Ruby and Sam were a couple feet behind.

"She was standing right here. Then this guy grabbed her." He scanned left and right, but there was no sign of her.

"Are you sure?" Sam said. "She didn't just duck down one of these side streets?"

Gerald didn't respond. He knew what he saw. He turned to the shopkeeper: "The girl who was here—where did she go?"

The woman shook her head. She didn't understand.

Ruby spoke quickly. "There are only two ways they could have gone. Back the way we came or up this alley. I say we split up."

Gerald knew there was no time to argue. He dived into the alley without looking back. Ruby and Sam would just have to keep up.

The crowd was thinner in that part of the market, and Gerald increased his pace, dodging left and right between the shoppers. He looked around in desperation, but all he could see was a line of stalls selling beads and sequins. He came to a crossroads: another alley cutting across his path. He looked either way and gazed up to the second- and third-story balconies stacked up over the market.

Nothing.

No sign at all.

His mind raced. What was Alisha wearing? Jeans and a gold T-shirt? Or was it white? He couldn't think clearly. How would they find a policeman in this jumble of stalls and people? And would they be understood? Or even believed?

Then he heard a cry.

He looked around and caught a glimpse of gold in the night shadows. At a point where a lane forked in two and a pool of light spilled onto the ground, Gerald saw them. Alisha was struggling with the figure in black, battling to free herself.

Gerald yelled out and, for an instant, the attacker looked around. The figure's head was swathed in a black scarf that revealed only a narrow strip across the eyes.

"You," Gerald whispered.

It was the same person who had been watching him at the airport the night before. But before Gerald could take a step, the lithe figure wrenched Alisha's arm and dragged her deeper into the maze of laneways.

Gerald set off. He had to keep up. He rounded a corner at speed to find a cow lying in the middle of the path: a cow with two curved horns poking straight at his ribs. Gerald only had instinct to save himself from a certain impaling. He stuck out a hand and pushed down hard on top of the cow's head. Momentum lifted his feet from the ground and he spun a full twisting pirouette in the air. The cow let out a startled bellow as Gerald zipped past her head and skidded down to his knees. He bounced back to his feet and scrambled on.

His sneakers bit the pavement as he danced around a cycle rickshaw parked on the curbside, its driver snoozing in the backseat. He was sure he saw the back of Alisha's head disappear around a bend. He slid sideways into the corner, upending a pile of baskets and sending their contents spraying across the ground. Ignoring the cries of the irate owner behind him, Gerald surged forward. He was gaining on them. He gulped in the hot night air. This is good, I'm almost there.

Then he ran smack into a wall of bodies. He'd wound his way into a lane so narrow that two people couldn't pass each other without turning sideways. Alisha and the figure in black were almost within reach, but between them and Gerald was a gridlock of maybe a hundred people all trying to squeeze through the bottleneck at once.

"Alisha!" Gerald yelled. "I'm coming!"

Alisha turned toward him, but her kidnapper was strong. She was dragged onward. The harder Gerald pushed the people in front, the tighter he was stuck in the crowd. It was as if he'd blundered into a tar pit like some feeble-brained dinosaur. The crush of bodies pinned his arms to his sides and his progress stalled. All he could do was watch in despair as Alisha's terrified face grew more distant in the lantern light.

Gerald looked frantically around him. There were no gaps in the mob, no way through.

Then he looked up.

The gap-toothed array of awnings and sun covers hovered above him. Just maybe . . .

Gerald heaved himself sideways, pushing past a middle-aged man in an orange turban to get to the brick wall between two storefronts. He freed his right arm and reached up. With an effort he grabbed a metal support rod that held up one side of a sheet of rusty corrugated iron. He wedged a foot into a gap in the bricks where the mortar had crumbled. Then he hauled himself off the ground and swung his other arm up to grab the rod. He pulled as hard as he could. But his hands were slippery with sweat. He needed more leverage.

He glanced down and saw the orange turban of the man beneath him. With a cry of "Sorry!" Gerald stepped onto the man's head with his left foot and scrambled up the wall, clambering onto the corrugated iron. He ignored the protests from below and jumped to his feet. A hotchpotch of iron and board stretched out before him like a line of stepping stones above the crowded laneway. Almost immediately Gerald spotted Alisha. She was only feet from the end of the alley where it opened onto a courtyard. At least five lanes twisted away in different directions. If they got much farther ahead, Gerald could lose them forever.

There was a gap of a yard and a half to the next awning. Gerald peered at the people below. The man in the orange turban was yelling at him, shaking his fist. Gerald took a breath, edged his toes to the end of the sheet of iron, and jumped. He soared over the gap and landed heavily on a section of plywood. The board shifted under his weight. He knew he was going to have to be quick to make this work. Without warning, the board dropped a foot and Gerald lurched backward. His arms flailed as he tried to keep balance. With a push off his back leg he drove himself forward. He thumped down on the next board and it too began to collapse. Keeping his momentum rolling, Gerald stretched out, leaping across the trail of overhangs, flying along the line of awnings like a never-ending triple jump. Behind him battered iron and plywood swung over the heads of the startled people below. A storm of dust and bolts rained down as Gerald scrambled the length of the alley. He made a final leap onto the last of the awnings, landing on both feet with a resounding clatter. For a second he balanced there, unsure how to get down. Then the metal sheared away from the wall. Gerald rode the sheet of iron like a snowboard, bouncing first off a stack of wooden crates that splintered under him, then onto a trestle table covered with T-shirts. The table crashed to the concrete, and shoppers leaped clear as Gerald's makeshift ride skimmed across the ground. He didn't dare look back at the carnage behind him.

Gerald ran through a tight corridor and almost straight past the entry to a side street, only sliding to a halt at the last second. He backed up and peered into the gloom.

It was a dead end, lit by a single lamp suspended from a pole halfway down the street. The dirty yellow light cast a pall across the ground. Buildings stretched up three stories on all sides, creating a box canyon of decaying bricks and mortar. Blank windows and balconies stared down like the unseeing eyes of the dead. Unlike the rest of the market, this area was deserted . . . except for the figure in black and the terrified girl.

They stood at the end of the lane. The bandit rattled on

door handles. All were locked.

Gerald took a few paces forward, stepping past a cycle rickshaw in the gutter. "Alisha," he said calmly, holding up his hands, "it's all right." Her face shone wet in the lamplight.

The kidnapper—agitated, boxed in like a trapped animal—yanked Alisha to another door, squeezing a sob from her.

"Let her go," Gerald said. "Let her go . . . and you can go."

Gerald took another step. He was only ten paces from them.

The bandit spun around to face Gerald, brandishing Alisha like a shield. A pair of eyes stared right through him and toward the only avenue of escape. In a blink, the figure whipped a hand from deep within folds of cloth. A glint of silver. A dagger. Pressed into Alisha's throat.

Gerald had no idea what to do. There was no way he could try to free Alisha while there was a knife held against her neck. But he also couldn't stand aside and let the kidnapper escape with her. He stared into those eyes, searching for a solution.

"You don't have to do this," Gerald said. "If you need money, I can give it to you. Put the knife down. Let her go. And we'll get some money. Okay?" Gerald took half a step closer. The bandit tensed, tightening the grip on Alisha.

The blade pressed into her skin.

A cry caught in Alisha's throat. Gerald could see the whites of her eyes grow large. He stopped. Then he sensed something move behind him.

"Gerald?" a cautious voice called.

He shot a glance over his shoulder. Sam and Ruby stood at the entry to the cul-de-sac. He turned back to face the figure with the knife. At least now he had numbers on his side.

The bandit started moving in a shuffle toward Gerald, with Alisha still gripped tight.

Gerald was distraught. How could he stop them?

The answer came too quickly for him to register. From a balcony up to his left a blur of movement shot across the alleyway. The figure in black fell backward and crashed to the ground. Another flash in front of Gerald's eyes exploded in a shower of dirt, plaster, and debris. Gerald blinked. Was that a flowerpot?

Someone up on a balcony was throwing potted plants, and one had connected with the kidnapper's head. Gerald grabbed a dazed Alisha by the hand.

"Come on!" he said. "Time to go."

They ran the short distance to join Ruby and Sam under the light pole. Gerald looked around to see the bandit stagger upright with a hand to his head. Another flowerpot smashed at the kidnapper's feet. All eyes shot up to the balcony where a figure stood in shadow, a pot in each hand.

The kidnapper turned to face Alisha, the dagger raised and ready. But before it could be launched, the knife was knocked out of the bandit's hand. Ruby crouched and picked up another rock from the ground. Her second throw missed the bandit's head by millimeters.

"Join in anytime you'd like," she said to the others.

Gerald and Sam sent a hailstorm of stones and broken flowerpots across the alley. The figure in black ducked and weaved. Then the bandit pulled something from a pouch. It looked like a ball on the end of a short rope. The kidnapper swung it in an arc and flung it across the lane toward the balcony. It split into a three-pronged sling that sliced fizzing through the air. The ropes snared around a bamboo prop under the balcony and snapped it clean. With a wrenching screech, the metal balcony tore off the front of the building, sending the figure with the flowerpots tumbling into the street.

The bandit set off like an Olympic sprinter, heading straight at them.

Gerald tensed, ready to make the tackle. But the bandit dodged to the right clean past him, then jumped onto the canopy of the cycle rickshaw and up onto a balcony. In the same fluid movement, the bandit grabbed onto the gutter and swung up onto the roof. In a blink, the figure in black was off across the rooftops.

Gerald turned to Alisha but she waved off all his questions with, "I'm all right. He didn't hurt me." She glanced at Ruby, who still held a rock in her hand.

Alisha opened her mouth but Ruby got in first. "It's okay," she said, letting the stone fall to the ground. "You don't have to say anything."

Alisha raised her chin an inch. "I wasn't planning to," she said.

Ruby's eyes crackled with lightning. "Why, you little—"

She was cut off by a moan coming from the wreckage of the collapsed balcony. Sam and Gerald rushed across to find a man splayed on his back amid a twist of rusted metal and shattered pottery. He wore a black polo shirt and dark trousers, and what looked like military-issue boots. There was another moan and the man eased up onto his elbows.

"Are you okay?" Gerald asked.

The man's dark hair was clipped short and he sported a neatly trimmed goatee. His arms extended out of his shirtsleeves like tree trunks. When he spoke from his mattress of pottery shards, it was with a French accent. "Thank you for your concern, Monsieur Wilkins, I am fine."

Gerald's head jolted. "How do you know my name?"

The man pushed back on his shoulders and bounced to his feet like a gymnast. "It is the job of Interpol to know such things," he said.

"You're with Interpol?" Sam said. "Inspector Parrott

said you'd be in touch."

"I was expecting a phone call," Gerald said. "How did you know we were here? Who was that guy?"

The man waved his hand at the boys, as if shooing flies. "Your questions can wait. I must speak with Mademoiselle Gupta." Ruby had stalked off into the shadows farther down the alley, and Alisha had assumed a pose of practiced indifference beneath the streetlight.

"Mademoiselle, I am Special Agent Leclerc. You are unharmed?"

"My arm's a little sore but I'm okay."

The man grunted. "You have a mobile phone?"

Alisha nodded and retrieved her phone from her handbag. The officer took it and stabbed his thumbs into the keypad.

"I'm afraid mine is out of battery. Now the local police will be looking for you," he said, tapping out a message. "I need to contact them about pressing charges."

"Don't you have to catch that guy before you can charge him?" Gerald said.

"I was referring to charges against you, Monsieur Wilkins."

"Me!"

"You caused a great deal of damage in your pursuit of Mademoiselle Gupta. But if you do as I say, you should avoid any time behind bars."

Gerald's eyes widened. He had no desire to witness the Indian criminal justice system from the inside.

Leclerc handed the phone back to Alisha. "The local chief of police is a friend of mine," he said. "That message should smooth things over until I see him. Now tell me, Mademoiselle Gupta, the man who attacked you—did he say anything? Anything that might provide a clue to his identity, where he was taking you?"

Alisha shook her head. "Nothing. Not a sound. One moment I was waving at Gerald and the next he was dragging me through the streets."

"He said nothing? Not even a threat?"

"Not one word."

Leclerc stroked his goatee and stared across the alley. *"Trop bizarre,"* he muttered.

"Who was he?" Gerald asked.

Leclerc squinted up at the balcony where the bandit had vaulted to freedom.

"Just some thief," he muttered. "The local police will track him down, I am sure. Now, Monsieur Wilkins, what are your plans? Do you intend to travel outside Delhi?"

"No plans, really," Gerald said. "Alisha's father was talking about some trip to a game reserve down south."

"Um, excuse me, officer," Sam said. "Inspector Parrott said he contacted you because of the thin man . . . you know, Mason Green's thug. What has someone trying to kidnap Alisha got to do with that?"

"I have been following you since your arrival in Delhi," Leclerc said. "Tonight was a lucky coincidence for your friend."

"Lucky?" Alisha said. "How can being dragged through this place by some madman be considered lucky?"

Leclerc sniffed. "Lucky that I was here to help you."

Sam knelt down and picked up one of the potted plants. "You're a good throw," he said to Leclerc. "But don't you have a gun?"

"Guns, Monsieur Valentine, have a nasty habit of producing corpses. I was trying to capture, not to kill." He pulled a scrap of paper from his pocket and handed it to Gerald. "My number," he said. "Please keep me informed of your movements. I will be in touch." Leclerc turned and limped out of the alley.

"What a cheery soul," Sam said. "So the guy who grabbed Alisha is just some random thief?"

Ruby moved into the circle of light. She held the bandit's silver dagger.

"I don't think he was that random," she said. Ruby pointed the tip of the blade to the ground. On the butt of the dagger's hilt, clear even in the dim light of the streetlamp, was the impression of a triangle, formed by three forearms. In the center burned a flaming sun.

"Seen this somewhere before?" she asked.

CHAPTER EIGHT

Gerald was dumbstruck. His family seal. Again. And this time on the handle of a kidnapper's knife.

"Still think it's all a coincidence?" he said to Ruby.

Gerald took the dagger and held it up to the light. It was about a foot long. The handle was a dark wood, set with colored stones. The blade glinted silver under the lamp.

"This could do some damage," he said, waving it in the air. He went to hand it back to Ruby, but she shook her head.

"Souvenir," she said.

Gerald nodded and pulled his backpack from his shoulders. He put the knife inside. He wandered across to the twisted pile of metal that was once a balcony and kicked among the debris. He stooped and pulled out a section of bamboo pole. Wrapped around it was the sling the bandit had used to bring down Leclerc. What Gerald had thought were three balls were actually flat river stones: gunmetal gray, smooth and cool to the touch. He held one in his palm. Carved into one side was the triangle of his family seal. He let the stones clatter to the ground. He lifted his head and stared into the heavens.

The night was still incredibly hot—hot enough to dry the sweat from his shirt after the drenching it received in his mad dash through the market. And hot enough to tip his simmering brain to the boiling point. A month ago he hadn't even known he had a family seal. Now it was turning up like mushrooms after rain.

He felt a tug at his elbow. "You might like to see this as well," Ruby said. She gave a nod in Alisha's direction. "I didn't feel like explaining everything to the princess." Ruby held out a black rectangular object.

"What is it?"

"It must have fallen from the kidnapper's pocket," Ruby said. "Open it."

Gerald looked down at the black notebook in his hand. He flipped open the cover. In childlike printing on the first page was written CONSTABLE D. LETHBRIDGE.

"Please don't say anything about coincidences," Ruby said.

"That was the guy who broke into Lethbridge's house?"

Gerald said. "And now he's trying to kidnap Alisha?"

Ruby held up her hands. "I don't have any answers. Let's find our way out of here."

Gerald slid the notebook into his backpack. He couldn't shake the feeling that Mason Green's tentacles were somehow tied up in the night's events.

Alisha was on her mobile phone calling Miss Turner, making up excuses as she led them to the main thoroughfare.

"Do you smell that?" Gerald asked.

"What?" Sam said. "The bit that smells like fried food, the bit that smells like Ruby's feet, or the bit that smells like cat's pee?"

"No. It's like after a really hot summer's day. It smells like . . . rain." Even in the middle of this chaotic city, the rich loamy smell of a looming summer storm was unmistakable. Gerald had a sudden pang for home.

They rounded a corner and could see there was a commotion up ahead. A group of people had gathered and there were shouts of alarm. Gerald and the others edged through a tight section between several stalls when the crowd split apart. People were diving in all directions, screaming in panic. In an instant, it was clear why. The crowd fell away to reveal an enraged elephant rearing up on its hind legs and trumpeting furiously into the night. The animal that had been blessing people so peacefully outside its temple had gone berserk. Its handler waved his bamboo pole and shouted. But he may as well have been a fly buzzing about the elephant's ears. With a flick of its trunk the elephant flattened a row of trestle tables, sending pots and skillets flying.

Gerald grabbed Alisha by the arm. "Quick," he shouted. "This way." They ducked into a tight alcove protected by stone walls on either side. They craned their necks around the corner.

"Sam! Ruby!" Gerald yelled. "Over here."

The Valentine twins were stranded in the middle of a torrent of people. Sam grabbed Ruby's hand and barged his way across the flow, straining to hold on as the frantic crowd swarmed past them. The elephant was only feet away, its eyes wide with fury. It head-butted a wooden cart into splinters. It trumpeted again. The sound ruptured the screams that filled the alleyway. Sam and Ruby were only steps away. But just as Gerald leaned out and grabbed Sam by the shirt to reel him in, a man blinded by fear slammed into Sam and Ruby's clenched hands. Sam's grip flew loose and Ruby was swept back into the mob. Then, as if a tap had been shut off, the flow of people drained away. Ruby was alone in the middle of the alley. The elephant was barely ten yards from her. For a moment they held their ground and looked at each other. It was not an even match. The elephant flattened its ears and lowered its head. And charged.

Ruby stood, dazed, unable to move. Sam cried out to

his sister. Gerald went to dive into the alley to grab her. But he was too late.

Alisha got there first.

She flung herself into the path of the elephant and tackled Ruby hard around the waist, sending them both into a stack of cane baskets on the other side of the lane. The animal rampaged past without breaking stride and disappeared into the maze of the marketplace beyond.

Gerald and Sam flung baskets out of the way and found Alisha facedown on top of Ruby with the tips of their noses centimeters apart. For a second, the girls just stared at each other.

"I guess this makes us even," Alisha said to Ruby.

She didn't reply.

The ground around Ruby's head was suddenly dotted with splashes of water. Fat, ripe raindrops spattered into the dirt. Within seconds the heavens had opened in a tropical downpour. The monsoon had arrived.

Sir Mason Green was taunting. Cajoling.

"Gerald, you risk missing out on a truly great treasure. It could all be yours. Don't you want it?"

"Not interested," Gerald mumbled.

"Really? Then why do you keep inviting me back?"

"I don't. You keep imposing yourself. You're just a figment of my imagination. So save your nonexistent breath. I don't need any more treasure. Billionaire. Remember?"

Green arched an eyebrow. "There is a difference between want and need, Gerald. And this treasure is unlike any you can imagine."

"If it's so great, then why don't you just take it? How come you want me to join in?"

Green paused and tilted his chin.

"So much more fun when there's a bit of competition. Wouldn't you agree?"

"Only if both people want to be in the race. And I don't."

"As you wish." Green turned to go, then paused. "But I thought you might be more curious to know."

Gerald refused to take the bait. He wasn't going to buy into his mind's folly. . . .

"To know what?" Gerald couldn't resist.

A smile showed on Green's face. "That you are so very close to one of the caskets."

Gerald shook his head on his pillow. "No. What about Egypt and France?"

Green's face started to shimmer and distort. "It's in India, Gerald. Just waiting for you . . ."

Again, Gerald woke to the sound of water. But this time it was the torrential rain sheeting down outside. He pulled back the shutters; he may as well have been on the inside of a waterfall.

He sat on the end of the bed and sighed. His dreams were becoming more ridiculous each night. Gerald dragged his backpack onto his lap. He reached in and pulled out Constable Lethbridge's notebook. He turned it over in his fingers and tried to work out what it could mean. The person who had broken into Lethbridge's house had also tried to kidnap Alisha. Sir Mason Green had to be behind it. But what would he want with Alisha? Or a police notebook?

Gerald flipped open the cover and leafed through the pages. They were filled with Constable Lethbridge's labored handwriting. Page twenty-three contained a description of the robbery of the Noor Jehan diamond, and page fifty-seven had interview notes with the porter from the Rattigan Club. Gerald grinned when he saw the porter had described him as a "young miscreant with a common accent."

Page after page of detail about the robbery and Sir Mason Green's involvement. But then Gerald noticed something. The notebook went from page eighty-four (a description of the Reading Room at the British Museum) to page eighty-seven (Lord Herring's strong desire to stop talking with Constable Lethbridge). A page was missing. Gerald folded the notebook back and ran a finger along its spine. A page had been sliced out with a sharp knife or razor.

"What's missing?" Gerald pondered out loud. He shoved

the book back into his pack.

Gerald found Sam in the lounge on his favorite pile of cushions, munching toast and jam.

"You know, Gerald," he said between mouthfuls, "this whole luxury thing—it's the way life's meant to be. People getting you breakfast, making your bed, picking up after you."

"Isn't that what parents are for?" Gerald asked.

"Yeah, of course. But servants do it with style. And they don't expect you to say thanks. Or help with the washing up."

"So you've found your place in the world, have you?"

"Oh yes," Sam said, stuffing more toast into his cheek and nestling back into the cushions. "This is where I belong."

Gerald poured himself some orange juice and took an apple Danish from a tray brimming with pastries. He picked up a remote, switched on the television that filled one of the villa's walls, and flicked through the channels, not looking for anything in particular. He settled on a music video station and dropped into a lounge chair with his breakfast.

"I've been thinking," he said.

"Always dangerous. What about?"

"We should look for one of the caskets."

"What!" Sam almost dropped his toast. "Are you insane?"

"It's obvious, isn't it?"

"What? Your lack of sanity?"

"No. My family seal. The way it keeps turning up. It must have something to do with one of the other caskets."

"Why would you think that?"

Gerald wasn't about to describe his imaginary conversations with Sir Mason Green after what Sam had said about his sanity.

"Just a hunch," Gerald said. He opened his backpack and pulled out the bandit's dagger. He rubbed the silver butt against his shirt. "Gaius Antonius had this symbol on his ring. He was the bearer of the diamond casket. It's on a knife that some bandit used to snatch Alisha off the street. And it's on this."

He retrieved the card that the fortune-teller had slipped into his pocket the night before.

Sam gave a "so what?" shrug.

"Don't you see?" Gerald said. "One of the caskets must be in India."

"But that map in Green's study," Sam said. "There was no link to India. And you don't care about the other caskets, do you?"

Gerald thought back to his dreams. Before this whole billionaire thing had happened, his dreamscape had been restricted to the terrain of his sketchbook—fighting dragons or rescuing girls. But ever since Sir Mason Green had started invading his sleep, the dreams had taken on a clarity he'd never experienced before. And he hated to admit it, but he was desperate to know what was in the other caskets. The power of the golden rod that had surged through him that night in Beaconsfield—he wanted to know what lay behind it. He *needed* to know. And if he was honest, there was something else as well.

He wanted to feel that power surge again.

"If we can find those other caskets, we'll stop Green from getting them," Gerald said to Sam, not very convincingly.

"Not worth interrupting a holiday for," Sam said, helping himself to pastries.

"Well, it is to me," Gerald said. "I think we should find the tower on this card."

They were interrupted by the sound of laughter. Shrill, uninhibited laughter. Gerald and Sam looked through the windows to see Ruby and Alisha holding hands and dancing in crazy whooping circles in the pouring rain.

Gerald looked back at Sam. "Are you seeing this?"

Sam shook his head. "They are from another planet."

The girls danced into the shelter of the porch and almost kicked in the glass doors as they tumbled inside. They were drenched through and still laughing.

"What's with you two?" Gerald said. "You're like a pair of—"

"What?" Alisha said. "Giggly schoolgirls?"

For some reason, Ruby thought this was the funniest thing that she had ever heard. She fell into the cushions on top of Sam.

"Hey! Careful," he yelped. "You're soaked."

"Yes," Ruby panted through gulps of air. "I think it's raining."

This time it was Alisha's turn to burst into a fit. They both rolled onto the silk rug in the middle of the room, giggling madly.

"Ruby wasn't like this before," Gerald said to Sam.

"There wasn't another girl around before," Sam said. "Alien species. May as well try to understand creatures from Mars."

"Or anything from Uranus!" Ruby blurted out. That was the end of her and Alisha for the next five minutes.

Gerald and Sam sat on the couch and continued eating while they waited for the hilarity to subside. Eventually, Ruby and Alisha squeezed out the last cackle and lay exhausted in a haze of tears and snuffles.

"Finished?" Gerald asked.

"Yes, I think so," Ruby said. She raised herself up on her elbows and smiled at the boys. "Everything feels better after a laugh."

Ruby was like a new person. It was the first time they'd seen her happy in days. She was wearing one of Alisha's white and gold robes—the girls had clearly been playing dress-up.

"Shouldn't you two be spitting poison into each other's eyes, cobra-style?" Gerald said.

Ruby grinned. "We sat up most of last night. We've sorted things out," she said.

"Like what?"

"None of your business," Alisha said. "Girl things. We understand each other now."

Sam looked at Gerald.

"Do you understand me, Gerald?" Sam asked.

"Why of course, Samuel," Gerald said. "I understand that you were hungry because you've just eaten a loaf of bread. And I understand that you are extremely ugly."

They both burst out laughing.

Ruby pulled Alisha to her feet. "I am so glad you're here, Alisha," she said. "I was getting tired of putting up with these two. Now, what are we going to do today?"

"Gerald wants to find a casket," Sam said, changing the channel on the television. "What do you want to do?"

Ruby looked at Gerald in exasperation.

"Gerald? I thought we agreed that it was pointless."

"I think you agreed for the both of us," Gerald said.

"Welcome to my world," Sam mumbled.

Gerald showed the fortune-teller's card to Alisha. "Do you recognize this?"

The picture showed a slender stone tower, rising five

stories and becoming narrower toward the top. Carved balconies ringed the structure at each level and there were small windows like finger holes on a tin whistle. The overall impression was of a giant pirate's spyglass.

Alisha studied the picture.

"It looks familiar. But there are so many monuments and temples. I'll ask Father. He'll know."

"Your father!" Gerald said. "I'd forgotten about him. After what happened last night there's no way he's going to let you out."

"That's not a problem," Alisha said with a dismissive wave of her hand. "He doesn't know."

Gerald looked dumbfounded. "Miss Turner must have told him about us running off," he said. "That's what the fun police are for."

Alisha smiled to herself. "I had a little chat with her last night. It doesn't look good that she and Mr. Fry lost us at the market. So we've agreed that Father needn't hear anything about it."

"Not even about the kidnapper?"

"They don't know anything about it, and I'm not going to let some common bandit, or my father, get in the way of me having some fun. That thug was just after money. People get robbed every day—it's no big deal."

Gerald took the card back from Alisha. "Good. It's agreed then. Let's find this tower."

* * *

Mr. Gupta held the picture under a gilded desk lamp.

"That's the Qutab Minar," he said. "It's a little south of here. Tallest brick minaret in the world. Would you like to see it?"

Gerald nodded and retrieved the card, slipping it into his shirt pocket. "Yeah. It looks interesting."

Mr. Gupta stood from his desk and walked across to wrap an arm around his daughter's shoulders.

"I'm delighted you're seeing some of our national heritage, Gerald. And getting Alisha interested as well. Until now, she preferred to spend her life in a shopping mall."

Alisha shifted under her father's embrace, as if cold porridge was running down her spine.

"So I can go?" she asked, through clenched teeth.

"Of course. As long as—"

"Miss Turner and Mr. Fry go along as well. Yes, I know." Alisha's voice was all sunshine, but Gerald could see her eyes were brewing a storm.

From the backseat of the Mercedes limousine, Gerald couldn't tell which was more frosty: the air-conditioning or the reception they received from Mr. Fry and Miss Turner.

"Shall we enjoy the pleasure of your company for the entire day or will young sir and his friends be attempting another suicide mission?" Fry's voice was carved from ice.

Gerald tried to keep a straight face amid the sniggering in the backseat. "Don't worry, Mr. Fry. You won't lose us today."

"Oh, joy," Fry said.

The choking traffic was no longer a novelty, and Gerald amused himself for the thirty-minute ride by trying to annoy his butler.

"Mr. Fry," he said. "I never found out. What's your first name?"

There was silence.

"Mr. Fry?"

The butler shifted in the passenger seat. "I choose not to divulge that information."

"Why not?"

There was another pause.

"Because any unnecessary familiarity between the master of the house and the staff will lead to an inevitable and irretrievable breakdown in discipline and the corrosion of the chain of command."

"What chain of command?" Gerald said. "This isn't the army."

"More's the pity," Fry muttered. "Nevertheless, it would be inappropriate for you to refer to me by anything other than Mr. Fry."

Sam leaned forward, a glint of mischief in his eye. "It's not because you're embarrassed, is it?"

Fry's jaw tightened. "I have nothing about which to be embarrassed."

Ruby chimed in. "I bet Miss Turner would tell us her name."

"It's Emily." The name popped from Alisha's mouth like a pip from an overripe cherry. She grinned. "Her name's Emily. Emily Turner."

Gerald glanced at the statuesque Miss Turner behind the wheel, her sunglasses reflecting the arc of the Mercedes's windshield wipers. Did he catch a flash of her eyes darting across to Mr. Fry? A single bead of sweat made a break from Fry's right eyebrow and tracked south along his cheekbone.

"I bet Miss Turner would like to know your name," Gerald said. "Wouldn't you, Miss Turner? Emily?"

For a moment all that could be heard was the *fwump-fwump* of the wipers, sweeping the rain from the windshield. Miss Turner didn't answer. But she did cast a glance toward Mr. Fry.

Fry's eyes swiveled a millimeter toward the governess. "I'll write it down," he said.

The four occupants of the rear seat tumbled back in triumph. Fry pulled a notebook from his breast pocket and scribbled in it with a pencil. He tore out a sheet and flicked it back over his shoulder. There was a bridesmaid scramble for the page before Gerald emerged the victor. He shielded the contents against his chest.

"Come on, Gerald," Sam said. "Let's see."

Gerald peeled back the corner of the paper. His forehead puckered. "Saint John?" he said.

Fry's nostrils flared. "It is pronounced *Sinjin*," he

sniffed. "It is an old family name."

Gerald blinked. "Your name is *Sinjin* Fry," he said. "Singe and Fry. That's too good." The backseat erupted in laughter.

Fry's ears turned a deep red.

Eventually the mirth died down and Gerald came up for air.

"Sorry, Mr. Fry," he said, catching his breath. "I don't feel so bad about being called Gerald now."

Gerald wasn't sure, but he thought he saw Miss Turner's lips edge up slightly at the corners.

The Mercedes turned into a parking lot near the entrance to the Qutab Minar complex. From behind a bank of trees they could see a cluster of ancient stone buildings.

The rain had eased to scudding showers. Before they could get out of the car, Miss Turner flicked a switch and the rear doors locked with a metallic clunk.

Alisha tugged at the handle. She swung around to face Miss Turner. "And?" she demanded.

Miss Turner drew a hand to her face and removed her sunglasses. Her eyes shone a not-to-be-messed-with blue. "There will be no running off. No silliness. No levity. Do I make myself clear?"

"Yes," Alisha said. "No fun. No laughter. No reason to live. Can we get out now?"

The blue eyes drilled into Alisha's face. "Need I remind

you, Miss Gupta, that all it takes is a word from me and your father will have you in lockdown until it's time to go back to school. We don't want a repeat of the Swiss incident. Do we?"

Alisha narrowed her eyes and glared back at her governess. "No," she said through strained lips. "We don't."

Miss Turner managed a smile. "Then we understand each other."

The door locks sprung open. The four of them climbed from the backseat and rushed to the shelter of a banyan tree while Mr. Fry and Miss Turner lined up for tickets at the admission gate.

"Those two make a good pair," Gerald said.

"Yeah," Sam said, "*Sinjin* and *whingein*."

"What happened in Switzerland?" Ruby asked Alisha.

Alisha glared across at Miss Turner. "I'd rather not talk about it," she muttered.

"Must have been big," Sam said.

"Put it this way," Alisha said. "If you ever need tips on starting an avalanche, come and see me."

They dodged some puddles and followed Mr. Fry and Miss Turner through a stone archway and into an expansive garden. They declined an offer from a man in an orange shirt for a guided tour and walked toward the stonework remains. Vaulted gateways of red sandstone the height of a five-story building stood among dome-topped temples and

the ruins of columns and courtyards. The site was domi-
nated by a singular structure that stood sentinel over it all.
The minaret, a work of art in red brick and white marble,
towered over them.

Gerald craned his neck to take in the scale of the building. "How old is this thing?" he asked no one in particular.

Ruby read from a plaque at the foot of the tower. "At
least seven hundred years."

Sam leaned up against a railing that circled its base.
"There's a lot of old stuff around here."

Ruby glared at her brother. "You're not much into history, are you, geography boy?"

"What do you mean?"

"Of course there's a lot of old stuff here. People have
been living here for thousands of years. This is home to
some of the world's earliest civilizations. What were you
expecting? People flying about with jetpacks?"

Sam reached into his pocket and pulled out a pack of
gum. He folded a stick into his mouth. "I dunno," he said,
chewing away. "Maybe a bit more new stuff."

Ruby closed her eyes and, judging by her lips, she was
counting to ten. Finally she took a breath and turned to
Gerald. "Either he is or I am."

"What?"

"Adopted."

Gerald fought back a grin. "Come on," he said. "Let's

see if we can find my family seal around here."

Mr. Fry and Miss Turner accepted their request to explore and seemed happy to keep at a distance.

Sam stayed beside Alisha as they wandered across a stone courtyard toward a domed building. Gerald nudged Ruby as they followed.

"Don't you think that's cute?" he said.

Ruby blew a raspberry. "Alisha would rather kiss the cat," she said.

They followed Alisha and Sam inside a temple. Light streamed in through arched openings on two sides. There was a tangle of bamboo scaffolding in one of the archways where workmen were busy with hoses and brushes, cleaning carvings on the inner edge.

"Your family seal might be among these patterns," Alisha said as Gerald stopped beside her.

He scanned the archway and the surrounding ceiling. There were countless designs cut into the red rock but nothing resembled a triangle of forearms.

He sighed.

"This is hopeless," he said to Alisha. He took the card from his pocket and studied the black ink sketch. What had the fortune-teller been trying to tell him?

Alisha reached out and squeezed Gerald's forearm. "Let's keep looking," she said.

They wandered back outside. "Where do we even start?" Sam asked.

Gerald, whose shoulders had curled into a despondent slouch, suddenly straightened. He pointed a finger toward a man in an orange shirt, standing near the base of the minaret. "We ask that guy," he said. And before anybody could say a thing, Gerald ran into the rain toward the man who had offered them a guided tour.

"Excuse me!" Gerald called from a dozen paces away. "Excuse me. Can you help us?" He skidded the final couple of feet across the wet paving to stop beside the middle-aged man.

"What can I do for you, sir?" the man said.

Sam, Ruby, and Alisha caught up with them as Gerald held out the card. "Have you ever seen this symbol anywhere here?"

The man took the card from Gerald and studied the drawing, then flipped it over to look at the other side.

"Where did you get this?" he said to Gerald.

"Last night. At a market. From a fortune-teller."

The man seemed satisfied with the answer. He glanced about, then asked Gerald, "Would you like a tour of the inside of the minaret?"

Gerald looked up at the tower.

"I'm afraid I can only take one of you as the stairway is very narrow," the man said.

Before he could answer, Gerald felt a firm hand on his shoulder and he was ushered through a squat opening at the base of the minaret. A heavy wooden door banged shut behind him and Gerald's vision went blank in the darkness.

"Allow your eyes to adjust," the man said. "The steps are steep."

The blackness lightened and Gerald was able to pick out the shape of stairs spiraling up to his right. He started climbing. The guide followed behind. Occasional beams of light cut across his path from the windows notched into the walls. Every few circuits they came to a landing that led out through double doors to a walkway around the tower.

"Not this one, sir," the guide said each time.

Just when Gerald thought they couldn't possibly go any higher they reached the top landing and doors lined with pressed gold.

"Open them," the guide's voice came from behind. Gerald grabbed a handle in the shape of an elephant's head and pushed. The doors swung open and Gerald emerged at the top of the minaret on a platform ringed by metal railings.

He took in the full expanse of the site below. Sam, Ruby, and Alisha waved up at him. In a small garden, he could see Mr. Fry and Miss Turner sitting together on a bench under a tree.

"Tell me how you found this card."

Gerald swung around. The guide was right behind him. The kindness in his voice had evaporated.

"I didn't find it," Gerald said uneasily. "A fortune-teller gave it to me."

The man's eyes tightened. "He handed it to you? Pressed it into your palm?"

"Well, no. He must have slipped it into my pocket. I didn't notice till after he ran away."

"Ran away? Why did he run away?"

Gerald was beginning to feel edgy. It was a long way down to the ground. He took a step back and felt the metal rail against his spine.

"I don't know why he ran," Gerald said. "He was mumbling stuff about making a choice and facing temptations."

The guide extended his hand. "The card. Please."

Gerald reached into his pocket and gave it to him.

The man looked at the card and studied Gerald's face closely.

"Do you know what this represents?" The man's voice rose in intensity. "What it means?" There was no way Gerald was about to reveal that it was his family crest. He shook his head.

"This is the symbol of a cult," the guide said.

"A cult?" Gerald repeated.

The man glared at him. "The deadliest cult in India."

Chapter Nine

Gerald was stunned. Cults were for the weird and the unhinged.

"What type of cult?" he asked.

"The type that would cut off your hand and steal your watch rather than bother asking you the time," the guide said, his face darkening. "The type that would slit your throat if you looked at them the wrong way. In short, the type you want nothing to do with."

Gerald's mind raced. Things started to fall into place. The knife in the alley. The kidnapper who tried to snatch Alisha—was that bandit a member of this cult? Had his family adopted its calling card from bandits that liked slicing throats open?

The guide's voice somehow penetrated Gerald's thoughts.

"You must not seek out this cult, young sahib," the man said. "No good can come of it."

Gerald couldn't deny that this was good advice. The run-in with the bandit the night before was proof enough of that. Was trying to beat Green to the hidden casket really worth the risk? That mattress of money he inherited was looking mighty soft and tempting. Surely better to lounge back on that than pursue Sir Mason Green across the globe?

"What do you know about this cult?" Gerald asked the man.

"Enough to give children nightmares," the man replied.

"How about secret caskets? Do you know of any stories about treasure hidden in a stone chest?"

The guide looked hard into Gerald's face. "Are you sure you want to take this path?"

Gerald nodded. The lure of defeating Sir Mason Green was just too strong. His curiosity about the secret behind the caskets was stronger still.

The man thought for a moment, then pointed to a cluster of flat-roofed buildings outside the main gates. "Do you see the bazaar down there? The building farthest on the right? They sell many things carved from stone. The owner may be able to assist you."

Gerald led Sam, Ruby, and Alisha along a broken pathway into the market, leaving Mr. Fry and Miss Turner enjoying a cup of tea together at a roadside stall.

Gerald had the overwhelming sense he was on the threshold of some great discovery—that he was about to avert a tragedy.

"... three ... four ... five ..."

"What are you doing?" Ruby asked.

"Counting gates," Gerald said. "The fortune-teller last night said something about the tenth gate—so I'm counting."

"Oh puh-leese," she said. "You believe anything that man said?"

"... seven ... eight ... you can scoff all you like. But I had a dream—"

"Yes, thank you, Martin Luther King."

"—and if I can find this casket, it might just save your life. So a little less snark, thank you."

Ruby stopped and glared at Gerald. He continued. "... nine ... ten." He halted outside a narrow opening, a rickety wooden gate across the entrance. He glanced back at the others, smug as a teacher's pet. "The tenth one," he said. "Just like the man said."

Across a squat courtyard, crowded with stone sculptures and weeds poking through the pavers, was a small building. Gerald led the way inside.

There was barely enough room in the shop for them all. Gerald squeezed between stands of sculpted elephants, lions, snakes, and cows. There were racks of trinket boxes and paperweights. Everything on display was carved from stone.

"What are we looking for?" Sam asked.

"Anything with my family seal on it," Gerald said. "Or a clue to where the caskets are hidden."

Gerald scanned the shelves and display cases. If they'd been searching for tiny statues of Ganesha or dancing goddesses, he'd found the right place. Nothing looked remotely helpful.

Then Alisha's voice sounded from across the shop. "How about this, Gerald?"

She pointed to a large rectangular stone box at the foot of the store's counter. Gerald blinked. Ruby appeared next to him and she saw it as well.

"Is that really it?" she said.

The box was identical to the diamond casket they had found in the burial chamber at Beaconsfield.

Gerald almost fell over a display of stone lions in his rush to get to it. He dragged the casket into the aisle, grunting with the strain, and gaped at what he saw. It was covered in a thick layer of dust, but the similarity was unmistakable. The same carved images of suns and moons, the same whorls and swirls. And on top of the lid was the familiar design of a muscled archer, his bow at full draw. The only difference was the shape of the indentation in the archer's abdomen. The casket beneath Beaconsfield had a hollow designed to accept the Noor Jehan diamond—Mr. Gupta's diamond. This one, however, had a sharp rectangular indentation.

Had the object of Sir Mason Green's treasure hunt been sitting neglected and forgotten at the back of a rundown souvenir shop in Delhi?

"You have a fine eye, young fellow."

A man dressed in long white trousers and a billowing shirt emerged from behind a curtain at the rear of the shop. He glided smoothly past the stacks of statues and carvings.

"One of our best pieces. Most of my customers are tourists looking for some cheap keepsake. Only a true collector would appreciate this."

Gerald could barely take his eyes from the casket. He crouched by it and ran his hands across its surface, clearing away the dust. "How did you get it?" he asked. "Where did it come from?"

The man's face wrinkled in a smile. "My family visits remote villages all over India searching for relics such as this. We buy only the very finest. This piece is from the south, from a fishing village on the Bay of Bengal. My son himself made the purchase. It had been in the owner's family for generations. Centuries even." The man nodded to himself. "You have a very fine eye."

Gerald couldn't believe it. He turned to Ruby. "Behind the tenth gate, just like the man said." He stood and looked at the store owner. "How much is it?"

The man wrote a figure on a piece of paper and handed it to Gerald. "How does one put a price on such beauty?" he said.

Gerald looked at the paper and swallowed. "You seem to have managed it," he said.

"It is a unique piece, sir," the man murmured to Gerald. "You must recognize its quality."

Gerald looked at the others and shrugged. "It's only money, right?" He pulled his wallet from his pocket and handed the man his black American Express card.

The man smiled warmly. "That will do nicely, sir."

As the shop owner processed the sale, Gerald struggled to lift the casket onto the counter.

Alisha looked at it doubtfully. "You should have haggled with him," she said. "That's a lot of money for a box."

"A *box*!" Gerald said. "Alisha, I have probably just saved our lives."

"What?"

"The dream I had—"

"It was a *dream*, Gerald!" Ruby was incensed. "You're talking like a lunatic."

"You don't recognize this casket?" He spun around to face her. "You don't see how we've been led here—the fortune-teller, my family seal. We've been brought to this place, at the tenth gate. I can't tell you why or what it means. But I've found it. And Mason Green loses."

Ruby clenched her jaw. "It was a dream. . . ."

Gerald turned his back. "Fine. Don't believe me. But be ready to apologize when we open this thing."

Gerald suddenly stopped and turned to the shop owner. "Does this come with a key? A gemstone, or something?"

The man looked puzzled. "There is no key. But I have many gemstones. Let me show you—"

"No, that's all right," Gerald interrupted. "We'll get it open. Sam, give me a hand."

Sam and Gerald hefted the casket out of the shop. Ruby and Alisha followed, whispering to each other.

They got halfway across the courtyard and set the casket down on a stone bench.

"Come on," Gerald said. "I want to open this thing now."

"Gerald, you realize that you're—"

He cut Ruby off. "I'm not interested in hearing it, okay? This is important. Nothing you can say will change that."

Ruby took a deep breath, then said quietly, "Fine."

Gerald gripped his fingers under the lip of the lid. "There's no booby traps around this one. We might not need a key." He jerked upward. Nothing moved. He tried again, straining against the weight. Nothing.

"It's bound to be a bit tight after a thousand years. Sam, try that end and we'll do it together."

Sam shrugged at his sister and clutched onto the lid.

"Okay. On three. One . . . two . . ."

They both lifted.

"It's moving!" Gerald said. "Try again."

The lid came off with a rush and they almost dropped it as it shot free.

"This is it," Gerald breathed. "Nothing will ever be the same again." He fixed a triumphant eye on Ruby, then reached inside the casket.

He pulled out a piece of paper, folded in half.

"Go on," Sam said. "Have a look."

Gerald opened it.

"It's a message," he said.

"What's it say?"

Gerald took another look, then closed his eyes. His hand dropped to his side.

Alisha plucked the page from Gerald's fingers. She unfolded it. "It says: 'This quality product was proudly man-ufactured by Kumar & Sons of Tamil Nadu, 2006.'"

"*What?*" Ruby said.

Alisha slipped the page back between Gerald's fingers. "They seem very proud of their work."

Gerald was devastated.

Sam nudged him on the shoulder. "Never mind. Come on, mate."

Gerald lifted his head. His eyes were ringed in red. The others made for the gate. He glanced at the window of the shop. The man in the white shirt was placing an identical casket at the foot of the counter.

Gerald sat hunched on the wooden bridge that straddled the fishpond in the Gupta compound like some giant garden gnome in the rain.

"I've just saved all our lives," he mumbled to himself. He couldn't believe he'd uttered the words in the first place. "Nothing will ever be the same again," he said in the same self-mocking tone. "What an idiot!" He screwed up his eyes and his chin drooped to his chest. He was drenched through and miserable. He'd lost track of how long he'd been sitting in the pouring rain, trying to rinse away his embarrassment.

Gerald was suddenly aware that the rain was no longer drumming on his skull. He lifted his head to find an umbrella over him.

"Are you going to stay here much longer? Because I can get you a fishing rod if you want." Ruby was grinning down at him.

Gerald stared at the rain-pocked surface of the pond. Even the fish had enough sense to keep their noses out of this weather. "I'm surprised you're talking to me."

"Why wouldn't I?" Ruby said. "You saved my life, didn't you?"

Gerald squirmed. "That's not fair."

"Actually, it's more than fair. You acted like a complete

prat. What possessed you to go on like that? And I can't believe what you paid for that casket—it would have fed an African village for a month."

Gerald lifted himself from the boards and wiped the rain off his face. "Want to come for a walk?"

They set out under the umbrella across the lush lawns in the teeming rain. Gerald was glad Ruby had come out. He didn't have the nerve to go back inside by himself.

"The dreams seem so real," he said. "It's like Mason Green is in the room with me. I think I really believed that finding that casket would save our lives, would stop Green from hurting us. You're right—I was possessed."

Ruby walked alongside him in silence, feet sloshing through the grass. They stopped by a white marble statue of a Greek god, a bow and arrow in his hands.

"But you're finished with it now," Ruby said. "We can get on with our holiday without you going nuts again?"

Gerald didn't answer straightaway. He knew Ruby was right. They were only dreams. He had acted like an idiot. But Mason Green's voice lingered in his ear: *It's in India, Gerald. Just waiting for you.* If one of the caskets was in the country, how could he deny its lure? How *could* he?

"Sure," Gerald said to Ruby. "Let's go see some tigers."

"You disappoint me, Gerald."

Sir Mason Green sat on a lounge in Gerald's bed-chamber, an ankle crooked over one knee, a gold-banded cigarette in the fingers of his right hand. His left cradled a tumbler of dark liquid, which Gerald assumed was whiskey—his father was fond of an after-dinner tipple. In fact, the rhythm of Green's sip-drag-exhale-sigh-sip was so similar to his father's nightly ritual it was as if he was lifting images from his own life and wrapping them around the figure of Sir Mason Green.

Gerald tried desperately to wake himself. But he was trapped in the binds of sleep. Sir Mason swallowed deep and swirled his drink. The ice tinkled like a crystal bell. He placed the tumbler on a side table and leaned behind the lounge to pull out a case, one that might contain a musical instrument—a clarinet perhaps, or an oboe. He flipped two brass clasps and opened the lid to reveal, cushioned in maroon velvet, the rod from the diamond casket. He placed his cigarette in an ashtray and picked up the scepter, cradling it like a newborn child.

"I'll make a deal with you, Mr. Wilkins," Green said, his eyes fixed on the golden rod in his hands. "You help me find the next casket and I'll tell you exactly what this beautiful relic is for—its glorious history"—Green paused to wipe a smudge from the rod's patina—"and its bountiful future."

Gerald tried to open his eyes but it was as if his lashes were glued. Yet he could see Sir Mason Green so clearly, smell the tobacco smoldering in the ashtray. Every moment he spent with this spectral Mason Green somehow made the man more real, his presence more tangible. Gerald *had* to wake up.

"What? First you threaten me and my friends and now you want a partnership?" Gerald said to his tormentor. "What's the matter? Can't you find it yourself?"

The man's eyes narrowed. He placed the golden rod back in its case.

"I am not used to being spoken to in such a manner by a child," he said, snapping the clasps closed.

"Who cares?" Gerald said. "It's not like you're real."

Green picked up his cigarette, took a long drag and allowed the smoke to pour from his nostrils.

"You should care, Mr. Wilkins," he said.

Sip-drag-exhale-sigh-sip.

"You seem to think my threat is not serious. I would hate for you to think that I am not a man of my word."

Gerald tossed in his bed, trying to shake the vision from his mind. But the voice resonated in the room.

"You had best be first to the casket, Mr. Wilkins," Green continued, his voice a rasp. He stood up from the lounge and drifted across to Gerald's bedside. He held up the cigarette and blew on the tip. It flared bright. "The lives of your friends depend on it."

Then he stabbed the cigarette into Gerald's face, right between his eyes. The red ember seared the skin, as hot as an iron. The pain was electric. Gerald struggled to sit up but his shoulders were pinned to the bed, some hidden force holding him down. Green's eyes grew wild. The old man pressed down on the cigarette. Its tip was, impossibly, still alight. A shriek of agony jammed in Gerald's throat. He lay there, unable to move or make a sound, his mouth framing a silent scream.

"Beat me to the casket," Green snarled. "It's your only hope."

Gerald's back arched at the torture. His eyes flew open as he finally broke the bonds of sleep. He sat up, his legs tangled in his sheets, sweat covering his body. His hand shot to his brow, certain he would find a weeping wound between his eyes. But the skin was smooth and flawless. He breathed deep and stared at the lounge across from his bed. The cushions were undisturbed. There was no ashtray on the side table, no whiskey glass to be seen. All was normal.

"Pah!" Gerald cried out loud. "Normal?"

He screwed his eyes tight. But he couldn't erase the vision of Sir Mason Green. In the fraction of a second it had taken for Gerald to open his eyes, to emerge from nightmare into shivering consciousness, the cigarette that Sir Mason Green was grinding into his forehead had transformed into the golden rod—an exquisite branding iron searing his flesh.

There was no more sleep for Gerald Wilkins that night.

Chapter Ten

Alisha didn't join them for breakfast. Sam was content to bundle his plate with a mountain of pastries and sink himself into his usual nest of cushions in front of the music channel.

Gerald took a single croissant and sat at a table out on the porch. The rain spilled over the gutters in a liquid curtain. He stared into the deluge and went over the details of his nightmare, still vivid in his mind. More than once his fingers strayed to the bridge of his nose to check on the state of his forehead. It had all seemed so real. The smell of the tobacco smoke, the whiskey. His own burning flesh . . .

Gerald knew he had to stop the dreams. He couldn't go through another night like that.

"Have a good sleep?"

Ruby dragged a chair across the tiled porch and sat down, a plate of fresh fruit in her hand.

Gerald peered at her through puffy eyes.

"I'll take that as a no," Ruby said. "More dreams?"

Gerald bit into the croissant and chewed. It was an effort. He knew what he was about to say would annoy Ruby no end.

"I've got a theory," he said, gazing out at the rain while trying to keep half an eye on Ruby's face. "About these dreams."

"Is that so, Sigmund?" Ruby said, keeping an equally careful eye on Gerald's expression. "Do tell."

Sigmund? Sometimes Gerald didn't understand Ruby at all. He tore off a corner of his croissant. "Would it be completely mental of me to think that Sir Mason Green is using the golden rod to insert himself into my dreams?"

Ruby didn't blink. She reached out, stabbed a slice of mango with her fork and popped it in her mouth. She chewed, then swallowed.

"Yes," she said. "You would be totally mental to think that."

"I knew you'd say that. But you didn't see what I saw. He was there in my room. Right there. And he stubbed his cigarette into my head, but it wasn't a cigarette, it was the golden rod. And it burned, and—"

Ruby held up her fork. "Gerald, I understand that these

nightmares are disturbing, but seriously, that's all they are. Nightmares. Sir Mason Green is not broadcasting himself into your dreams, all right." She wasn't looking for a reply.

Alisha opened the glass door to the guest villa. The hammering of rain followed her inside. She looked like she'd been arguing with her father again.

"The tiger safari is organized," she said flatly. "We fly down in the Archer jet the day after tomorrow."

"Great!" Sam said. "Love that jet."

Ruby clicked her tongue at her brother then turned to Alisha. "Is something the matter?"

Alisha tossed her head back. "Father insists that Miss Turner and Mr. Fry come with us."

"You must have expected that," Sam said. "The usual escort."

"I know. Miss Turner will be shackled to me until the day I die. But there's something else."

"What's that?" Gerald asked.

The answer came with a sharp rap at the door. Gerald looked up to see a meaty face staring in at them. Sweat poured down the man's cheeks and he looked about as happy as a penguin in a sauna. It took them a second to recognize Constable Lethbridge of the London Metropolitan Police.

"Flipping heck," Sam said. "What's he doing here?"

Gerald pulled open the door. Lethbridge stood on the porch and closed his eyes as the waft of air-conditioning swept over him. He let out a strangled "arrgghhhh."

Gerald ushered the constable inside. Lethbridge collapsed into the nearest armchair, a physical wreck dressed in a T-shirt, Bermuda shorts, and sneakers. While the long summer had given Gerald, Sam, and Ruby a honey tan, Lethbridge's skin had apparently gone from Arctic white to shocking pink in a matter of hours. He looked like he was about to expire.

Ruby offered him a glass of lime juice, which he took in both hands and gulped down. "More," he gasped. "More . . ."

"Bit hot for you?" Sam said. "Don't worry. It only gets hotter."

The constable slumped back and took in slow breaths of cool air.

"Flew in last night," he gasped. "Nobody told me it was going to be this hot." He glanced at the windows and the torrential bucketing that was going on outside. "Or wet."

Gerald handed him another drink and Lethbridge snatched it and tipped it down his throat.

"Look, constable, it's nice to see you and all, but why are you here?" Gerald said. "Surely Inspector Parrott hasn't sent you all this way."

Lethbridge caught his breath. "Not as such. I'm in India

162

as a guest of the IPF—I'm here to attend a very high-level conference in an official capacity."

"Wow!" said Ruby. "The Indian Police Force."

Lethbridge cleared his throat. "Uh, no. The Indian Pigeon Fanciers. A most prestigious association. Very much respected in the world of pigeon fancying. I'm the general secretary of the East Finchley branch of the Royal Pigeon Racing Association."

"There's a world of pigeon fancying?" Sam said, failing to stifle a giggle. "Sorry, it doesn't sound too interesting."

"Not interesting! It's fascinating. Pigeons are very intelligent creatures. You can take them thousands of miles from their home and they still find their way back. I've had them since I was a lad and I love 'em. When you've got a pigeon, you've got a friend."

Lethbridge looked at them with such earnest sincerity that it was difficult to respond.

"They invited you to a conference," Ruby said to fill the silence.

"All expenses paid," Lethbridge said with undisguised pride. "Air France—first class! Sat next to a very nice man—very good English, for a foreigner."

"You haven't traveled much, have you?" Alisha said.

"First time," he said. "How did you know?"

"Lucky guess."

"And you're still in all the papers," Lethbridge said to

Gerald. "The man on the plane was reading about you in the *Independent*. We had a good chat about it. You're quite famous, you know."

Gerald blushed. He hated the idea of being the topic of other people's conversations.

"You'll be leaving quite soon for this conference," Gerald said. "I mean, you won't be hanging around here for long."

"I'll be off the day after tomorrow. The conference is in Chennai, in the south."

Gerald looked at Alisha. "That's not so bad."

"Tell them about my father's brilliant idea," Alisha said to the police constable, a grim look in her eyes.

"It is brilliant, isn't it? Mr. Gupta said that since you're flying south I should hitch a lift."

"What!"

"It's only a three-hour flight," Alisha said. "And only a little out of our way. For some reason Father thought it was a great idea."

"Bit of extra security expertise," Lethbridge said, puffing his chest out. Gerald couldn't help notice his similarity to a pigeon. "I'm meeting a local pigeon fancier later today. I can tell you all about it on the flight."

"I can hardly wait," Sam said.

Lethbridge got up to go, then paused. "Almost forgot. The reason I dropped by." He ferreted around in his bag. "The inspector asked me to give you this."

He pulled out a stack of envelopes and handed them to Gerald. "They were in Sir Mason Green's room at the Rattigan Club. It seems they're yours."

Gerald leafed through the envelopes. They contained the remainder of the news clippings and other documents that the thin man had stolen from the house in London, including the letter his great-aunt Geraldine had left him.

But something else caught Gerald's eye. "What's this?" he asked. He pulled out a sealed envelope, with a blue Interpol insignia on the front. Typed on a label in capital letters was: INVESTIGATION INTO SIR MASON GREEN AND CERTAIN HISTORIC ANTIQUITIES IN EGYPT, FRANCE, AND—

"India!" Gerald said, his eyes popping.

Lethbridge looked at the envelope with surprise. "Don't remember that being in there. Must have picked it up by mistake. Never mind." He reached across and plucked it from Gerald's fingers. "I'll send that back to the inspector."

Gerald emitted a sound that a six-year-old might make if he dropped an ice cream in the dirt.

Lethbridge put the envelope into his bag. "I'm really looking forward to flying on your jet," he said to Gerald. "I'll go out to the airport with your butler and check it out ahead of time. Security, you see. Till then, there's pigeon business to attend."

Lethbridge took a deep breath, opened the door to the

porch, and took off up the covered walkway to the main house.

"Did you see that?" Gerald said, before the door had swung closed. "Egypt, France, and *India*. One of the caskets must be here. The fortune-teller was right."

Ruby dismissed the idea in an instant. "Agent Leclerc didn't mention it," she said. "He's the local Interpol guy. It must be a mistake."

Gerald wasn't listening. "And I don't believe Lethbridge for a second. What a load of . . . pigeon business."

"You think he's lying?" Alisha said.

"Of course. It's a bit much, isn't it? Five seconds after we get here he turns up with some rubbish story about a pigeon conference. You wouldn't invite him for coffee, let alone fly him down here to join some bunch of bird nuts."

"Flock," Sam said. "It would be a flock of bird nuts."

"Flock, then. I've never trusted Lethbridge anyway, not after the diamond went missing while he was guarding it. Think about it. His notebook with all the evidence from the case—supposedly stolen—just happens to turn up in India in the back pocket of a guy who tries to kidnap Alisha. And now Lethbridge is here to attend some pigeon conference and he just happens to have an Interpol report in his bag. He must be tied up in all of this."

"How would some junior police officer get involved with Sir Mason Green?" Ruby said.

"I don't know. But I bet that Interpol report has some answers."

Ruby peered at Gerald with suspicious eyes. "And what do you mean by that?"

"Nothing," he said. "I wonder which hotel Lethbridge is staying at."

CHAPTER ELEVEN

The lobby of the Colonial Hotel in Delhi is one of the city's standout meeting places. Beneath its crystal chandeliers and art-clad walls, the elite of India gather to sip tea and nibble tiny sandwiches, the crusts removed. While the city is a bustling metropolis of trade and commerce, the lobby at the Colonial is a cool oasis of calm and whispered conversations.

Alisha led Gerald, Ruby, and Sam through the hotel's revolving glass doors shortly before seven o'clock in the morning.

"What if he's already had breakfast and gone back to his room?" Sam said.

"Then you better think of plan B," Ruby replied. She surveyed the plush surroundings. "The Indian Pigeon

Fanciers must be doing okay to put Lethbridge up in this place."

"So you agree with me?" Gerald said. "Lethbridge's story doesn't add up."

"Don't get ahead of yourself, Sherlock," Ruby said. "I'm just humoring you. Once you've done what you need to do here, we're going to look at tigers." She took Gerald by the arm and looked into his eyes. "Right?"

Gerald grinned. "Whatever you say. Now, how are we going to do this?"

It was Alisha's turn to smile. "My father does more business in this lobby than in his office. This is my second home. Follow me."

She set off toward the concierge desk, the others trailing after her.

"Are you going to keep Lethbridge's notebook?" Ruby said to Gerald.

"I'll give it back eventually," he said. "But until his story checks out, I think it's safer in our hands. If that bandit in black is working for Green, there must be something in that book worth having, and I wouldn't mind betting the missing page holds some interesting information."

"That's a lot of ifs," Ruby said.

Alisha was talking to a slender man in a dark suit—he had a telephone in one hand and was jotting something on a pad with the other. He tore off a page and handed it to

Alisha with a polite nod. She sauntered back to Gerald with a triumphant smile.

"He's on the ninth floor—room number 912. He hasn't been down for breakfast yet. If we wait on that lounge over there, we can keep an eye on the elevators and make our move when he appears."

"I thought all that stuff was supposed to be private," Ruby said.

"I've known the concierge here for years. I said Constable Lethbridge was an old family friend and we wanted to surprise him."

"Isn't she incredible?" Sam said.

"No," Ruby said. "She is smart. You being able to walk and talk at the same time is incredible."

Gerald ushered them over to the lounge and made sure Sam and Ruby sat as far apart as possible. They didn't have long to wait. Constable Lethbridge rolled out of one of the elevators and made for the restaurant.

"Judging by his size he'll be eating for a while. We should have plenty of time," Gerald said. "You got the package?"

Ruby patted her bag. "I'll give you ten minutes, then I'll send it up."

Two minutes later Gerald and Sam stepped from the elevator and counted down the rooms until they stood outside number 912.

Gerald checked his watch. "We've only got a couple of

minutes. We've got to time this right." He glanced to his left. "You take the door. I'll do the talking."

Sam nodded and continued up the corridor, away from the elevators. There was a cleaner's cart against one wall and he ducked behind it.

Gerald went back past the elevators to the far end of the corridor. He reached a set of fire stairs and poked his head inside. "Perfect," he said. As he entered the stairwell, a *ding* signaled the elevator door was opening. He peered around the doorjamb as a hotel porter stepped out of the elevator and headed toward room 912. He was carrying a small parcel wrapped in striped paper.

The porter knocked and waited. When there was no reply, he slipped a key into the lock and stepped inside. The moment the porter disappeared into Lethbridge's room, Gerald moved. He scampered down the corridor until he was three doors from 912. He glanced at the cleaner's cart farther down the hall. Sam was invisible.

Moments later, the door opened and the porter emerged. The moment Gerald saw him, he called out, "Excuse me?"

The porter looked up and gave a polite smile. He paused in the doorway, his hand still on the open door.

"Yes, sir," he said. "How may I help you?"

Gerald knew the next five seconds were crucial.

"Can you help me with some directions, please?" he asked and pulled a folded street map from his pocket.

"Certainly, sir."

The porter stepped toward Gerald, releasing the door. It started to swing to, the automatic closer drawing it in. Gerald tried not to look over the porter's shoulder as Sam scuttled along the wall like a mouse on the skirting. The gap in the doorway narrowed. Sam was still yards away. The porter peered over the top of the map in Gerald's hands.

"Where was sir wanting to go?"

The space inched tighter and tighter.

"I'm trying to find the museum."

The gap narrowed to a sliver.

"Which museum, sir? There are many."

"Um . . ."

At the last second, Sam dropped onto the carpet in a baseball slide and shot out his foot, jamming the toe of his shoe into the door. A judder shot up the wooden frame. The porter started to turn his head at the sound.

"The National Museum!" Gerald was almost shouting, rattling the map under the porter's nose—anything to distract him from the boy struggling onto his hands and knees and crawling into Lethbridge's room.

The porter turned back to Gerald. His description of the short walk to the museum from the hotel forecourt was detailed and entirely accurate. Gerald didn't take in a word of it.

"Thank you so much," he said, as the porter entered the

elevator. The man held the door for Gerald, an inquisitive look on his face.

Gerald waved a hand. "Um, no thanks," he said. "I just remembered I need to"—his mind went blank—"um, wash my hair."

The porter looked surprised, then gave a courteous nod as the elevator doors closed.

Seconds later Gerald was tapping on the door to room 912. It opened a crack and a blue eye appeared in the gap. "Is that room service?"

Gerald shoved on the door and it banged into Sam's head. "Don't muck around," Gerald said. "We don't have time." He pushed his way inside.

Lethbridge's king-sized bed was unmade and there was a pile of soggy bath towels bunched on one end. A sideboard bore the remains of a midnight feast: chocolate-bar wrappers and potato-chip packets. A bowl of fruit remained untouched. A large black suitcase sat on the floor with its lid propped open. Gerald made for it. Sam followed, still rubbing his head.

Gerald lifted folded shirts and trousers out of the way, careful not to disturb things too much, but there was no sign of the Interpol report. He eyed a pile of underwear. It wasn't clear if it was clean or dirty. He took a deep breath and was about to sink his hands into the middle of it when Sam spoke.

"What's this?"

He was pointing at a large rectangular shape near the foot of the bed. It was covered with a dark cloth. Could Lethbridge have found something already?

Gerald knelt down and grabbed a corner of the cloth. He was about to lift it away when a something stirred underneath. They both jumped.

"Holy cow!" Sam yelped.

Gerald glanced at his friend then back at the box. He took a tentative hold of the cloth between finger and thumb, and pulled. The covering came away and Gerald was suddenly nose-to-beak with a speckled . . .

"Pigeon!"

Four gray-and-white birds blinked at them from inside a wooden frame covered in chicken wire. They cooed and pecked at the gaps in the mesh. Each bird had a red band around one leg and a tiny metal tube attached to the other.

Gerald and Sam leaned back on their heels. "Maybe Lethbridge was telling the truth after all," Sam said. "He's not going to bring this lot with him if he's helping Green search for one of the caskets."

"Maybe," Gerald said. "But what's the point of bringing them at all? They're hardly going to find their way back to East Finchley from here."

Then Gerald saw the bag. The one that Lethbridge had with him when he was in the villa at the Gupta compound.

He scrambled on hands and knees to grab it. He pulled the handles apart and peered inside. At the bottom was a bundle of documents held together with a rubber band. Gerald pulled it out and started flicking through.

"Airline ticket, itinerary, travel insurance . . . here it is!" He pulled out the envelope with the Interpol insignia.

"How are we going to look at the report if it's sealed?" Sam asked.

Gerald turned the envelope over. "It's not sealed anymore," he said. "Lethbridge must have opened it." With a quick glance at his friend for reassurance, Gerald pulled out the document. It was about a dozen pages long, stapled at the top. He scanned the front page. But it just seemed to be a summary of their discovery of the diamond casket. He flipped over the next few pages. There were sections headed "France" and "Egypt," and finally, he came to a page with "India" at the top.

"This is it," he said to Sam. His eyes tried to drink in the words on the paper but, in his rush, the letters seemed to melt into each other. Finally, near the bottom, he found something.

"Listen to this," he said: "'Though there is no hard evidence to support such a claim, local legends speak of a magical casket that was buried in an ancient coastal city, possibly late in the fourth century. The casket was supposedly under the protection of a dangerous religious cult, aspects of which survive to this day.'"

Gerald took in a sharp breath. "A cult! That's my family!"

Sam looked puzzled. "What are you on about?"

After the disappointment of the stone casket at the bazaar, Gerald had almost forgotten about the link between his family seal and the deadly cult. "Tell you later," he said. He read on:

"There are myths of a magnificent metropolis, boasting six temples. The location of the ancient city was forgotten after it was inundated by rising seawaters more than a thousand years ago. However, the recent tsunami has uncovered the ruins of what appears to be a large township, buried for centuries under the Bay of Bengal. Local fishermen claim it is the lost city of the legends."

Gerald grabbed Sam by the elbow. "The casket must be there!" he said, his eyes wide with excitement.

"Where is it?"

Gerald looked at the bottom of the page. "The town of Ma—"

The phone on the bedside table burst into life.

"Far out!" Gerald cried. He dropped the report. "Do we answer it?"

The ring continued. Loud. Insistent.

Gerald reached up, gave an anxious look at Sam, and lifted the handset.

"Hello?"

"Lethbridge is on his way up!" It was Alisha.

Gerald dropped the phone back into the cradle and dived on the report, which had fluttered under the bed. He struggled to straighten it out and get it back into the envelope.

"Lethbridge!" he hissed at Sam.

He jammed the bundle of documents back into the carry bag and they raced for the door. Sam was about to open it when a chorus of cooing struck up behind them.

"Pigeons!" Gerald spun back and flung the cloth over the birdcage.

They burst out into the corridor as the elevator doors slid open. To their horror, a foot appeared on the carpet.

They were in the middle of the hallway.

The cleaner's cart had gone.

There was nowhere to hide.

Gerald shoved his hand into his pocket. The street map. He just managed to unfold it in front of their faces as Lethbridge stepped out of the elevator. They kept their heads down and scurried past the constable, ignoring his greeting of "Good morning." Gerald stabbed at the elevator button, stopping the doors from shutting and they fell inside. He poked an eye back into the corridor and saw that Lethbridge had reached room 912—just as the automatic closer pulled the door shut. Lethbridge jerked his eyes back toward the elevator. Gerald snapped his head inside and hammered on the button for the lobby.

"Come on."

The doors slid together and the elevator started its downward journey.

Gerald waited until Mr. Gupta's butler had finished laying out the lunch buffet in the casual dining room and had pulled the double doors closed behind him.

Sam had been bursting to let Ruby and Alisha know about the Interpol report, but Gerald insisted they hold on until he could get some food into his belly. Mostly he had wanted some time to get everything straight in his own mind.

He started by telling them about the cult.

He'd been chewing over why his family would adopt the symbol of a murderous gang of thugs but had got no further than the theory that it was just a pretty cool design.

"Don't worry about it, Gerald," Alisha said. "Whatever the reason, it all happened centuries ago."

Gerald and Sam then took it in turns to retell what they'd seen in the hotel room.

Ruby couldn't get past the pigeons.

"That settles it, as far as I'm concerned," she said. "Lethbridge must be telling the truth. No one is going to bring a box of pigeons with them as cover for some secret mission."

"Well, what about the Interpol report?" Gerald said. "It named the town where the casket might be hidden. The dates are about right. Professor McElderry said the three Antonius brothers left Rome with the caskets around AD 400. One of the caskets must be in that town."

"Shame you can't remember the name of it then, isn't it?" Ruby said.

Gerald glared at his plate. He'd been in such a rush to get the report back inside the envelope.

"Anyway, a tale of a lost city uncovered by tidal waves is all a bit far-fetched, don't you think?" Ruby said. She picked up a chicken leg and took a bite. "You've had your fun, Gerald. Who's in favor of going to look at tigers?" She raised her hand and looked at the others.

Alisha raised her hand. Sam looked first at Gerald, then at Alisha. He gave Gerald a shrug then put his hand in the air.

Ruby turned to Gerald. "You promised," she said.

Gerald bit his bottom lip. Then he slowly raised a hand.

After lunch Gerald assured Ruby that he had abandoned any plan to find the missing casket. He didn't mention that he'd phoned Agent Leclerc, trying to find out more about the Interpol report. It was only after the third call went through to an answering machine that Gerald gave up and settled on chasing tigers.

They spent the afternoon lounging around the Guptas' indoor swimming pool. The monsoon lashed down outside, sluicing over the clear, barrel-shaped roof high above. Sam was entertaining them with a variety of poorly executed dives from the high board.

"This one I call the dying swan," he said from ten feet up. He launched off the platform as if he'd just been shot and landed in an explosion of spray and limbs.

"More like the brain-dead twin," Ruby said. Her raft bucked in the wash. Sam launched himself up from the bottom of the pool and torpedoed her into the water.

He was halfway up the ladder to the diving platform when Mr. Gupta wandered into the pool enclosure. He was followed by Mr. Fry and a sheepish-looking Constable Lethbridge.

"I'm afraid there's been a change in plans," Mr. Gupta announced.

Alisha looked up from her deck chair. "What's happened?"

"It appears the Archer jet is no longer available."

"What!" Sam spluttered from the ladder. "Why not?"

Mr. Fry gave Lethbridge a sideward glance. "Shall you tell them?" he said. "Or shall I?"

Lethbridge swallowed. Somehow, even with a lobster-colored complexion, he'd gone pale. "I was at the airport with Mr. Fry," he said. "Giving the plane the once-over. You know, for—"

"Security." Sam finished the sentence. "Yes, we know that. What's happened?"

"I was on the tarmac, see. Walking around the plane, just checking for anything unusual. The pilot had the engines on, warming them up, I guess. Then, over on a patch of grass, I see the pigeons. . . ."

"Pigeons?" Ruby said.

"Beautiful, they were. Lovely birds. Very intelligent, you know. They can fly huge distances back to their homes. Never get lost. Did I mention that?"

"So you thought you'd take a closer look," Mr. Fry said, his eyes dark as death.

"Must have been fifty or more of them," Lethbridge continued, his voice dreamlike. "Each one a beauty."

"Get on with it," Fry said.

"I only wanted to have a look." Lethbridge choked. He couldn't go on.

"He got too close, the birds took off, and the whole lot got sucked into the engines," Fry said. "Feathers and drumsticks everywhere. The plane's grounded for a week for repairs."

Lethbridge looked devastated.

But not as devastated as Sam. "A week!" he said. "How are we getting to the tiger reserve now?"

Mr. Gupta puffed out his chest and a smile spread across his face. "I have an excellent solution," he said. "There are many commercial flights to the south—"

"So we have to fly in a normal plane?" Sam whined.

"No," Mr. Gupta said. "You don't get a real feel for a country from thirty thousand feet in the air. Now that Alisha is taking a greater interest in her heritage, I was thinking of an alternative means of transport."

"What's that, Mr. Gupta?" Gerald asked.

"The train."

"The train!" Sam was horrified. "How long will that take?"

"Oh, no more than forty hours. It will be quite the adventure for you."

"Forty hours!" Sam lost his grip and fell off the ladder into the pool. He surfaced still speaking. "On a train. Are you serious?"

"It sounds fun," Ruby said.

"Sure, why not?" Alisha said. "We can make some stops along the way. It's not like we're in a hurry."

Gerald swam over to where Sam was clinging to the side of the pool. His face was a picture of desolation. "I'm sure the train will be very comfy," Gerald said.

Sam was lost in his misery. "The plane . . . the beautiful plane . . ."

Chapter Twelve

The New Delhi Train Station at night is a beehive of activity. Eighteen platforms back to back, bustling with thousands of people in the draining summer air. Trains from across the country arriving and departing by the minute. A bubbling curry of families, hawkers, beggars, porters, guards, soldiers, Hindus, Muslims, Sikhs, Jains, Christians—all going, coming, or just staying put.

Gerald, Ruby, and Alisha clambered down the covered stairway onto the platform, brimming with anticipation, their packs over their shoulders. Sam lagged behind, his face as long as the journey that stretched out before them. They were followed by Miss Turner and Mr. Fry, who also carried backpacks and kept a wary eye on their charges.

"What's more funny?" Gerald asked as they wound

their way along the platform. "Sam being such a grump or Fry in shorts? He looks like an overinflated boy scout."

"I think the funniest thing is Miss Turner," Alisha said, glancing back at her guardian.

"What about her?" Gerald asked.

"Haven't you noticed? She fancies Mr. Fry."

Gerald let out a disbelieving, "You're kidding!"

Sam caught up. "What's so funny?" he said.

"Alisha reckons Miss Turner's got the hots for Fry," Gerald said.

"The ice queen and the king of dull?"

"Haven't you seen how she acts when he's around?" Ruby said. "Can't keep her eyes off him."

Sam gagged. "I may need a bucket."

They threw their packs into a heap and sat on the concrete to wait for their train. A pack of scrawny dogs, the color of melted ice cream, sniffed around the tracks, scavenging for scraps among the litter. A loudspeaker announced the arrival of a train on the platform behind them. The engine drew into the station and people gathered their belongings. Gerald watched Sam's face fall further and further at the sight of carriages stuffed to overflowing. People were leaning out the open doors and faces were pressed against the iron bars of the glassless windows.

Sam was horrified.

"We traded a six-star private jet for forty hours in a

sardine tin?" he said. "This is insanity."

"Maybe our train won't be so crowded," Gerald said.

A scrum formed around the doorway to one of the carriages. Bags and bundles were tossed over heads in the race to get inside.

Sam groaned.

"Where's your sense of adventure?" Ruby said. "Anyway, that's a second-class carriage. Mr. Gupta would have booked something more comfy."

All eyes turned to Gerald's butler. Mr. Fry unzipped a pocket in his shorts and pulled out some papers.

"We have seats in the chairman's carriage," he said.

"Well, that sounds all right," Ruby said, staring at the tangle of bodies inside the train opposite. Sam didn't look convinced.

"There's one consolation," Alisha said.

"What's that?" Sam grumbled.

"Constable Lethbridge won't be hitching a ride with us now."

Gerald pulled a water bottle from the side of his pack and took a sip. "Lethbridge seemed his normal goofy self at the house yesterday. You don't suppose he suspected anything?"

"That's the problem with your master criminal," Ruby said, pulling a face at Gerald. "You can never tell when they're acting dumb to disguise their insane brilliance."

Alisha laughed, but the smile froze on her face. Ruby looked her way. "What's the problem?"

Alisha pointed down the platform.

They turned to see a porter struggling toward them through the crowd with a large suitcase balanced on his head.

"What's that on top of the case?" Ruby asked.

Sam and Gerald recognized it at once.

"Pigeons," Gerald said.

From behind the porter emerged Constable Lethbridge, cheeks pink in the heat. He was dressed like he was about to star as an extra in a Tarzan movie: boots with long socks hiked to his knees, khaki shorts, and a shirt with an array of pockets and epaulets. The only things missing were a pith helmet and an elephant gun.

The porter placed the suitcase and the box of birds at Gerald's feet and accepted a handful of notes from Lethbridge.

"This is a bit of fun, isn't it?" Lethbridge said, clapping his hands together. "Think I've acclimatized now. Really looking forward to this trip. We can get to know each other a bit better. Oh, hello. We haven't met." He held out a fleshy paw to Miss Turner and shook her hand vigorously. "We'll all be best of pals." Miss Turner's expression indicated she thought that outcome was highly unlikely.

Gerald was mortified. "You're coming with us on the train?"

Lethbridge parked his frame on his suitcase. "Mr. Gupta's idea," he said. "He thought I'd enjoy the experience."

Gerald turned to Alisha. "Your father is full of good ideas."

She stared at the ground between her feet. "Isn't he just," she mumbled.

"But won't you be late for your conference?" Ruby said. "I thought it started tomorrow."

Lethbridge pulled a handkerchief from one of his pockets and wiped his forehead. "As luck would have it, I phoned the organizers, and the opening day has been put back. I'll have plenty of time."

"That is a stroke of good luck," Gerald said. He gave Ruby a look that showed he didn't believe a word.

"And it means the birds don't have to go in a plane. Funny thing, that. They don't like to fly. Not unless they're flying, of course. You see, with pigeons it's a matter of . . ."

Lethbridge droned for the next half hour about the intricacies of pigeon keeping, until the announcement that their train would arrive in four minutes.

"At last," Miss Turner said. She had positioned herself as far from Lethbridge as possible during the wait. She turned to Alisha. "Stay where I can see you."

Alisha flashed a scowl at her. "Can you please stop treating me like a child?"

Miss Turner pulled a pack onto her shoulders. "The day you stop acting like one."

Alisha fumed and turned her back on Miss Turner. She whispered to Gerald, "She drives me crazy. How do you put up with Mr. Fry?"

Gerald glanced across at his butler. He was trying to convince Miss Turner to let him take her pack. "I don't think my personal development is high on his list of concerns," Gerald said.

An engine barreled into the station at the head of a long line of dull green carriages. People scurried in all directions with their mountains of bags and bundles, looking to secure seats.

"Which one's the chairman's carriage?" Ruby asked. "They all look the same."

Gerald spied a train conductor and was about to go ask him for directions when a voice sounded in his ear.

"Excuse me, sir, would you be Mr. Gerald Wilkins?" The clipped English accent belonged to a solid man wearing an ivory-colored turban and, despite the heat, a black suit and waistcoat. He boasted a superb beard and moustache.

"Um, yes," Gerald said.

"Most excellent," the man replied. "And these are your friends? On behalf of the chairman of Indian Railways, welcome to New Delhi Train Station." The man clicked his fingers and a team of porters appeared and started picking up their bags.

"Your carriage is at the rear," the man said. "Please do come this way." He took off down the platform, and Gerald, Ruby, Sam, and Alisha, together with Mr. Fry, Miss Turner, and Constable Lethbridge, scampered after him.

"Did you say the chairman of Indian Railways sent you down here?" Gerald asked the man.

"That is correct. Apparently he and Mr. Gupta are old school friends. The chairman wanted to make sure you would be comfortable."

"My father called him?" Alisha said. "Why can't he let me live my life without interfering?"

They stopped at the end of the train. Sam took one look at the last carriage and whistled long and low. "Just this one time, Alisha, let's be thankful he made the call."

The chairman's carriage was like a rolling palace. Even from the outside, it was obvious that they were going to enjoy a level of comfort far above anyone else on the train.

The man in the turban climbed up to the door and swung it open. They clambered in and stared agog at the interior. Swathed in silks and hand-loomed rugs, the inside of the carriage was a scene from the Mughal era. Sam threw himself into a pile of cushions in one corner and squirmed around until he was comfy.

"Feeling better now?" Alisha asked.

Sam closed his eyes and burrowed back into his nest. "If you have to take the train, this is the way to do it," he said.

The porters lifted the bags on board. Lethbridge's box of pigeons was the last item to be stowed. Within minutes the train was moving. Gerald leaned out the open door and watched as the few remaining passengers ran for their carriages. The last of the porters squeezed past him and stepped down to the platform. A long blast of the train whistle signaled they were on their way.

Gerald closed the door and wandered into the air-conditioned carriage. Mr. Fry and Miss Turner were preparing bunks in a sleeping compartment while Ruby and Alisha sat at a table and flicked through Ruby's travel guide. Constable Lethbridge was checking on his pigeons.

"Alisha's arranged for us to stop in a town called Agra for a day, just to break the trip," Ruby said.

"Why Agra?" Sam asked.

"To see the Taj Mahal, of course," Alisha said. "And an ancient fort."

Sam wriggled upright. "Of course I know all about the Taj Mahal," he said. "But, just for Gerald's sake, what is it again?"

Alisha raised her eyes to the ceiling. "The Taj Mahal was built by one of India's greatest Mughal emperors, Shah Jehan. He was so devastated when his wife died he constructed the most beautiful building in the world to be her eternal resting place."

Lethbridge looked up from a seat in the corner of the carriage. "Shah Jehan was an enthusiastic pigeon breeder, you know." No one paid him any attention.

"It's a very romantic story," Ruby said.

They were interrupted by the sound of giggling. Miss Turner, a hand over her mouth, was laughing at something Mr. Fry had said. Fry was looking extremely pleased with himself.

"That's all we need," Sam said. "More romance."

The smell of freshly cooked bacon and eggs enticed Gerald from one of the best sleeps he could remember having. With the drum of rain on the roof and the comforting sway of the carriage, Gerald, wrapped in cool cotton sheets with his head nestled on a goose-down pillow, had fallen into a bottomless sleep. And this time, his dreams were blissfully free of Sir Mason Green. Instead, he'd been transported to an underwater world, where the liquid atmosphere made everything bulge and distort into the most bizarre of shapes. He had been trying to pick up a seashell that kept melting through his fingers when the fortune-teller from the market in Delhi came into view. The man took Gerald's hand and, in time with the *clackety-clack* of the train, recited over and over: "*Nothing is certain, nothing is certain.*" Then the man hoisted Gerald off the ground till his feet were pointing straight up. With a gentle push, Gerald floated into the liquid sky, turning and twisting as if in the vacuum of space. The fortune-teller grew smaller and more warped the higher Gerald rose. The ground beneath the man's feet began spinning like a pinwheel, with patterns forming and dissolving in an interlocking mosaic of colors and forms. It was only the whiff of bacon fat that brought Gerald back to the train carriage.

"That smells so good," he said, wiping sleep from his eyes. "I'm starving."

The others were already seated around the table, tucking in to breakfast. Mr. Fry, an apron strung around his waist, was dishing up generous servings onto fine bone china. He took an extra second to make sure Miss Turner's meal was particularly well presented. She smiled at him.

"What's that on your head?" Sam said to Gerald as he pulled up a chair.

Gerald patted his forehead.

"Oh, this," he said. He peeled off a large adhesive bandage from his forehead. "Just something to help me sleep."

Ruby shook her head. "Whatever works," she said. "I don't want to hear any more about your dreams."

"You having some funny dreams?" Lethbridge asked through a mouth full of eggs.

"It's nothing," Gerald mumbled.

He tucked into breakfast and, despite himself, was

impressed that Mr. Fry could prepare such a delicious meal in the cramped confines of a rail carriage. Then it occurred to him—they weren't moving.

He stood up from the table and went to the door. He swung it open and a plume of hot air was sucked inside as he leaned out. The rest of the train was gone. The chairman's carriage stood by itself in a station siding three sets of tracks from the nearest platform. People were milling in scores along the length of the station among the clamor of food vendors and hawkers. Gerald pulled the door shut.

"We seem to have lost our train."

Ruby and Alisha were stacking plates and helping clear the table. Constable Lethbridge washed up in a small sink, trying unsuccessfully to strike up a conversation with Miss Turner.

"I told you," Ruby said. "We're spending the day in Agra. We'll hook onto the next train south tonight."

There was a knock on the door. Mr. Fry opened it, and a man with the largest handlebar moustache Gerald had ever seen climbed on board.

"On behalf of the mayor of Agra, welcome," the man said, bowing deeply. "The mayor extends a personal invitation for a private night viewing of the Taj Mahal this evening."

"A private viewing?" Ruby said. "Fantastic."

"Excuse me, sir," Alisha said. "Did my father have

anything to do with this?"

The man with the moustache waggled his head. "I believe the mayor and Mr. Gupta were at university together."

Alisha exhaled loudly.

"Don't worry about it, Alisha," Gerald said. "A private tour of the Taj sounds pretty good."

"And at night," Ruby said. "Now we can spend the whole day shopping."

Sam spoke from his mound of cushions. "Or we could poke out our eyes with knitting needles. Whichever."

Alisha's mood lifted with the prospect of a day at the markets. Gerald and Sam tried everything to wheedle their way out of the shopping trip but with no success. Alisha landed the knockout punch when she laid a hand on Sam's forearm and said with a smile, "It wouldn't be as much fun without you."

Even Mr. Fry rolled his eyes at that.

Alisha and Ruby had advanced the farthest along the narrow bazaar, making strong headway through the rows of clothing and shoe stalls. Behind them Miss Turner and Sam were trying to convince Mr. Fry to buy a new hat, Sam doing his best to keep a straight face as he suggested increasingly ludicrous options. Gerald found himself bringing up the rear with Constable Lethbridge. They straggled along under leaden skies and stifling humidity.

Lethbridge stopped at a stall crammed with cane baskets that were filled with colorful spices, nuts, and seeds. He pointed to a mound of sunflower seeds, and the vendor heaped two scoops into a paper bag. "A little treat for the pigeons," he said to Gerald, handing the man some coins.

"Bit of an effort," Gerald said. "Bringing those birds all the way from London."

"They're not my birds," Lethbridge said. "Mine are in a loft in East Finchley. That pigeon fancier in Delhi lent them to me. He can't make it to the conference, poor chap, so he asked me to send a few messages to let him know how it's going."

"Using the pigeons?"

"Of course. They'll fly straight to his house. Far quicker than sending a letter. How else would you do it?"

"I don't know—telephone?"

Lethbridge gave Gerald a look of deep sympathy. They wandered on in silence.

"Miss Turner seems very nice," Lethbridge said a few moments later.

Gerald let the comment pass. The notion of any attraction between adults made him queasy. "There's something I've been wondering about," Gerald said. "Your notebook— why would someone want to steal that?"

Lethbridge paused to flick through a rack of T-shirts. "No idea. All it had was interview notes from when the diamond was nicked from the museum."

"Did you speak to many people?"

"Lots. The professor, of course, and Mr. Gupta. Sir Mason Green and people from the Rattigan Club."

"Do you think the inspector is any closer to finding Sir Mason Green?"

"He could be. He doesn't tell me everything."

"No," Gerald said. "I guess he wouldn't."

They caught up with Sam. He was helping Miss Turner choose some new sunglasses.

"Where's Fry?" Gerald asked.

Sam nodded farther up the line of stalls. Gerald spotted his butler buying a bottle of water. He was wearing an outlandish purple-and-gold–checked hat.

"The things they do for love, eh?" Sam snorted. He and Lethbridge wandered farther on but Gerald felt a tug at his elbow. It was Miss Turner.

"I'd like a word with you, please," she said. Her eyes were masked behind her new sunglasses.

Gerald stopped in his tracks. It was the first time Miss Turner had spoken to him without Alisha, Sam, and Ruby around.

"Yes?" He swallowed.

"Do you mind if I call you Gerald?" The voice was sharp, authoritative.

"No, that's fine," he squeaked.

"Gerald. Does Saint John have a, you know, *special* friend?"

It took Gerald a moment to absorb the question, then another to realize who Miss Turner was talking about. He had absolutely no idea what to say. He was having difficulty with the concept of Mr. Fry and a friend, special or otherwise. He shook his head. "No, he's pretty much a lone wolf, I think."

Miss Turner nodded decisively, the way a lioness might when picking which zebra to take down for lunch. Gerald couldn't change the topic fast enough.

"Miss Turner, have you worked for the Guptas for long?"

"Mr. Gupta hired me the week before Alisha was born," she said.

"He doesn't let her do much, does he?"

Miss Turner picked up a carving of an elephant from a display table and asked the price. After a minute of haggling she paid the stall owner and slipped the statue into her bag. "When Alisha was very young, maybe twelve months old, there was a terrible car accident," she said to Gerald. "Alisha's mother was killed. Mr. Gupta was devastated. Since then Mr. Gupta has had only two interests in life: his daughter and his gem collection. And he will do anything to keep both of them safe."

They found Alisha and Ruby inside a handicrafts emporium. At that moment the store offered Gerald everything he desired: air-conditioning, somewhere to sit, and a drink.

A merchant and his assistants were laying out handwoven saris for Alisha and Ruby to inspect. The others were spread out on a rug in a corner of the shop. Across from them a young woman sat on a stool, working a loom.

Whether it was the presence of Miss Turner, the relaxing cup of tea, or the sheer exhaustion from a day's shopping, Mr. Fry's manner seemed to be thawing. Gerald thought it might be a good time to ask some questions.

"Mr. Fry," he said, "you worked for my great-aunt for a long time—did she mention me much?"

Fry sipped his tea and accepted a top-off from one of the shop assistants. He was enjoying being on the receiving end of some service for a change.

"Your name came up whenever your mother telephoned," Mr. Fry said. "Miss Archer would ask your mother about your health. Mind you, not as often as your mother asked Miss Archer about hers."

"Mr. Fry!" Gerald said. "You didn't listen in on the phone, did you?"

Fry looked suitably aloof. "I may have, on occasion, picked up the phone in error when your great-aunt was speaking with your mother, but that is hardly an offense."

Miss Turner smiled at him. This had a significant impact on Mr. Fry. He cleared his throat. "Uh, I seem to recall there was one occasion, when I was cleaning the telephone—"

"Cleaning it, were you?" Sam said.

"Yes, that's right, cleaning the telephone, when I chanced to overhear Miss Archer speaking about you. It was to do with something called the fraternity, I think."

"What? Speaking with my mother?" Gerald asked.

"No. It was a man. I didn't recognize the voice. It was a long-distance call and the line wasn't clear."

"Maybe you didn't clean the phones properly," Sam said.

"Fraternity?"

It was Ruby. She and Alisha had taken a break from their browsing and had wandered across. "Wasn't that the word written on one of the envelopes your great-aunt left you, Gerald?"

"What is a fraternity, anyhow?" Sam asked.

"It's a group of people who share a common bond, isn't it?" Gerald said. "What did Geraldine say about it?"

"The man on the phone asked if you were ready," Mr. Fry said.

"Ready? Ready for what?"

"That I do not know."

Gerald sighed. "There are times when I'd enjoy a simpler life."

The shop assistant returned and offered Gerald some more tea. "Can I interest sir in a handmade rug?"

Gerald didn't look too enthusiastic, but the man was insistent.

"These are a treasure for life," he said. "Owning one lets the soul roam free."

Sam looked skeptical. "How so?"

The man smiled. "Have you ever felt your life is a constant conflict—between following what the gods have decreed for you and living what's right in front of you?" The man pointed to the woman at the loom. "Watch as she creates the carpet. Each thread is planned, the color and design known from the beginning."

Gerald watched the woman's hands skip across the loom. Colored threads fed into the machine from all directions to form superb order.

"It is a masterpiece from conception," the man said. "At the end you will have a piece of art. A rug that will last a lifetime. But you know the fate of every rug?"

"What's that?"

"People walk all over them!" The man let out a raucous laugh. "Maybe sometimes, sir, it's best to adjust to life's changes as they come along. Let it be the rug that remains steadfast—and allow your life to be free."

The man nodded his head. "After all," he said. "In life, nothing is certain."

It was fortunate Gerald was already sitting down; otherwise he would have fallen over.

CHAPTER THIRTEEN

The dinner at the rooftop restaurant was excellent. Gerald noticed that Constable Lethbridge made a point of sitting next to Miss Turner and butting into her conversation with Mr. Fry at every opportunity. The air was alive with insects and Gerald spent half the meal swatting at mosquitoes. He was chatting with Sam when an enormous brown cockroach flew right into the lamb curry in front of the police constable. Before Gerald could shout a warning, Lethbridge had scooped up a forkful of rice, curry, and cockroach and shoveled it into his mouth.

"Here, this food's good, isn't it, Miss Turner?" he said, biting down with a moist crunch. Gerald and Sam watched goggle-eyed as Lethbridge's expression registered the odd taste. He ran his tongue over his lips, then smiled. "Just like home cooking, this is."

After dinner they walked the quarter mile to the west gate of the Taj Mahal, past cycle rickshaws, camel carts, and peddlers trying to extract some last business for the day.

They were greeted by the man with the enormous handlebar moustache. "You need to be back at the station by one A.M. Your carriage will be coupled to the next train south and will leave with or without you on board," he said.

He ushered them through a clutch of hawkers and into the peaceful confines of a courtyard garden.

"Through those gates," the man said, pointing to an enormous red stone structure with a huge archway in the center. "I do hope you have a pleasant time." He waved farewell and left them.

The crowds were gone; the entire complex was theirs to explore.

Alisha led the way across the red and white checkerboard paving and through the archway.

On the other side of the entry they stopped in their tracks. A symmetrical garden stretched out before them. It was divided down the middle by a narrow reflecting pool. Lamps dotted throughout the shrubs and trees gave the scene a fairyland quality. But the greenery and the water features fell away before the structure about three hundred yards in front of them—the fabulous white marble domes of the Taj Mahal.

"That. Is. Amazing," Gerald said.

"It's so much bigger than I imagined," Ruby whispered. "And so beautiful."

"It's like the world's biggest onion," Sam said.

Alisha glared at him.

The pale white skin of the building's domes glowed in the evening light. Ruby and Alisha scampered into the garden. Gerald and Sam followed. They were two-thirds of the way to the Taj when Sam called out.

"Check the lovebirds."

Gerald glanced back and saw Mr. Fry and Miss Turner sitting side by side on a stone bench near the reflecting pool. They were deep in conversation. Constable Lethbridge was hovering in the background.

"That is so sweet," Ruby said.

Sam gagged. "Where's that bucket?"

Gerald laughed.

"You know," Ruby said, "every so often you remind me just what little boys you are." She and Alisha turned and stalked off toward a set of stairs that led up to the main buildings.

"What'd we do?" Sam asked.

"Who can tell?" Gerald said.

They followed the girls and emerged at the top of the

stairs onto a paved area the size of several football fields. At the center stood the Taj Mahal. There was no sign of Ruby or Alisha.

Gerald's boots clattered across the white marble tiles as he wandered to the far end of the platform. He leaned over a railing.

"There's a river down there," he called to Sam.

Lights from a small settlement shone from the opposite bank. Fingers of smoke from cooking fires crept up into the sky. The river lay black and mysterious.

"Do you think there are any wild animals around here?" Sam asked.

"Could be snakes," Gerald said. "Or monkeys, maybe." He paused, then said in a hoarse whisper: "Or . . . rats!"

Sam flinched. "I think I saw something move down there."

Then, from behind them, a cutthroat-razor shriek sliced the night air.

"That's Ruby!" Sam said. "It came from inside the Taj."

They sprinted across the tiles and rounded to the front of the white-domed building. Gerald shot a glance into the garden. The bench where Fry and Miss Turner had been sitting was empty. There was no sign of Constable Lethbridge.

Gerald trailed Sam as they raced inside. They skidded across the floor into a large octagonal chamber. Ruby stood on their left, fists clenched by her thighs, her face a mask of fury. Two men, dressed in black robes with scarves wrapped around their heads, held Alisha by the arms. A third figure pointed a handgun at Sam and Gerald.

"You!" Gerald said.

"Alisha?" Sam called. Her cheeks were wet with tears, her eyes beseeching.

The bandit nodded to the others and they dragged Alisha across the floor. She kicked and flailed, straining to free herself. But her captors simply lifted her until all she was kicking was air. Gerald took a step forward, but the bandit whipped the weapon around and aimed at Alisha's head. Gerald froze. The three kidnappers bundled Alisha into the night.

Ruby rushed to her brother. "They just came out of the dark," she said. "There was no sound at all."

"We've got to get help," Gerald said. "Fry. Miss Turner. Lethbridge. Anybody."

They bolted outside. There was no sign of the butler, the governess, or the policeman. Gerald turned to his left. A movement in the garden caught his eye.

"There!" he shouted. "Alisha." He ran across to the top of the stairs, took them three at a time, and leaped to the bottom. About thirty paces in front of him one of the abductors had Alisha over his shoulder. He was climbing over the side of what appeared to be a well. They disappeared over the edge.

Gerald came to a skidding halt. The bandit was clambering after Alisha but paused, one leg over the low brick wall. The gun was pointing straight at Gerald's chest. They stared at each other, motionless. Then Gerald took a step. The bandit pulled the trigger.

Gerald hit the ground.

The crack of the shot reverberated through the trees, startling hundreds of birds from their slumber. The night sky filled with a dark confetti of feathers and screeches.

Sam and Ruby raced to Gerald. He was facedown on the pavement, his arms splayed and right leg bent.

"Gerald!" Ruby cried. She grabbed his shoulders and rolled him onto his back. Vacant eyes stared up at her.

"No . . ." she whispered.

Then Gerald sucked in a breath. "That was a bit close," he said.

He ignored Ruby's sob of relief and rolled back onto his stomach. "They went down that hole," he said.

Sam got there first and peered over the edge. A rope ladder disappeared into a dark void. "Do we go down after them?" he asked. He already had a foot on the top rung.

"We don't have any light," Gerald said. "It'd be hopeless." He ran a hand over the top of his head. How did this happen? What did this cult want with Alisha?

"This drain must empty out somewhere," Gerald said. He turned to Sam. "The river." He sprinted toward the main gate, Ruby and Sam on his heels.

The three of them burst onto the street. The place was deserted, the carts and hawkers gone home for the night. The road split in two—one avenue wound around toward the river.

"They'll have to come out onto the road to get away," Gerald said.

"Unless they have a boat," Sam said.

Gerald started running down the road. "Let's hope that they don't."

He'd only gone fifty yards when a bicycle bell rang behind him. He looked over his shoulder to see Sam in the driver's seat of a cycle rickshaw, pedaling like fury. Ruby was in the back.

"Hop in," Ruby said, stretching out a hand for Gerald to grab.

Gerald made a running dive into the backseat. His head bobbed up behind Sam's shoulder.

"I borrowed this," Sam said, responding to the look on Gerald's face. "Hope the owner doesn't mind."

The road sloped downward and they picked up speed.

They'd gone about a mile with no sign of Alisha or her captors. Gerald was starting to get anxious that he'd made the wrong call, when Ruby shouted, "There!" She stabbed a finger into the darkness. "It's them."

A hundred yards ahead, four figures emerged from the

river side of the road. It was definitely Alisha slung across one of the abductor's shoulders. But now she was not resisting.

"Is she okay?" Ruby asked.

Sam eased off the pedals and coasted. "Let's see where they go."

The kidnappers jogged along the roadway. They seemed to be unaware they were being followed. The path began sloping upward and Sam had to ride standing on the pedals to keep up. They came to a roundabout that was choked with motorcycles, scooters, taxis, and rickshaws. The bandits ducked through the traffic and into the forecourt of an enormous building. Gerald had been concentrating so hard on keeping Alisha in sight that he hadn't noticed the structure loom out of the night shadows.

"What is this place?" he asked.

They stared up at the outer ramparts of an ancient fortress. Red stone walls stretched out of sight to the left and right. In the middle, a broad pathway led into the stronghold.

Sam searched for a break in the traffic. "We're going to have to leg it from here," he said. They abandoned the rickshaw. Gerald was about to chance his luck running across the road when he was grabbed from behind. He whipped around to find a young boy had him by the sleeve.

"You stole my rickshaw!" the boy yelled through his

gasps for breath. He'd chased them all the way from the Taj. He was barefoot and couldn't have been more than nine years old.

"Sorry," Gerald said. "It was an emergency. Here . . ." He fumbled in his pocket and pulled out a handful of notes and gave them to the boy. "Go get a policeman. Someone's been kidnapped and taken inside the fort."

The boy looked at the money then back at Gerald. "I don't know . . ."

"Just do it. It's our friend."

The boy shoved the cash into his pocket and jumped onto the rickshaw.

"I'll wait for you," he said. "My name's Pranav."

"No, no. Get a policeman."

The boy shrugged and set off up the road. Gerald was certain they wouldn't see him again.

Ruby grabbed his hand and hauled him out into the traffic. "Come on, or we'll lose them."

The three of them scooted across the road and into the deserted forecourt.

The walls of the garrison stood over them like a disapproving teacher. Gerald slowed to a walk, his eyes struggling to adjust to the shadows. They entered a crowd-control barrier shaped like a funnel. It led onto a bridge and then over a moat. The path cut to the left and stopped at a tall archway pinched to a point at the top and blocked by a wooden drawbridge. Gerald peered up to the top of the wall. Archers' battlements loomed above them.

"This thing was probably built to keep out war elephants," he said. "How are we going to get in?"

Iron chains ran down either side of the drawbridge from notches high up in the wall. Gerald tugged hard on one. It didn't budge. He turned to Sam and Ruby. "Any ideas?"

Ruby stood to one side of the drawbridge and looked up.

"I don't think this thing is closed properly," she said. "It's tilting out a bit."

"You're right," Sam said. "There's a gap at the top. If someone can get up there, they might be able to wriggle through."

"What do you think, Gerald?" Ruby said. "You're the rock climber."

Gerald inspected the stone facing around the drawbridge. It was as smooth and featureless as a pane of glass. There were no gaps to gain a foothold.

"Don't think I can climb this one," he said. Then he had an idea.

"Ruby, remember how you got into the house at Beaconsfield? That gymnast jump?"

Ruby sized up the height of the drawbridge. "That's got to be twenty feet to the top," she said, shaking her head. "I'd need a trampoline to even think about it."

Sam paced across the courtyard and looked back at the arched entryway.

"What if we did a totem pole? Gerald on the bottom, me on his shoulders?"

Ruby considered it for a second. Then she grabbed Gerald and shoved him against the drawbridge. "Don't sneeze," she said.

Gerald braced his back against the timber. Sam placed a foot on Gerald's thigh then pushed up onto his shoulders. Gerald winced. He was still tender from the thin man's attack weeks before. The thought of that cadaverous face unsettled him. Even if they were able to breach the fort's defenses and find Alisha, what would they do against three armed members of a deadly cult? Gerald took a deep breath. He had to concentrate.

"You can come up anytime you want," Sam called to Ruby.

He was met by silence.

"What's the problem?" he asked. He was facing the drawbridge and couldn't see back to the courtyard.

"You're too short." Ruby's voice was plain and to the point. "Here, try this." She held up a plastic chair.

Sam clambered back to the ground, squeezing another wince from Gerald on the way down. Gerald placed the chair by the drawbridge and he and Sam reassembled their human ladder. Again, there was a pause.

"Still not high enough," Ruby said. "Hold on, there might be something over here."

Soon Gerald was back standing on the chair, which was now balanced on a wooden crate. Sam scaled up and perched on Gerald's shoulders, extracting more gasps of pain. There was a slight wobble between the chair and the box but they held.

"Do you want to try anytime soon?" Sam called down, running out of patience.

"Feeling the strain, are we?" Gerald muttered under his breath.

Ruby clambered up to be face-to-face with Gerald. "Muscle up, Mack. Yertle the Turtle is coming through." She clamped a foot on his sore shoulder and pushed up. Gerald grimaced but held tight. Within seconds he heard Ruby exclaim a triumphant "Ta-dah!"

"Is she through?" he called up.

"Not yet," Ruby called back. "But I've got a hand in the gap. Just need to push up a bit more . . ."

Gerald's heart skipped a beat. A leg of the plastic chair was starting to buckle. He didn't have time to open his mouth and shout a warning. The platform under his feet toppled. His right shoulder hit the stone ground hard, igniting a flash of pain, which surged throughout his body. He took a boot to the face as Sam crashed down on top of him.

Gerald clamped a hand to his mouth, the warm tang

of blood on his lips. They both ended up on their backs, gazing at Ruby dangling by her hands, gripping the top of the drawbridge.

"Hold on!" Sam yelled.

"Thanks for the advice," she grunted.

Ruby drew her knees up to her chin and planted her feet flat on the wooden boards of the drawbridge. She pushed out. Her head raised above the gap between the massive door and the stone wall.

Gerald glanced at Sam. "We might have to catch her."

"I heard that!" Ruby called down.

She swung a leg through the overhang and before they could shout any more encouragement she squeezed through to the other side.

There was an uncomfortable silence. Then came the sound of iron chains clattering through the notches in the wall. The drawbridge was coming down. Gerald shoved Sam hard and they both rolled clear as the wooden door slammed onto the ground.

Ruby appeared in the archway. "Sorry," she said. "That got away from me a bit."

The three of them crossed the drawbridge and entered the fortress.

Chapter Fourteen

The skies opened and rain pelted down as Gerald, Ruby, and Sam trudged up a steep path into the fort. Stone walls rose high on either side. Gerald guessed that even if they were on the back of a rampaging war elephant, archers from centuries gone by could still fire down on them with ease. This castle had been built to stand strong.

They reached the top of the rise and found a wide grassed area boxed in by more stone walls. There was no one else to be seen.

"Keep close," Gerald said. "If they don't know we saw them, we may be able to snatch Alisha back."

They made for the nearest wall and followed the edge of the gardens toward a set of gates. The archway was wide open and they ran through.

Gerald ducked into a cloister that ran around the outskirts of a large rectangular garden. The others followed him. They stopped in the shadows, relieved to find some shelter from the downpour, and watched as the rain gathered intensity. Water gushed from spouts jutting from the roof onto the path in front of them.

Gerald nursed his injured shoulder and ran his tongue along the inside of his bottom lip. A lump was forming where Sam had kicked him. He spat a glob of blood onto the stonework at his feet and shook his head with frustration.

"Now what?" It was Sam. He sounded defeated. "This place is enormous. They could be anywhere."

"So you want to quit?" Gerald snapped. "You want us to leave Alisha?" He was tired and sore.

Sam turned on him. "I didn't say that." He shoved Gerald in the chest. Gerald fell heavily against a pillar, sparking a fresh burst of pain through his shoulder.

"Hey!" Gerald cried. "You stupid—"

Ruby threw herself between the boys before the first punch could be thrown. She grabbed her brother.

"Stop it!" she hissed. "What's the matter with you?"

Sam glowered at Gerald but said nothing. He pushed Ruby aside and flopped next to a column a short distance away.

Ruby was furious. "We've got to find Alisha," she said.

"You two can kill each other after that."

Gerald stared out into the rain-soaked night. He took a deep breath and exhaled. He was tired of everything going wrong. He wanted to forget about his fortune, about his family history. He wanted to go . . .

Home.

Gerald blinked back tears. His eyes stung. He told himself it was because of his shoulder. He exhaled again and repeated the advice he'd given himself before: Concentrate. All the other stuff could wait. Including arguing with Sam.

Gerald could make out the silhouettes of a number of buildings on the far side of the gardens, maybe a hundred yards away. There was no sign of any people. If they were going to find Alisha, they were going to have to start exploring.

"We need to look for her," he said to Ruby. His words were almost lost in the noise of the rain. Ruby nodded, then went to her brother and spoke in his ear. Sam remained seated for a moment, scowling into the night. When he dragged himself up, he refused to meet Gerald's eyes.

Gerald led the way along the cloisters to their left, keeping well inside the roofline. They reached a doorway that led through the rain to the ground floor of a large rectangular building, set around a central courtyard. They ducked inside. A line of arched windows, set close to the ground, looked inward across a patchwork of shrubs toward the opposite wing.

Gerald knelt by the nearest window and peered across the garden.

"There!"

He pointed to the opposite side. "Do you see it?" he asked Ruby. "That yellow glow."

Faint and barely visible through the sheets of rain was a dull lamp inside one of the ground-floor rooms.

"That's got to be them," Ruby said. "So what do we do?"

Gerald looked to Sam, who was staring into the shadows. "What do you think?"

Sam didn't move. "Whatever you want."

Terrific. Gerald shook his head. "We better see what we're up against," he said.

A ribcage of stone columns ran the length of the building. The internal walls had decayed or been demolished long ago. Gerald, Ruby, and Sam jogged to the end of their wing, keeping in the shadows. They reached the final turn, then pulled up short. A huge pile of rubble blocked their path. A section of the first floor had caved in.

"Great," Sam said. "Now what are we going to do?"

Gerald looked at the ceiling. The section closest to the inner wall had fallen through, but the outer part was intact. It was supported by three rows of columns, forming a mezzanine that overlooked the ground level.

"We can use this," Gerald said. "If we can get to that ledge, we should be able to sneak along the length of the building and spy down on them."

Ruby studied the edge of the collapsed ceiling. "How do we get up there?"

Gerald eyed the nearest arched window and traced a path up the wall to the window above that. "Follow me," he said. "And don't look down."

Gerald took a running jump at the window frame and vaulted up the wall. In one flowing movement he jammed his fingers into a cavity in the stonework, tucked his knees to his chest and pushed off against the wall to the second-floor window. Without pausing, he turned to the crumbling section of ceiling and launched himself into free air. He soared across the void, landing on the mezzanine in a rolling tumble. Seconds later he was lying on his belly and peeking over the edge at Sam and Ruby. He couldn't hide the grin on his face.

Ruby shot him an admiring look. "I don't think I can do that," she said.

Sam said nothing.

Gerald considered his options. "I'll go see what's going on. Probably better to have only one of us up here anyway."

"And what do we do?" Sam asked, his voice sour as week-old milk.

"You can stop laughing, for a start," Gerald said. "And keep out of sight."

Gerald pushed himself to his feet and headed in the direction of the lamp. His eyes had adjusted to the dark fairly well and he could make out a path ahead. It looked like the inner section of the first floor had collapsed for the length of the building, giving him a clear view of what he hoped was Alisha and her kidnappers.

Gerald crept along as fast as he dared. He picked his way through leaf litter and crushed plastic bottles, trying not to make a sound. The farther along the building he got, the slower and more cautious he became. Every breath sounded like a wind tunnel in his head. The rain pounded down outside but still he moved like a cat.

After slinking through a number of rooms he entered a large chamber at the end of the building. The floor collapse had been more extensive there, with a framework of columns below propping up nothing but air. Then Gerald saw them: three black-cloaked figures huddled close together in the room beneath him. They appeared to be in a heated discussion about something. The bandit with the gun was shorter and more wiry than the others but was obviously in charge. The leader jabbed a finger toward the door and the other two ran outside. Gerald melted into the shadows and scoured the space below for any sign of Alisha. She must be down there somewhere.

Gerald sank to his haunches. He needed to get the remaining bandit out of the building so he could get to the ground floor and find Alisha. He needed a diversion. All he could see in the shadows were piles of vegetation and rubbish.

He stood up and took a half pace backward. A howl erupted at his feet. Gerald jumped in panic as something grabbed his ankle. Two arms clutched at his calf. Then there was the sensation of something biting his boot. Hard. Again and again, teeth piercing the tough fabric. A dusty brown creature had wrapped itself around his leg. The beast drew its head back and bared needle-sharp fangs. Gerald kicked out and sent the animal sliding on its belly across the floor. It splayed out like a ragdoll, then sprang to its feet and glared death back at Gerald. A monkey. It sat on its bottom and nursed its right hand, its tail pounding the air in anger. Gerald must have stepped on it while it was sleeping. Two other monkeys emerged from the shadows amid a chorus of chattering. They crossed to their companion. One put an arm around its shoulder; the other stared at Gerald and launched a fang-bared screech. If monkeys could swear, this one was turning the air blue.

Gerald cringed at the noise, not just the way it tore at his nerves but because of the warning it must be sounding to the bandit below. The three monkeys, apparently satisfied they'd got their point across, turned and launched themselves, one after the other, off the edge of the broken floor and into the void. The first monkey latched onto an iron ring fixed into the stone ceiling and swung out to land on top of the nearest column. It then leaped out to grab another ring before swinging across to the neighboring column. In a bounding procession, his friends followed, and the three of them in turn landed with a thump on the windowsill opposite, then disappeared into the rain outside.

Gerald held his breath. If the screeching hadn't been enough to warn the man in black, then the sight of three angry monkeys leaping across the array of columns in a game of aerial hopscotch should just about seal it. He counted to fifty, then, to be sure, counted to fifty again. In that time he spotted six other monkeys about ten paces away. One of them held a water bottle, like a small hairy man on the way to the gym. The others scuttled about, piling bottles into a heap. That explained the scores of old bottles on the mezzanine. The monkeys must collect them.

He was still no closer to figuring how he could get to Alisha.

Gerald flattened himself against the floor and wriggled as close as he dared to the edge. As more of the ground floor was revealed, he spied the bandit. Far from being alarmed at the monkey activity, the figure in black was squatting casually on the floor, apparently talking to someone. As Gerald edged further out he finally spotted Alisha. She sat with her back against a column and a dark cloth bag over her head. Her hands appeared to be bound behind her.

As he stared down at the forlorn image of Alisha, he had an idea.

Chapter Fifteen

Gerald scurried back to where he'd left Sam and Ruby. Along the way he collected as many water bottles as he could carry. A couple of monkeys had followed him, screeching in distress at the loss of their treasures, but they kept their distance. Gerald poked his head over the edge of the collapsed ceiling and the twins emerged from the shadows.

"I've found Alisha," he said. "But I need you to lure the man in black outside."

"How are we supposed to do that?" Sam asked. "And what about the other two gorillas?"

"Funny you should mention gorillas," Gerald said.

Ten minutes later Gerald was back in his hiding place overlooking the chamber. He eyed the top of the nearest column. It must have been five yards away from the edge of the collapsed ceiling and a good four yards above the stone floor below. Gerald knew the margin for error in his plan was close to zero. He glanced at his watch. Only a few more seconds to go.

There was a volley of shouts from outside the room below. Gerald peered down to see the bandit reach around and pull out a handgun. Sam and Ruby were screaming up a storm, their cries piercing the rain. Before the figure in black could take a step to investigate, a hail of water bottles rained in through the windows. Scores of bottles, weighed down with rocks, bounced into the room and skittered across the flagstones. One hit the bandit in the stomach and others smashed into columns. They pelted the room like a mortar storm. Then the barrage ended. The shouting ceased. The sound of rain again filled the chamber. The floor was covered with plastic bottles. The kidnapper picked up one of the containers.

What happened next was highly dangerous for Sam and Ruby but it was a gamble they had agreed to take. The bandit raised the pistol and took a step toward the door.

Then the monkeys arrived.

Twenty dusty brown monkeys poured into the chamber. Some leaped through the windows; others jumped from the mezzanine and clambered down the sides of the columns. They pounced on the bottles, snatching them up two at a time, howling and screeching with each new find. Then to Gerald's astonishment and delight, they threw them into a heap in a corner of the room. He had hoped the monkeys would cause just enough distraction to delay the pursuit of Sam and Ruby for a few moments, but this had worked a treat. The kidnapper stood rooted to the spot as the monkeys scurried about the place, little furry garbage men clearing the floor of rubbish. They were a blur of fur in motion. One leaped up to snatch the bottle from the bandit's hand. Finally the figure in black regained focus and rushed out the door.

Gerald didn't have long. He crossed to where the monkeys had jumped from the crumbling edge of the floor. He looked at the top of the nearest column, then up at the iron ring set into the ceiling. He took a breath, stepped back a few paces, and ran. Pebbles sprayed over the edge as his feet left the platform and he flew across the gap. His eyes never left the iron ring. He grabbed it with both hands and a stabbing pain shot through his right shoulder. But with a heave from his arms and a swing of the hips, he sailed onto the top of the column, landing in a squat on his feet and hands. But his momentum carried him forward. He flipped over and clung desperately to the top of the column, his feet flailing in the air. Gerald allowed himself a second, then started to shimmy his way down. He reached the ground, stepped past a large monkey that was collecting the last of the bottles, and rushed to Alisha.

He pulled the bag from her head. A piece of gaffer tape covered her mouth. Her eyes bulged.

"Don't worry," he said. "We're getting out of here."

Alisha's ankles and wrists were bound with cable ties. Gerald pulled the bandit's knife from his backpack and sliced through the binds. Alisha massaged her wrists while Gerald grabbed the ties around her feet. But before he could cut them a sudden blow to his ribs knocked him sideways, driving the air from his lungs. The knife flew from his hand as he tumbled across the ground. Gerald grappled with his attacker, thrashing out with his fists. But the bandit was fast. Gerald's punches were batted away with ease. He was thrown onto his back, his shoulders held down by the bandit's knees. He gazed up at his attacker sitting astride his chest and holding a gun to his forehead.

Gerald sucked in air, trying to pump up his flattened lungs. His assailant, face still swathed in black, stared at him with piercing dark eyes.

"Who are you?" Gerald groaned.

His attacker may have been about to respond, but never got the chance. Alisha bludgeoned the bandit across the side of the head with a lamp. The blow sounded a hollow *clang* and sent the figure sprawling. The handgun spun free and skidded across the floor. Gerald drew in another breath and scrambled onto his hands and knees, like a puppy running on linoleum, to where the bandit was slumped on the ground, hands nursing an injured head. With the last of his energy, Gerald rolled his attacker over and straddled his foe.

The bandit stirred and Gerald shoved his hands hard onto the man's chest to pin him down.

Gerald's eyes shot wide open. "Holy cow!" he yelped.

He recoiled as if he'd just grabbed a live wire. He stared at the bandit's chest in disbelief. He reached out and whipped the scarf away from his attacker's head.

"You're a . . . *girl!*"

Gerald was sitting on a girl aged fifteen or sixteen. Her dark hair was cut short and she had a face that belonged on a Bollywood movie poster: flawless skin, a button nose, well-defined jaw, brilliant white teeth. Sculpted eyebrows, perfect cheekbones.

Gerald was appalled. After everything this person had put them through—the attack at the markets, the abduction at the Taj—she was a *girl*.

The bandit pressed a hand to the side of her head. A trickle of blood seeped from a graze near her temple. Then she smiled at Gerald—a gleaming smile that illuminated her face.

Gerald was still in shock. He finally found his voice. "What do you want with Alisha?"

The girl's smile widened. Her eyes traced every feature

on Gerald's face. Alisha stepped beside them. She held the gun in her hand.

"A common bandit," Alisha spat. "After ransom. The police will deal with her."

The girl's eyes locked with Gerald's. Her lips parted.

"You are in great danger, Gerald Wilkins," she said. "You must not trust this Gupta."

CHAPTER SIXTEEN

Gerald was stunned. "How do you know my name?"

"How could I not know your name?" she replied, her eyes never shifting from his.

A sound to his right forced him to break his gaze. He turned to find Alisha training the gun on him.

"Alisha?"

"Why would you listen to her?" Alisha said with venom. "She's a thief. Low born. Worthless." Gerald couldn't believe what he was seeing. Was Alisha actually pointing the gun at him?

"Gerald?"

It was the girl's voice. Almost musical. She tilted her head, beckoning him to lean in. Gerald gazed down at her, bewitched. He bent closer.

"The Guptas are no friends of the fraternity," she

whispered. Then she lifted her chin and planted a soft kiss on Gerald's lips.

The kiss caught Gerald off guard and the girl pushed up from her hips, bucking him back over her head. Gerald went flying, legs cycling through the air. He landed flat on his back on the stone floor. He rolled over to find Alisha, her eyes pumped with fear, pointing the gun at the bandit.

The girl was on her feet like a panther. She flashed a smile at Gerald. "Remember my warning," she purred. She then launched into a string of cartwheeling flips across the floor, spinning right over the top of Alisha and knocking the gun from her hand. Without pausing, the bandit girl dived out the window and into the night.

Gerald dragged himself upright. Alisha stood with her hands by her sides, her body shaking.

"Are you okay?" he asked.

Alisha managed a nod but no words would come. They turned at the sound of feet splashing through the rain. Sam and Ruby burst through the doorway.

"Come on!" Ruby cried. "Those gorillas are coming back."

"This way," Sam said. "We've found somewhere to hide."

Gerald scooped up the bandit's knife from the floor and they followed Sam back through the crumbling building, monkeys howling after them as they disappeared into the shadows.

* * *

"The man in black is a *girl*?" Ruby was astounded.

Sam snuffled to himself. "Fighting with girls now, are we?" he said to Gerald.

Gerald rubbed his ribs, still sore from where the bandit had tackled him.

"She didn't feel like a girl," Gerald grumbled. "Well, bits of her did. But she fought like a guy."

They were in a basement cell in a barracks near the fortress gates. The battered lamp emitted a sorrowful glow. Alisha spoke for the first time since their escape.

"Gerald, whatever she told you, it's not true—"

"We'll talk about it later," Gerald said. "Right now we need to get as far from those thugs as possible." Gerald's head was still spinning from the girl's warning about the Guptas. And if he was honest, the kiss had him shaken up as well.

Sam checked his watch. "It's forty minutes till the train leaves," he said.

"Where do you think Mr. Fry, Miss Turner, and Constable Lethbridge are?" Ruby asked.

"Our crack security team? Probably at the station waiting for us," Gerald said. "That's our best hope. Get back to the train—there'll be heaps of people about—and it takes us out of town."

"Do you think the bandits are still out there?" Ruby asked.

Gerald forced a grin. "Only one way to find out."

The rain had stopped when they emerged from their hiding place and the pathways were slippery. They stole along a line of stone walls in single file, keeping close to the shadows, and soon came out near the large grassy area at the top of the fortress entrance. They were halfway down the path leading to the front gate when the first shouts broke out above them.

They looked up to see two of the bandits sprinting along the top of the battlements about to round the corner and descend on them.

Gerald couldn't see the bandit girl and he wasn't about to wait for her. "Run!" he yelled.

They raced down the path, feet skidding across the stones, over the drawbridge and out into the forecourt. Even though it was past midnight, there were autorickshaws parked by the roadside. Gerald's shouts jolted the drivers from their slumber. A man rolled groggily behind the handlebars of one as Gerald and Alisha dived into the back. Sam and Ruby leaped into another. Gerald was about to yell instructions when a young boy raced up to them.

"It's me! Pranav," he called. "I waited for you." He pointed to his vehicle. His eyes were full of hurt.

Gerald shook his head. "Sorry, it'll be too slow," he said. "What about the police? Did you tell them?"

The boy pointed to a livid mark on his cheek. "They

didn't believe me," he said. Gerald shot a look over his shoulder back toward the fort. He dug into his pocket for more rupees and shoved them into Pranav's hand.

"Men are coming," he said, jabbing his thumb back at the gates. "Slow them down, okay?"

The boy nodded. He peeled off half the notes and gave them to the autorickshaw driver, all the time speaking in rapid-fire Hindi. The man jumped from his driver's seat and ran toward the boy's rickshaw.

"I'll drive," Pranav said, climbing behind the handle-bars. "I'm good at shortcuts."

Ruby called from the back of the other autorickshaw. "Hurry! They're coming."

The first of the bandits appeared in the forecourt. It took him only a second to gauge what was going on. Gerald shouted to Pranav, "Train station. Fast!"

The autorickshaw shot out into the street. It bounced hard off the gutter, horn blaring, and swerved to avoid a horse and cart. Ruby and Sam were close behind. Gerald swiveled around and strained to see out the back. The cycle rickshaw ploughed straight into the mouth of the crowd-control barrier, like a cork jamming into a bottle. It blocked the bandits' exit. Gerald knew it wouldn't hold them for long—every second was vital.

He leaned forward and spoke into Pranav's ear. "We need to go really fast."

The boy opened the throttle and the engine roared. The rickshaw surged forward, sending Gerald tumbling back into his seat beside Alisha. "Hold on tight!" Pranav called over his shoulder.

Gerald pulled himself upright. Alisha stared straight ahead, stony faced.

The rickshaw carrying Sam and Ruby pulled alongside. Ruby leaned out and shouted, "They're on motorbikes! They're catching up!"

Gerald craned his neck and caught sight of the two bandits weaving their way toward them. Pranav was driving hard and blasting the horn even harder. Ruby and Sam suddenly swerved to the left as the two rickshaws parted to go around a cow lying in the middle of the road. They scooted past cyclists and handcarts, but Gerald knew it was only a matter of time before the bandits caught them.

A break in the traffic opened up behind and within seconds the two motorcycles were at their rear bumpers. Pranav leaned out and let fly with a stream of what Gerald guessed was swearing in Hindi. But before Pranav could duck his head back inside, the rickshaw hit a pile of rubbish, knocking them onto two wheels and sending Alisha tumbling into Gerald's lap. The rickshaw veered toward the footpath. Pedestrians dived for cover. The rickshaw mounted the curb with a jolt, bouncing itself back onto three wheels. Pranav wrestled control, bashing his way through stacks of cardboard boxes and sending crates of drink bottles shattering across the ground. A bandit drew up on Alisha's side. Like a striking cobra, the man lunged in and grabbed Alisha by the arm. She screamed and Pranav jammed the steering to the right. Gerald threw himself across Alisha and hit out with his fists, landing at least one good punch to the bandit's jaw. But the man held on. He reefed his handlebars to the left and half dragged Alisha out of the rickshaw.

"Pranav!" Gerald shouted. "Steer away. Steer away!"

The rickshaw bounced at speed toward a row of ragged stalls. They were entering a narrow market area of shops closed and shuttered for the night. Gerald was on top of Alisha, trying to release the bandit's grip. But the bucking of the rickshaw made it impossible.

They crashed over a bump and Gerald sprawled across the floor. His head was poking out the opposite side of the rickshaw.

His nose tingled. They were heading straight toward a row of cane baskets lined up against a brick wall. Gerald threw his hand out and thrust it under the cover of the closest basket. He scooped up a fistful of bright orange powder. He clenched his jaw, launched himself back across the rickshaw, and drove his hand into the bandit's face, smearing the powder across the man's eyes and nose. The bandit howled as the spice burned. He clawed at his blinded eyes. In a blur of movement, the front wheel of the motor-cycle jackknifed and the man went somersaulting over the handlebars, crashing into the metal roller door of a shop front. Pranav sped on. Gerald tumbled back to the floor by Alisha's knees.

"Are you all right?" he panted.

Alisha slumped back into her seat. "What was that you rubbed in his face?"

"No idea." He sniffed his hand and flinched. "But it'll take your head off."

Gerald pulled himself into the backseat and patted the driver on the shoulder. "Good driving, Pranav. Incredible."

The boy turned and flashed a smile. "Told you I knew some shortcuts." A second later Pranav was flying, hands outstretched toward the pavement. The other bandit had shot up beside them and leaped from his moving motorbike to shoulder-charge the boy out of the rickshaw. The bandit now sat at the speeding rickshaw's handlebars, with Gerald and Alisha in the back.

The bandit pulled to the footpath and leered over his shoulder. Alisha responded with a pert smile of her own. She then drove the heel of her right hand hard up under the man's chin. The jolt sent his head snapping back and knocked him senseless. He slithered out the side of the rick-shaw and flopped onto the asphalt.

Gerald was stunned. "Where'd you learn to do that?"

Alisha grinned. "The benefits of a classical education," she said. "It's not all Greek, Latin, and polo ponies at boarding school, you know."

Gerald clambered into the driver's seat. "That must be some school." He looked at his watch. "We better get a move on."

He took hold of the handlebars and gave the throttle a twist. They bounced forward. He did a tight U-turn and drove back to where Pranav was sitting on the roadside, rubbing his shoulder. Alisha helped him into the back and they sped out of the market.

They found Ruby and Sam back at the main road standing beside their rickshaw.

"Hop in," Gerald called. "We've got to get that train."

Sam and Ruby squeezed into the back. Gerald floored it and took off, following Pranav's shouted directions.

"As soon as you disappeared up that alley the guy who was chasing us went after you," Ruby said. "It's Alisha they're after."

"They must really need the cash," Sam said.

Gerald concentrated on driving. He had the feeling there was more to it than ransom money. He pushed the rickshaw as fast as it could go, and soon the Agra train station came into view.

Gerald gave Pranav a massive tip and they ran the last hundred feet, up the steps and onto the station concourse.

Alisha stopped a railway employee and he pointed to platform four.

"Come on," she said. "The train leaves any minute."

They bolted up a set of stairs to an overpass, sprinted to the far side, and looked down to see their train beginning to pull away from the station.

"Come on!" Gerald shouted. He planted his backside on the banister and slid all the way down to the platform.

The chairman's carriage was at the end of the train. The man with the huge handlebar moustache was standing in the doorway, waving at them to hurry. Gerald dug deep. His boots pounded the pavement and he finally reached the man's outstretched hand. He latched on and was hauled inside. He landed with a thud and watched as, one after the other, Alisha, Sam, and finally Ruby piled on board. The man with the moustache stepped down to the platform. Sam swung the door closed and they all collapsed on the floor.

Gerald glanced at his watch. Two minutes past one in the morning. The train was right on time. Then he looked down the length of the carriage and realized something. Mr. Fry, Miss Turner, and Constable Lethbridge were nowhere to be seen.

CHAPTER SEVENTEEN

The rattle and sway of the carriage changed tempo. Gerald was instantly awake. For some reason he felt incredibly alert: as sharp as a blade and seeing the world with a clarity he didn't usually achieve that early in the day, if at all. He peeled the adhesive bandage from his forehead, sat up, and looked at his traveling companions. In the bunk beneath him, Sam was wrapped in a sheet like a cheap Egyptian mummy. Robust snores signaled he was still asleep. Across the aisle, Ruby was in the top bunk. She faced the wall, her blond hair spilling across the pillow. The sheet resting over her shoulders raised and lowered in the peaceful ebb and flow of slumber. In the bed beneath her was Alisha. She lay on her back, her head to the side. Her face was cleaned of makeup and without blemish. She rested peacefully, apparently unaffected by two abduction attempts.

It was those two attacks that were occupying Gerald's thoughts at that moment. He tried to recall every detail from the previous night, especially the bandit girl's warning.

The Guptas are no friends of the fraternity, she'd said. And she'd kissed him. Gerald's eyes glazed over at the memory of that: the cushioned softness of the lips, the perfume of her skin, the musty warmth of . . .

Gerald rattled his head. No! He had to concentrate. How did the bandit girl know about the fraternity? Not that he knew anything about it, apart from an empty envelope and some overheard phone conversation between his great-aunt and a stranger. How could a teenage member of some murderous death cult know anything about it?

Was he ready?

Then a thought strayed into his head, like a wandering puppy that had turned into the wrong front yard. Gerald tried to shoo the thought away. But it lingered. It lingered, sniffed about, and threatened to lift its leg against the letterbox. He stared again at the sleeping face of Alisha. Gerald had a desperate urge to wake Ruby. But the train's rhythm shifted again, and the groans of stirring teenagers drifted through the carriage.

"What time is it?" Sam stuck his head out from inside

his cotton sarcophagus and immediately hid it away again.

"Almost eight, I think." Gerald swung down onto the floor and looked for his boots. He found them under a pile of wet clothes that he'd peeled off the night before.

Ruby stuck her chin over the edge of her bunk. "I'm starving. What's for breakfast?"

"We're coming into a station," Alisha said. "Let's get something there."

Gerald pulled back a curtain to reveal an overcast sky. The train slowed as it moved into a built-up area that was dotted with industrial workshops and brown-brick buildings in various stages of collapse. Gerald walked to the end of the carriage and swung open the heavy metal door. The heat of the morning greeted him like a slap in the face. He stood on the top step and leaned out. As ever, the station was a riot of activity. Porters pushed handcarts piled high with bags and bundles, and passengers positioned themselves to do battle for seats. Dotted along the platform were a number of food vendors toiling behind hot plates and pans of bubbling oil. Gerald was joined at the open doorway by the others.

"Alisha, why don't you see if you can get some mobile coverage here while Ruby and I get the food?"

Alisha checked her phone. "Okay, but it still looks like we're out of range. I'll try Miss Turner again if I can get a signal."

"And what do I do, since you're giving the orders?" Sam had sulked off to bed the night before without saying good night, and it looked like he was determined to keep the grudge simmering.

"You could watch over our stuff to make sure no one nicks anything," Gerald said.

Sam didn't respond. He slouched back inside the carriage.

Gerald nudged Ruby in the ribs. "Come on," he said. "Let's see what the food's like down here." He pushed his way along the platform and joined a crowd around a small cart. The aroma of something delicious cooking on a hot plate wafted around them.

"I need to talk to you," Gerald said.

"I figured that. You may as well have shoved Sam back onto the train and told Alisha to run away. What's up?"

Gerald took a deep breath. "I'm worried about Alisha."

"No kidding. We all are. Someone's tried to kidnap her twice."

"No, not that," Gerald said. "That bandit girl. She said something to me."

Ruby's brow wrinkled.

"It was a warning," Gerald said. "A warning that the Guptas couldn't be trusted."

"What? That doesn't mean anything. A criminal will say anything to get out of trouble."

Gerald shook his head. "You don't understand. The girl whispered to me . . . said it so Alisha couldn't hear."

"Said what, precisely?"

"She said the Guptas were no friends of the fraternity."

Ruby stared hard at Gerald while she took in what he'd just said.

"How could she possibly know about that?"

"Exactly," Gerald said. "She couldn't know about it—unless . . ."

"Unless what?"

"Unless the fraternity and the cult are the same thing."

Ruby gazed off toward the end of the platform. "You're saying that the fraternity—the group your great-aunt wanted you to join—is a death cult?"

"It's too much of a coincidence that the cult has the same symbol as my family seal," Gerald said. "This just nails it. The people who are trying to kidnap Alisha are directly linked to my family."

They reached the front of the line. Gerald pointed at a dozen different fried pastries and concoctions. "We need to be careful around Alisha," he said. He paid for the food and they turned to head back to the carriage.

"You think Alisha is hiding something?" Ruby said.

"You don't think it's strange that her father invites us all the way out here? The man who owns the diamond that started this whole fiasco. And for what? A thank-you? And then our fantastic bodyguard Fry somehow misses the train and we're all alone?"

"What? You think Miss Turner was making goo-goo eyes at Fry so she could get him out of the way?"

"Well, it couldn't be because she fancies him."

Ruby walked in silence, dodging through the crowd. "So the cult that dug that burial chamber under Beaconsfield, the three brothers who took the caskets out of Rome, the girl who tried to kidnap Alisha, and the fraternity that wants to know whether you're ready . . . they're all part of the same thing?"

"That's my guess," Gerald said.

"So this whole trip has been a setup?"

"Sure. Who's to say that Mr. Gupta isn't looking for the other caskets himself? He's a businessman. Maybe he wants a part of the action. And he's got Alisha tagging along with us in case we find anything."

"What about Lethbridge?" Ruby asked. "It was Mr. Gupta's idea that he tag along."

"Exactly. Silly old Lethbridge. Maybe he's not as dim as he seems."

"And you think they're all working for Sir Mason Green?"

Gerald shook his head. "I think Green and his scrawny mate are a separate nightmare altogether. Our danger is much closer."

They broke out of the crowd and saw Alisha at the far end of the platform still tapping away at her phone.

"And don't you think it's odd that her phone can't get any reception here?" Gerald said. "How do we know she's not texting her dad or Miss Turner or even Lethbridge to let them know what we're up to?"

Ruby didn't respond.

"We just need to play it cool around Alisha, okay?"

Ruby stopped walking and Gerald bustled into her. She spun around and there were tears in her eyes. "I don't believe it," she said. "Alisha's not like that at all." She turned and ran ahead, leaving Gerald and his accusations alone on the platform.

"Still no signal," Alisha said to Gerald when he got back to the carriage. He grunted a reply. They climbed inside as the train started to move off.

"I don't understand why Miss Turner wasn't waiting for us at the station," Alisha said.

"Maybe she and Fry had better things to do," Ruby said.

"Well, what about Constable Lethbridge?"

"I think wherever you find Miss Turner you'll find Constable Lethbridge," Ruby said.

Gerald laid the parcels of food on the table. He looked at Ruby, but she refused to catch his eye.

They tucked into a feast of pickles, chapatis, parathas, and samosas, eating in silence. Ruby, Sam, and Alisha still seemed to be half asleep. But not Gerald. If people could be overtired, he was overawake. He wanted some answers. And he wanted them now.

"Alisha, why did that bandit girl say the Guptas couldn't be trusted?" Gerald said. "Is there something you're not telling us?"

"Gerald!" Ruby's eyes blazed. "Don't you dare!"

Alisha opened her mouth to respond, then stopped. It looked like she was fighting back tears. After a moment she tried again.

"Someone has tried to kidnap me. Twice. They've used a knife and a gun. And they haven't been gentle." She rolled up her shirtsleeve. Dark purple bruises ringed her upper arm. Ruby gasped at the welts. "And you take the word of that thug over mine."

Gerald was aware of the accusing looks he was receiving from Sam and Ruby. But he was determined. "Why would she warn me about you?"

Ruby pushed away from the table. "I can't believe you're doing this." There was a break in her voice.

Alisha straightened in her chair and composed herself. "My father is a wealthy man," she said quietly. "Gerald, you should know what that means. You become a target."

Gerald's mind flashed back to the days after he inherited his great-aunt's fortune, and the turmoil that it caused among his relatives and in the media. He felt a little uneasy.

"My family dates back to the Gupta kings of the fourth and fifth centuries," Alisha said. "They ruled over the golden age of the Indian empire. There was art, poetry, and culture like the world had never seen. My father says I have no appreciation of my history. He is wrong. I am very proud to be a Gupta. But over fifteen hundred years we have attracted enemies, some who can bear a grudge for a very long time. And now you come here. You impose yourself on my family's hospitality and you accuse me of treachery."

"I'm imposing on you?" Gerald said, his voice rising.

"Besides, Gerald," Alisha said coolly, "I'm more interested in why some common bandit is calling you by your first name and kissing you on the lips."

"What!" Ruby and Sam chorused.

Alisha sat back with a look of triumph in her eyes.

Gerald blushed. "She caught me by surprise," he mumbled.

"No kidding, stud," Sam said. "Did you manage to get her number? Or were you too busy playing tonsil hockey while we were out in the rain dodging the bad guys?"

"It wasn't like that."

"Really?" Sam was up for the fight. "Because that's exactly what it sounds like."

Gerald looked to Ruby for support. She stood at the end of the carriage, her arms held tight across her chest, her face a portrait of disappointment. "I can't believe you kissed her," she said.

Three sets of eyes drilled into Gerald. He lowered his head onto the table. This hadn't gone the way he'd hoped at all.

For the next few hours the chairman's carriage played host to a three-cornered sulk-off. Ruby and Alisha hunkered down on an L-shaped couch and spoke nonstop in a buzz of low whispers. Sam retreated to his bunk, wrapped himself inside his mummy's tomb, and went back to sleep. Gerald stayed seated at the table where his friends had abandoned him.

He couldn't understand why Ruby didn't believe him. The more he thought about it, the more he was convinced. Alisha was with them to discover where the second casket was hidden. Whatever it contained, it was valuable enough to attract Mr. Gupta's attention.

And what about this fraternity, or cult, or whatever it was? His great-aunt had wanted him to join—that much was clear—and Professor McElderry's discoveries under Beaconsfield all pointed to it as well. His family and the fraternity were linked across a history spanning the millennia. If the fraternity thought the Guptas couldn't be trusted, maybe Gerald had to consider that possibility as well. And that bandit girl? Gerald pressed his fingers to his lips—she'd been pretty convincing too.

The day wore on and everyone stuck to their corners. The train pulled into a number of stations. Occasionally,

Ruby and Alisha left their nest to venture out into the heat to stretch their legs. But mostly they remained huddled together talking. Sam alternated between his bunk and pacing the length of the carriage. Gerald spent most of the time lying on the pile of cushions, sketching. All the drawings were of Sam in various medieval torture devices. Lunch was the leftovers from breakfast. No one was hungry.

The train rattled across endless fields, gray and muddy under the downpours that continued throughout the day. Tiny farms, little more than patches of tilled earth, and a few stone buildings flashed past. Every so often, a lightning strike and clap of thunder would puncture the boredom. By the time night fell, the tension in the carriage had reached toxic levels.

Ruby finally spoke. "Twelve hours to go." She paused. "I'm bored. Come on, Alisha, let's go exploring." She and Alisha went to the end of the carriage and through a door that linked them to the rest of the train.

Sam and Gerald were alone.

The silence lay over them like a scratchy blanket.

Gerald glanced across at his friend. "You hungry?" he asked.

Sam grunted. "Not really."

There was an awkward moment. "This bandit girl," Sam began. "Good kisser?"

"I was fighting for my life," Gerald said.

"Fighting for breath, more like."

Gerald stood up. "You don't have to be here, you know!" he shouted. "You can leave anytime you want."

Sam leaped out of his bunk and flung himself upright, nose to nose with Gerald.

"Sounds good to me!" he said. "But right now I'm stuck on a train. And I don't have access to my personal helicopter to take me to my nearest palace."

"Is that what this is about?" Gerald said. "You're jealous?"

Sam pressed his lips together. Then looked away.

That was the end of it for Gerald. He'd had enough of Sam and his whingeing.

He picked up his backpack and stormed out of the chairman's carriage, straight into the stifling fug of an airless alcove. He gagged at the sudden change in atmosphere but continued on. He grabbed the handle of another door and pushed hard, exposing a narrow corridor to a sleeper carriage. Bunks were stacked up three high on either side. There were bodies and limbs everywhere. Men, women, children, babies—lying, sitting, standing, lounging, talking, coughing, eating, laughing, praying, singing, crying. It was a compressed sausage of life stuffed into a sixty-foot-long metal tube and cooked at one-hundred-nine degrees Fahrenheit.

Gerald squeezed down the corridor. People smiled

and made way for him. He reached the end and the door opened. Alisha and Ruby walked in. They said nothing as they brushed past on their way back to the chairman's carriage.

"So that's the way it's going to be," Gerald mumbled. He blundered farther along the train. It was getting late and the main ceiling lights had dimmed. Parents were bundling their children into bunks. There was no need for blankets or sheets. Gerald paused in the entryway to the next carriage, by the toilets. The unfamiliar diet of the last few days gurgled deep within. He had the sudden urge to go. He shouldered the door and stumbled into a compartment that consisted of a battered metal sink on the wall and a hole in the floor. Gerald took one gulp of the rancid air and thought about retreating. But his belly told him otherwise. He unbuckled his pants, balanced on footpads either side of the hole, clutched a handle bolted to the wall and squatted. The train jolted and jerked from side to side. He glanced down at the ghostly image of rail sleepers flickering past beneath him as he made his contribution to the Indian countryside. He washed his hands and looked at his reflection in the mirror. He was shocked.

There were bags under his eyes and his face was pulled into a natural scowl.

He pushed back into the carriage and fell into the nearest vacant space on a bench seat. He dropped his backpack between his feet and his head into his hands. The woman sitting next to him was doling out dinner to her children and husband. She handed each of them a round piece of bread dolloped with a bright orange pickle. Two girls not quite in their teens and a boy aged four or five munched on the food. Between bites the girls played peek-a-boo with their brother, who giggled.

The sight of these people enjoying a family meal left Gerald hollow. His parents had dumped him the moment the inheritance came through. He wasn't likely to have a meal with them anytime soon. And he had just spent the day killing off pretty much the only friendships he had. All the money in the world wasn't doing him too many favors at the moment.

He felt guilty. Ashamed at the way he had treated Alisha. How could he have been so stupid? Ruby was right. There was no way Alisha could be acting as some sort of spy. And Sam? Sam had saved Gerald's life when he was attacked by the thin man—how could he ever fight with Sam?

The door to the carriage opened and two men rolled in with the sway of the train. They were selling food and Gerald suddenly felt very hungry. One man carried a tray of fried pastries and the other had a stainless-steel pail sloshing with a watery stew. The man placed the bucket on the floor and Gerald asked for some samosas. He rattled a hand inside his backpack looking for his wallet.

"Sorry," Gerald said, "it's right at the bottom. Hold on." He pushed his drawing pad to one side and Ruby's travel guide to the other. There was his wallet, wedged under the bandit's knife. He balanced the dagger on his lap and pulled out some rupees. The train took a sudden lurch as it rounded a bend, jostling Gerald from his seat. The knife splashed into the bucket of stew.

The food vendor cried out. Heads turned the length of the carriage.

Gerald was aghast.

"I am so sorry," he said. "I'll pay for it." He peeled off more notes, painfully aware that he looked like a rich tosspot throwing his money around. The vendor seemed happy with the deal, and people's heads returned to their business.

But the knife.

Gerald peered into the bucket of gray soup. Chunks of random vegetable floated on the oily surface. He steeled himself to stick his hand in to feel about when, out of the depths, the image of his family crest bobbed up among the carrots.

Gerald arched an eyebrow. "Interesting," he said. He clamped a thumb and forefinger around the butt of the dagger and plucked it out of the stew. The vendor gave him a cloth to wipe it clean and then moved on up the carriage. Gerald laid the dagger across his palm, weighing it as if on a pair of scales.

"Too heavy to float," he muttered. "Unless . . ."

He inspected the image of his family seal on the end of the wooden handle. There was a fine line running around the circumference of the insignia. Gerald gripped the butt and twisted. The end came off in his hand.

He glanced about. No one was paying him any attention. He peered inside the handle of the dagger. It was hollow and dry. He poked a finger in the opening and felt something—a piece of paper. Gerald slid it out and flattened it on his knee. It was covered in childlike writing and at the bottom was printed a number: 85.

"The missing page from Lethbridge's notebook," Gerald breathed. "We've had it all this time." His eyes scanned the front. Then the back. And then locked on a single sentence.

His mind started buzzing. He reached into his pack and found the three envelopes that he'd taken from Green's desk. Then he pulled out Ruby's travel guide and flicked to the index. He turned to a map and ran a finger down the page. Then stopped.

"Mama the ram," he laughed. "How about that."

He folded the page into his shirt pocket, shoveled everything else into his pack, and barged out of the carriage.

Gerald reached the end of the train at a run and heaved the door. There was a light on at the far end near the lounge area. He passed the bunks and saw they were all empty. That's good; everyone's still awake, he thought. Because he had some serious talking to do.

He stepped into the main section of the carriage. Sam was facedown on his favorite pile of cushions. But there was something about the way he was lying that wasn't quite right. Next he noticed Alisha. She was sitting stiffly on the lounge, her hands in her lap. Her wrists were bound together with black tape. And then he saw Ruby. She was sitting at the table. Her hands were behind her back and a large red cloth was stuffed into her mouth. Seated next to her was a man. He was holding a pencil-thin dagger to her throat. The man was dressed in a black suit with a black shirt buttoned at the neck. A broad-brimmed black hat cast a shadow across his face. And even though it was approaching midnight, he wore sunglasses of the darkest shade imaginable. He was achingly thin, little more than a skeleton wrapped in a skin of a deathly white. A stench of bleach wafted from him.

"Mr. Wilkins," the thin man hissed. "I was wondering when you would make an appearance."

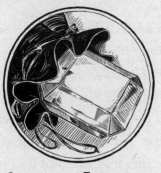

CHAPTER EIGHTEEN

Fear gripped Gerald's stomach with both hands and twisted. For a few seconds he forgot to breathe. The thin man was alive. Alive and holding a knife at Ruby's throat.

Gerald's eyes darted around the carriage. Sam was still motionless on the floor.

"He'll wake up . . . eventually," the thin man said. Gerald shivered at the voice. "It appears Mr. Valentine is quite attached to Miss Gupta. He took some exception to my tying her up." The thin man turned his head to look at Sam's immobile body. "A temporary solution to a permanent problem."

Alisha sat unmoving on the lounge, her head held high. If she was afraid, she hid it well. Ruby, however, was all belligerence. She bit down on the gag in her mouth with undisguised fury.

"A pity he's asleep," the thin man continued. "I have so much to thank him for." He raised a gloved hand and removed his hat. Gerald gagged. He was staring at something straight from a 1950s horror film—one side of the face was scarred beyond recognition, a melted and twisted mask in its place. The hair was a burned stubble. Ruby recoiled, but the thin man snatched hold of her upper arm and jabbed the dagger point under her chin.

"I have been in a great deal of pain lately so I may not be my usual pleasant self." He lashed out with a boot and collected Sam in the ribs. A low moan came up from the cushions.

Gerald fought to keep calm. "What do you want?" he said, his voice as steady as he could keep it. "Green got what he was looking for. Wasn't the golden rod enough?"

The thin man released Ruby and launched himself across the carriage. His hand shot out and gripped Gerald's right shoulder, wrenching out a howl of pain.

"After what you and your friend did to me, I think the niceties are no longer necessary."

He hauled Gerald up off the floor until their noses touched. The stench of bleach was overpowering. Gerald cried out in agony. The thin man answered with his own wide-eyed wail of torment from behind a ragged curtain of cauterized skin. The strain on damaged flesh was there for all to see. Gerald was flung onto the floor. The thin man dropped on him with a knee to the chest and the tip of the dagger against his side.

"Tell me about the emerald casket," he demanded. "Sir Mason doesn't have time to waste."

"Emerald casket? I don't know—"

The first slap knocked a chip from Gerald's front tooth. The next two were even harder.

"When you and your friend set me on fire, Mr. Wilkins, my face was not the only thing to melt away—I've lost my patience as well." He grabbed Gerald's hand and slammed it to the floor.

The thin man raised the dagger and held it above Gerald's palm.

"This will hurt . . . a lot." The thin man tensed, ready to drive the dagger down. Gerald stared in horror at the knifepoint.

A voice rang out. It was Alisha. "It's in the temple!" she cried. "In the lost city. The Temple of Surya."

The thin man didn't move his eyes from Gerald's terrified face. "Where in the temple?" he demanded.

"Under a stone slab. Buried beneath the main shrine, below the statue of the dancing goddess." Alisha looked spent.

"You knew about this all the time?" Ruby had managed to spit the rag from her mouth. She was appalled. "You've been lying to us?"

Alisha straightened herself and resumed her born-to-rule posture. She addressed the thin man as if speaking to a servant. "I have told you where to find the emerald casket. You must go now."

The thin man sneered. He raised himself from the floor, thrusting a knee into Gerald's ribs. "You're not at home ordering the help around now, sweetie. It's hours till we reach the next station. Plenty of time for me to enjoy some revenge." He stabbed a boot under Sam's body and rolled him over. Sam lolled onto his back. A low groan came from his lips. The thin man glared down at him and his distorted features warped into a sick smile. His hand tightened around the hilt of the dagger.

Gerald threw himself up from the floor and around the thin man's neck, knocking him against the table and driving out a yowl of pain. The villain slashed around with the blade, missing Gerald's cheek by millimeters. A jolt of the train threw them both to the floor. Gerald landed on his back. He looked up to find the thin man hovering over him, the dagger pointed at his heart. The knife drove home, piercing through cloth and skewering the backpack that Gerald had whipped across to shield himself. The thin man fell upon him, wrestling to extract the knife. Gerald grabbed him by the wrist and they rolled on the floor in a desperate battle.

Gerald kicked his way free, sending the thin man sliding

on his back toward the door. The villain stumbled to his knees and turned to Gerald. Blood was smeared across the welts on the thin man's face.

Lying on the floor next to the thin man's leg was a black velvet bag. Half spilled out was a large rectangular gem of the deepest green.

"The emerald key," Gerald whispered. Without thinking, he made a dive for it. But the thin man was faster. He scooped up the gem and jammed it into his pocket. Gerald shouldered into the thin man's side and sent the villain flying.

Then Ruby spoke.

"The train's stopped."

The thin man paused to check his senses. Gerald dragged himself to his feet and looked about. Ruby was right. The carriage was still. But they weren't due at the next station until dawn.

The thin man edged back, never taking his eyes from Gerald, and pulled open the carriage's interconnecting door. Over the man's shoulder, Gerald could see the endless blackness of night and what appeared to be a red taillight on the back of the train shrinking into the distance. They'd been cut free.

At that moment four bandits smashed into the carriage. Two came through the windows on either side, one dropped through the skylight, and one swung feetfirst through the door. A pair of ankles wrapped around the thin man's neck and wrenched him out into the night. The bandit girl swung back inside and landed on the rug with the elegance of a cat jumping from a table.

She switched on a one-hundred-watt smile. "Hello, Gerald," she said. "Nice to see you again." A second later everything went black.

Gerald couldn't move or see a thing. He was trussed up tight and seemed to have a bag pulled over his head. He was lying facedown across the back of something that, judging by the smell, could only be a horse. The beast didn't seem to be in any hurry. Gerald was starting to feel seasick from the constant rise and fall. He could hear whispers but didn't recognize any of the words. He had no idea if Sam and Ruby were close by. Or Alisha. Not that he ever wanted to see her again.

Gerald stayed quiet. He didn't want to draw any attention to himself. The last thing he could remember with any clarity was when the lights went out on the train. That and the smile on the bandit girl's face. *That smile.* No! He had to concentrate. If she was glad to see him, he'd hardly be tied up and thrown over the back of an old nag in the middle of the night a million miles from anywhere.

The horse ambled onward. Gerald tried to think of something other than the churning sensation in his stomach. It looked like his suspicions about Alisha had been correct. What a lying cow she'd turned out to be. She'd known the location of the second casket all along. An emerald casket.

And Sir Mason Green was back—and not just in some weird dream.

Gerald shuddered. What was Green up to, and why did it always seem to involve him? Gerald's mind cast back to the wall in the Green Room at the Rattigan Club, the silver letter opener stabbed into his throat and the hole burned into his forehead.

And on top of all that he now had a deadly cult of violent bandits to worry about, including one whose kisses set the pit of his stomach on fire. *No! Must concentrate!*

Why couldn't his holidays be more like other people's?

After what seemed an age, he came to a halt. Two sets of hands grabbed him and pulled him down to his feet. The binds around his ankles were cut and a sharp push between the shoulders propelled him forward. His boots scuffled across rocky ground. He staggered along, glad to get some feeling back into his legs.

Fifty paces later, another shove in the back sent Gerald sprawling to the ground. Rough hands rolled him over and his wrists were cut free. The bag was pulled from his head.

He was in a tent—a big army-style tent, all heavy canvas and olive green. The back of a large man with shoulders like a bison disappeared through a flap in one wall.

"Gerald!"

Ruby's voice rang out. She and Sam were crouched in a corner and they raced across, lifting him to his feet.

Gerald was relieved that Sam had recovered from his ordeal with the thin man. And Sam was quick with an apology.

"I'm so sorry," he said. "I was so messed up with this whole Alisha thing. I couldn't believe what you were saying. But you were right. She knows exactly where the casket is hidden."

"No, it's my fault," Gerald said. "I got carried away with the idea of getting even with Mason Green." He looked from Sam to Ruby.

"We're good," Ruby smiled. "But what's with these bandits? If this cult is tied up with your family, they've got a funny way of showing it."

"It's hardly the red carpet," Gerald said. "Did you see what happened to Alisha, or the thin man?"

Ruby shook her head. "Last thing I saw was the lights going out and someone shoved a bag over my head."

"There's a few things I'd like to ask Alisha," Gerald said.

Ruby's face darkened. "There's a few things I'd like to tell her too."

"But there's one good thing," Gerald said.

Sam laughed. "You mean apart from the beating from the thin man and the train getting hijacked?"

"Yes," Gerald said. "I know how to find the lost city."

Ruby and Sam stared at him, mouths open.

"No time to explain now," he said. "First we have to find a way out of here."

He surveyed the inside of the tent. It was cluttered with piles of camping gear: sleeping rolls, tinned food, jerricans. Then he saw something familiar.

"Our stuff from the train," he said. "They must have cleaned out the carriage."

Gerald tossed bags out of the way and turned up his backpack. He rifled through it and pulled out the bandit's dagger.

"This could come in handy," he said.

Ruby looked at the dagger doubtfully. "You're not going to fight your way out," she said.

"Maybe not. But we may need to defend ourselves." Gerald unzipped a pocket in one leg of his pants and slipped the knife inside. "What else can we use?"

They scoured through the bags—Gerald was about to upend Mr. Fry's backpack when he saw a bright color in among the blacks and greens.

"Alisha's handbag," he said, diving to get to it.

"So?" Sam said.

"Mobile phone."

Ruby and Sam crowded over Gerald's shoulder while he tipped out the bag. In among the perfume, lip gloss, and moisturizer he found it. They stared at the screen.

"Still no signal," Sam said.

Gerald glared at the piece of plastic in his hand. He was about to toss it away when he heard a light rustling behind him. Then came the lilt of cooing. Gerald spun around to see Lethbridge's pigeons in a corner of the tent.

A spark went off in his brain.

"Ruby," he called. "Look in my backpack for a piece of paper and a pencil. Lethbridge might have done something useful for once."

Gerald stabbed at the buttons on Alisha's phone and after a second found what he was looking for. "Okay," he said to Ruby, "write this down." He read off a series of numbers and letters.

"What's that?" Sam asked.

"Navigation coordinates, geography boy. We don't have any mobile coverage but Alisha's phone can still pick up the global positioning satellite."

"Yes, very interesting," Sam said. "But not much good to us if we can't phone somebody and tell them."

Gerald grinned. "Ever heard of pigeon post?" He took the cover off the birdcage. "There's only three here—Lethbridge must have already sent one to his friend in Delhi."

"Or eaten one," Sam said.

Ruby tore off two more pieces of paper and copied the coordinates again. She wrote a message for help at the bottom. Sam rolled the notes and slid them into the metal tubes on the pigeons' legs.

Gerald stole across to the tent flap and lifted an edge. His view was blocked by the back of a large man dressed in black.

He retreated into the tent. "We're not going out that way," he said. "Let's try over here." Sam carried the box of birds to the rear of the tent. Gerald pulled the knife from his pocket and stabbed through the canvas wall, slicing a neat line up, then across. Sam shoved the first bird through, and the others close behind.

"Think this'll work?" Ruby said. They peered out through the opening as the pigeons took flight.

"If they're as smart as Lethbridge made out, they should fly straight to his pigeon fancier mate in Delhi," Gerald said. "Hopefully he'll call the police."

There was a sound behind them and they spun around to see the large bandit filling the entryway. A white dressing covered his chin.

"Come," he said. It was a tone that suggested he wasn't going to ask twice. The bandit wrapped cable ties around their wrists, binding their hands in front of them.

He led them to a rough bush camp in the middle of a glade of trees. Three logs formed a triangle around a central campfire that burned a bright hole in the night. About twenty yards away Gerald could make out another cluster of tents, and beyond them some horses grazed in a tight bunch.

The bandit nodded toward one of the logs, and Gerald,

Sam, and Ruby sat down. A moment later, a lithe figure, slim, toned, and dressed in a set of fitted black overalls, emerged from a tent and walked toward them.

"Heads up," Sam said. "Looks like your girlfriend's on the way."

"She's not my girlfriend," Gerald said. "Will you quit it?" For the first time in a long time, Sam grinned. Gerald was glad to see it.

The figure walked into the light of the campfire. Her sleeves were rolled to her muscled biceps and she wore a black scarf around her head. She unwound the cloth to reveal the weathered face of a woman well into her forties.

"Jeez Louise!" Sam yelped. "You kissed *her*?"

The woman raised an eyebrow. "You must be the one who's not so bright," she said.

A svelte girl dressed in identical overalls stepped from the shadows. To Gerald's disgust, his heart started pounding the moment he saw her.

"That would have been me," the bandit girl said. "Hello, Gerald." She winked at him. Gerald felt his cheeks redden.

Ruby glanced at the expression on his face. "Oh, *puh-leese*."

"Ah! My daughter," the woman said, shaking her head. "Not as modest as one would hope. But teenagers these days, what can you do?"

"A mother-and-daughter bandit team?" Gerald said, trying to keep his gaze away from the girl.

"I thought you would have realized by now," the woman said. "We're all about family."

"You don't act like it," Gerald said. "Where are we? And where's Alisha?"

The woman turned and whispered to her daughter, who nodded and half walked, half ran toward the collection of tents.

"The Gupta girl is quite all right," the woman said. "But you will not see her again."

The woman said this with such finality that it made Ruby gasp. "What are you going to do to her?"

The woman's face was like stone. "The Guptas are no friends of the fraternity," she said flatly.

A triangle of light appeared at the front of one of the tents as a flap was thrown open. Two people emerged; judging by their shapes, one was the bandit girl and the other a man. The man led the way across the glade, his rolling gait accentuating his round shape. There was no doubt in Gerald's mind that this was the leader. The man burst into the firelight and stopped. He fixed his fists to his hips and a scowl to his face.

Gerald's mouth dropped at the sight of the man and the fury on his face. He could barely form the words that fell from his lips.

"Mr. . . . Hoskins."

Chapter Nineteen

The man who stood before them was definitely Mr. Hoskins, but his expression bore no resemblance to the man who had collected them from the airport days before. He got straight to the point.

"What have you told the Gupta girl?" His tone was cold, demanding an answer.

"Told her?" Gerald said. "I don't understand. Told her what?"

Hoskins chewed the inside of his bottom lip. "About us."

Gerald was mute, unsure what to say. He was horrified at this transformation.

"Why are you being like this?" Gerald asked.

"Because there's too much at stake to be any other way." Hoskins turned toward Sam and Ruby. "And you think you can trust this pair?"

"'Course I can trust them. What are you saying?"

Hoskins maintained his gaze on the Valentine twins. "How long have you known these two? A few weeks?"

Gerald pulled his shoulders back and glared at the man. "I'd trust them with my life."

"Good. Because that's exactly what you're going to have to do." Hoskins jerked his head at the bandit girl. She unsheathed a knife from a scabbard at her waist. She grabbed Ruby roughly by the shoulder.

"Hey!" Gerald yelled. Hoskins caught him by the shirt before he could move. The bandit girl cocked her head at Gerald and flashed him another one of her smiles. She then sliced through the bindings at Ruby's wrists. She did the same to Sam but stopped in front of Gerald and took hold of his hands.

"You need to relax," she whispered, then cut through the cable tie with a flick of her blade.

"Kali!" the bandit woman snapped. "Enough." She sat on a log and muttered about teenagers.

Kali gave Gerald a coy smile, then sashayed across to her mother.

Gerald gazed after her as if in a dream. *She likes me. . . .*

He suddenly realized Ruby was standing right in front of him. She smacked him across the forehead with a sharp *thwack.*

"Oi!" she said. "Concentrate."

"Yes," Gerald said. "Yes, must concentrate."

Hoskins glowered at them. "Now, Gerald, what have you told the Gupta girl about the fraternity?"

"Nothing. How could I?" Gerald protested. "I don't know anything about it myself."

"Think!" Hoskins said. "This is important."

Gerald's mind was awash with too many questions to be coming up with any answers.

"Alisha knows that the fraternity wants Gerald to join them." Everyone looked at Sam. He sat staring into the embers.

"We were talking about it when you two went to get food at the train station," Sam said. "She was fiddling about with her mobile phone and said it was kind of neat that Gerald was going to join a fraternity. Then she asked if I knew much about it. I didn't think anything of it, but—"

"Of course," Gerald said. "She would have heard Fry talking about it in the shop at Agra."

Hoskins muttered under his breath. "And what exactly did Mr. Fry have to say, the great pillock?"

"He mentioned a phone call he'd overheard between Great-Aunt Geraldine and some man. About whether I was ready. Or something."

Hoskins turned his back and bellowed a ten-second curse-laden tirade into the dark. Gerald, Ruby, and Sam stared at him with eyes like dinner plates.

"Trust bleedin' Fry to be listening in," Hoskins said.

"That was you on the phone?" Gerald said. "You're the one who wanted to know if I was ready."

Hoskins studied Gerald's face in the firelight. Over near the tents, one of the horses whinnied. "Well? Are you?"

Gerald couldn't believe his frustration. "Ready for *what*?"

Hoskins squatted and picked up a stick. He prodded the base of the fire. Sparks arced into the air. He laid another log across the top.

"You've got this far on your own," he said at last. "You're ready enough."

Gerald bounced to his feet. "Ready for WHAT?"

Hoskins retrieved a beaten rectangular tin from his pocket. He popped the lid and tossed a peppermint into his mouth. All the time, he didn't take his eyes from Gerald's face.

"Ready to keep a promise," he said at last.

Gerald looked like he was ready to explode.

Hoskins held up a hand. "I'll tell you what I know. Then, if you want, you can scream at me till your tonsils pop."

He settled on the third log in the triangle and stared into the flames.

"We're part of a promise," he said. "A promise that was

made a long time ago. Your great-aunt. You. Even your rotten cousins—you're all part of a family pledge that has stretched across sixteen centuries."

Gerald thought about the cousins he'd met for the first time after his great-aunt's funeral—Zebedee and Octavia. He shuddered to think he shared any DNA with them.

"The story my father told me is the one that his father told him," Hoskins said. "And the one that I will tell you now."

"Does that mean we're related?" Gerald interrupted. Trying to keep track of his family was becoming increasingly difficult.

"Very distant cousins," Hoskins said. "There's some happy news for you."

Sam snuffled and grinned. "Think you can contain yourself, Gerald?"

Hoskins transferred his glare to Sam. "The question is, can you contain yourself? Or do I have to find a container for you?"

Sam swallowed and huddled back onto the log.

Hoskins's face glowed red in the firelight. Shadows danced in the pouches under his eyes and his voice dropped to a ghost-story whisper.

"The tale my father told me has enough holes in it to sink a supertanker. Most of it is probably wrong and the rest highly inaccurate. But it's all we've got."

The fire crackled and spat. All eyes were focused on Mr. Hoskins.

Ruby spoke. "Is this the story about Quintus Antonius and his sons? And how they escaped Rome with three caskets after some secret mission for the emperor went wrong?"

Hoskins jolted in his spot. "How did you know about that?"

Ruby tried to keep a straight face. "Professor McElderry told us. He and some friend at the Vatican Library figured it out."

Even in the firelight, Gerald could tell that Hoskins's face had gone white.

"You know about the three caskets?"

"Yep. And how one of them came to India and is now buried in a lost city on the coast," Gerald said.

"Your great-aunt knew the legends better than me," Mr. Hoskins said. "For some reason she saw fit not to share that knowledge. And now a lot of the story has gone with her to the grave."

Gerald sensed Hoskins wasn't entirely happy with Great-Aunt Geraldine.

"The fraternity was forged by the three sons of Quintus," Hoskins continued, "Gaius, Lucius, and Marcus. Three brothers, three arms. It was Marcus who came to India, about AD 400, on a Roman trading ship. He was on the run. He jumped ship when he found a quiet fishing village in southern India. All he had with him were the clothes on his back and a casket."

"An emerald casket," Gerald said. "At least one that's opened with an emerald."

"He hid it with great care," Hoskins said. "Marcus wanted to lie low—you don't cross a Roman emperor and expect to live for long. He became a stonemason, married, and had a family. But even so, the story of the Roman visitor was well known in the region. For many years they lived in peace. But then another boat came to the village. And this time no one on board looked like a merchant. The moment Marcus heard of its arrival he called his children together and told them the family secret."

Gerald interrupted. "Family secret? Mason Green said something about a family secret in the chamber under Beaconsfield."

Hoskins's face darkened. "Sir Mason Green is remarkably well informed."

"So what is it?" Gerald asked. "What's the big secret?"

Hoskins again prodded at the fire, seemingly mesmerized by the bend and twist of the flames.

"I don't know," he said.

"What!" Sam said. "Why not?"

"Because it's a secret, bonehead. That's the point. Marcus told his children about the casket, about how he'd smuggled it to India and hidden it. He made them swear never to reveal its location. And they never did. The only thing the fraternity members needed to know was that the contents of the casket had to be protected."

"That boatload of Romans," Ruby said. "They were after the casket, weren't they?"

Hoskins nodded. "And after Marcus. On the orders of the emperor himself, the story goes. Something must have gone wrong back in Rome. That's why the brothers left in a hurry. The emperor sent a band of assassins to hunt them down."

"What's in the casket?" Gerald asked.

"No one knows," Hoskins said.

The bandit woman spoke up from her place by the fire. "It's the mantra. All the myths point to it."

"Rubbish," Hoskins said. "You listen to too much gossip."

"What mantra is that?" Ruby asked.

"The Sanjivini mantra," the woman said in a hushed voice. "Once recited, it has the power to—"

"Bring the dead back to life!" Ruby said. "Remember, Gerald? It was in my travel guide."

"Is that what Green's after?" Gerald said. "The secret to eternal life?"

"Well, you thought the Holy Grail was hidden in the diamond casket," Ruby said.

"And I was wrong, wasn't I? Be serious—a mantra that

brings the dead back to life! What's Green going to do? Raise a zombie army to take over the world?"

Sam's eyes widened. "That would be so cool!"

Gerald and Ruby stared at him. His smile faded. "Sorry," he mumbled.

Gerald turned to Hoskins. "The fraternity was formed to protect the secret. Okay, I get it. But what have you got against the Guptas?"

"Plenty," Hoskins said. "Before the assassins arrived in the village, their leader visited the palace of the Indian king, as an emissary from Rome. That king was Chandra Gupta the Second."

"Alisha's relative?" Sam said.

"He'd heard the stories of the Roman who settled in one of the southern villages. When he was told that Marcus had some great treasure, Chandra Gupta led the assassins straight to him on the promise of a share of the spoils. Marcus was captured and tortured. But he never revealed the location of the casket."

The bandit woman spoke from the other side of the fire. "The leader of the assassins was the emperor's favorite killer. A man named Octavius Viridian. By all accounts, he was a heartless beast. He slaughtered Marcus and went after his children. But they escaped and the location of the casket became lost in the centuries." She spat onto the dirt in disgust. "The Guptas are no friends of the fraternity."

"I don't understand," Ruby said. "What could be so valuable that you'd die rather than give it up?"

Gerald thought of the golden rod that had been hidden in the diamond casket.

"I've got something to say. . . ."

For the next five minutes the only thing to be heard around the campfire was Gerald's voice as he described in quiet detail the brain-splintering vision that he'd experienced when Green touched the rod to his forehead. He tried to give a sense of the subatomic annihilation, of his very core being atomized and sprayed throughout the universe. He maintained eye contact with a spot a foot in front of his boots for the duration of the story.

When he finished, there was silence.

Gerald looked to Hoskins. "I'm a direct descendant of one of the original fraternity members, of Gaius. The visions I've been having, the effect the golden rod had on me, you asking whether I'm ready or not—does this mean I'm some sort of chosen one?"

Hoskins looked Gerald long and hard in the eye. Then he burst into laughter.

"Chosen one!" he howled with glee. "Bit full of yourself, aren't you, sunshine? *Chosen one* . . . pffft!"

"I just thought that, you know, since you wanted to know if I was ready, and you didn't ask my cousins to do it, that I might be—you know—special?"

Hoskins pulled out a handkerchief and wiped his eyes. His belly still heaved.

"Special? We didn't ask Zebedee because he's as slow as a fat woman in the biscuit aisle. And we didn't ask Octavia because she couldn't find her own bum using two hands."

"What? So I was last man standing?"

"Basically, yes." Hoskins saw the hurt in Gerald's eyes. "Oh, get over yourself. I'm a descendant of Marcus Antonius and you don't see me jabbering on about special powers. Your great-aunt thought you were destined for great things, that the gods had plans for you. That's why she paid for you and your parents to migrate to Australia just after you were born—to keep you out of harm's way. But I don't hold truck with all that nonsense."

"Why didn't you tell me this before?" Gerald asked. "What's with all the riddles and mystery? Where's the trust?"

"Don't talk to me about trust!" Hoskins bellowed. "Your flamin' great-aunt wasn't a big one for trusting anyone, excepting herself. And look where it got her. I guarantee Geraldine knew the location of the lost city, but she wasn't telling. Wouldn't pass on the family secret. We could be there now, protecting the casket from the marauding hands of Mason Green. Sixteen hundred years it's been hidden and now we're going to lose it. Thanks to her." Hoskins glared at Gerald. "That is, unless you've got some amazing insight you'd like to share with us, chosen one."

There was a shocked silence around the campfire. Ruby moved to put an arm round Gerald's shoulders. "I believe you, Gerald. We've seen you go into a trance. You are kind of special."

"I think he's very special," Kali purred from behind a curtain of flame and sparks.

Gerald looked at the bandit girl smiling at him with controlling eyes, then across at Hoskins still seething in the smoke. He had a growing sense of being used. It was time to take the lead.

"So the fraternity doesn't know where the casket is hidden?" Gerald said.

"It could be anywhere in southern India," Hoskins said.

Gerald turned to Kali. "And you've been trying to find out how much the Guptas know about it."

She raised a finger to her chest, all innocence. "Who? Me?"

"It was you who broke into Constable Lethbridge's house and stole his notebook. You wanted to know what Mr. Gupta told the police after the Noor Jehan diamond was stolen—whether he gave any hint about another casket. And you found something, didn't you?"

The smile vanished from Kali's eyes, but she said nothing.

"Something in that notebook convinced you the Guptas

must know about the emerald casket. But you needed to find out more. So you decided to kidnap Alisha. Maybe ransom her in exchange for some information from her father. But you didn't count on Interpol following us. And when Agent Leclerc helped free Alisha, you dropped this." Gerald unzipped his pocket and pulled out the dagger.

Kali gasped. Her face lit up. She took a step toward Gerald.

But Gerald wasn't handing anything over.

"Then you thought you better have another crack at Alisha at the Taj Mahal. Where you also thought it was okay to shoot at me."

Kali was unrepentant. "Did I hit you?" she asked.

"No."

"Then you've got nothing to complain about."

Gerald stared at the girl across the fire. "But we escaped. So finally you hijacked the train. And here we all are. One big happy family."

No one around the campfire was smiling.

"Instead of kidnapping Alisha and taking potshots at me, why didn't you just tell us about the fraternity?" Gerald said. "We could have worked together."

Hoskins scowled into the fire. "You were too close to the Gupta girl. I didn't know if you could be—"

"What? Trusted?" Gerald interrupted. Hoskins refused to meet his eye. "Tell me," Gerald continued. "What did you do with the thin man?"

Kali sat up stiffly. "We left him by the carriage. He'll have a headache when he wakes."

"And a treasure map straight to the casket, thanks to Alisha," Ruby said.

"And the key to the emerald casket in his pocket," Gerald added. "We could have had that."

Kali shrugged. "Some things can't be helped."

Gerald tossed the dagger into the dirt at her feet. She seized it. But before she could twist off the end Gerald pulled the folded paper from his shirt pocket.

"This page you cut from Lethbridge's notebook convinced you that the Guptas were close to finding the emerald casket. Lethbridge writes like a kid but he takes good notes. Let's see: 'Mr. Gupta said coming to London following the theft of the Noor Jehan diamond has caused him considerable inconvenience. He is about to buy a big gem in India and can't afford to be away. He has been trying to locate it for many years—an emerald.'"

The crackling of the embers was the only other sound as those around the fire took in Gerald's words. He continued: "'Mr. Gupta said the emerald would join the diamond as one of the key pieces in his collection.'"

"Key pieces," Sam said. "To open a lock, maybe?"

Mr. Hoskins tossed another peppermint in his mouth. "When Kali found that in the constable's notebook, we knew Gupta was after the casket. We had to find out more."

"You should have just turned over the page," Gerald said.

"What do you mean?"

Gerald held up the piece of paper and flipped it over. "It's Lethbridge's notes from his interview with Sir Mason Green," he said. "It makes for interesting reading."

Chapter Twenty

G erald laid the page on his knee. It flickered in the yellow firelight.

"Lethbridge's interview has all the usual stuff, but then there's this one sentence: 'I asked Sir Mason whether he would be available for any further questions and he said other than chairing a meeting for an Indian tsunami relief charity, he'd be at his desk all day.'"

Sam looked at him blankly. "What does that tell you?"

"On its own, not much. But remember the report from Interpol we found in Lethbridge's hotel room? It said the casket was hidden in a village that had been buried under the sea and only recently revealed after the tsunami. I didn't get to see the name of the town because Lethbridge was coming back. Then I saw in Lethbridge's notes that Green was going to be at his desk all day. Do you remember that old detective movie, and what we found on one of the envelopes? 'Mama la ram.'"

"That still doesn't help me," Sam said.

"When I saw that Green was interested in the area affected by the tsunami, it sort of clicked into place. Ruby's travel guide lists only one town starting with M-a-m-a: Mamallapuram. Or, minus a letter or two, Mama la ram."

Hoskins almost choked on his peppermint. "Mamallapuram! That's a fishing village on the Bay of Bengal, about a hundred and twenty miles from here. It was almost wiped out in that tsunami."

"Exactly," Gerald said. "Ruby's guide said the town is recovering by attracting tourists. They go there to see a famous temple but also the local stone carvings. And then I remembered this." He pulled another piece of paper from his pocket.

"What's that?" Ruby asked.

"The paper we found in the fake stone casket in Delhi."

"You kept that?"

"I keep all sorts of things," Gerald said. "The casket was identical to the one we found under Beaconsfield. How could that be? Unless the people who made it had access to some designs. Read the line at the bottom."

Ruby took the paper from Gerald. "'This quality product was proudly manufactured by Kumar & Sons of Tamil

Nadu.'" She shrugged and went to hand the paper back.

"No," said Gerald. "The small print at the bottom."

Ruby squinted in the dim light. "It's an address," she said. "In Mamallapuram!"

"The artists of Mamallapuram have probably been selling those caskets to tourists for hundreds of years," Gerald said, "with a design based on a casket that arrived there around AD 400."

"The emerald casket is in Mamallapuram." Hoskins shook his head in wonder. "After all this time." A look of determination set in his eyes. He clicked his fingers at Kali and jerked his head toward the tents.

"Go get the Gupta girl," he said. "It's time to ask her some questions."

Gerald could tell this wasn't going to be a conversation that Alisha would enjoy.

Alisha sat on the log as if it was an imperial throne. She faced all the accusations hurled at her with an air of contempt worthy of any king's daughter.

"That man was about to stab you through the hand," she declared to Gerald. "The only way to stop him was to tell him what he wanted to hear."

Ruby wasn't convinced. "You know exactly where the casket is hidden. You've known it all along."

Alisha cast an imperious look at Ruby. "It's called using

your imagination. You should try it sometime. And it worked. Otherwise Gerald might not be alive now."

"What? From nowhere you just happened to pluck out the name of the temple as the hiding place. What was it? Surya?"

Alisha couldn't hide a glimmer of pride. "The sun god," she said. "I have no idea if such a temple exists, but I was so much more convincing with that little detail, don't you think?"

Murmurs swept around the fireplace.

"I believe her," Sam said.

"There's a surprise," Ruby said. "You were out cold—you didn't hear her."

"I thought you two were best friends forever."

"Well, things change."

Gerald had been silent during the interrogation, leaving Ruby and Hoskins to take turns playing bad cop and even worse cop. Alisha had been composed, but the last comment from Ruby seemed to pierce her armor. The hint of a tear formed in one eye. It budded, blossomed, and rolled down her cheek.

Ruby glared at Alisha, then turned her back.

"Alisha," Gerald said. She lifted her chin and looked at him. "Answer me honestly."

"Of course," she said.

"When was the first time you heard that the casket has an emerald key?"

"When that man in the train was about to stab you."

"And the emerald that your father was trying to buy for his collection—does it have anything to do with the casket?"

"He has never said anything about an emerald. He never discusses that sort of thing with me."

"There was no emerald in the display case at your house where he keeps the Noor Jehan. Does that mean he never bought it?"

"That is the only place he keeps his gems as far as I know."

"And you swear that you're telling the truth."

Alisha blinked up at Gerald's face. Her cheeks were bathed in tears. "I swear."

Gerald turned to Mr. Hoskins. "We should leave for Mamallapuram in the morning."

"That's it?" Ruby said. "You say she's telling the truth and everything is magically okay?"

Gerald stood and stared down at Ruby. "I think Alisha's father has been searching for an emerald that forms part of a collection of three gems. The Noor Jehan diamond is one of them—all three are the keys to the caskets smuggled out of Rome by my family. My guess is Mr. Gupta never got the emerald because Sir Mason Green beat him to it. And now Green has the key and the location of the lost city. But he doesn't know where in Mamallapuram to find the casket."

Gerald took a deep breath and lowered his voice to a

determined whisper. "My great-aunt was murdered on the orders of Mason Green. He tried to kill us too, remember? Somewhere in that sunken city is a casket that Green wants. I don't care if it's a magic zombie formula or a pile of gold that would choke a horse, I am going to stop him from getting it."

He turned and walked toward the tents. He was exhausted. He needed all his strength if he was going to beat Green to the casket. And the prospect of seeing the thin man again did not bode well for a good night's sleep.

Gerald woke to music. He sat up from his bedroll of a rough gray blanket and ran his fingers through his knotted hair. He stuck his nose under an armpit and sniffed. The recoil almost cricked his neck. He reeked. Sam was still snoring on the other side of the tent.

Ruby was curled up beside him. Gerald pulled on his boots and crawled out through the tent flap. It had rained through the night and the sky promised more for the day.

The campsite sang with the sounds of early-morning preparations. The horses, hobbled under a tree, feasted at their feedbags. The hollow thwack of an axe echoed from near the fire. Hoskins was converting a block of wood into kindling with a few practiced strikes. A blackened pot sat in the embers, and Kali stirred the contents with a long-handled ladle. Fingers of smoke trailed into the morning air. But it was the music that captured Gerald's attention.

In a clearing, away from the tents and the horses, Kali's mother sat cross-legged on a mat, her back perfectly straight. She plucked a stringed instrument that rested against her knee. Gerald was amazed at what he heard—it was a musical tapestry, notes weaving together in superb patterns.

The woman's eyes were closed and her head nodded in time with the music. Her fingers danced up the neck of the sitar, teasing the notes from the strings. Gerald could have listened for hours.

"That sounds amazing."

The woman looked up. "Thank you. Clears my mind for the day."

"It's a nice thing to wake up to."

"I'm Neeti," the woman said.

"Kali's mum?"

"And, for better or for worse, wife of that grumpy so-and-so over there."

"You're married to Mr. Hoskins?"

"I know. The sacrifices you make." She started another tune, a lilting concoction of sounds. Gerald was amazed at how much music she could create from just one instrument.

"You don't trust us, do you?" Neeti said.

"It's not a matter of trust," Gerald said. "It's just so much to take in. This whole fraternity thing."

The woman nodded. "For what it's worth," she said, "we

trust you. And your friends do too." Her fingers skipped across the frets.

Gerald was surprised by the remark. Then he realized the others must have been talking about him after he went to bed.

"Yeah, maybe," he said. "But I can't ask them to come along for this next bit."

Neeti shrugged and went back to her music. "As you wish."

Gerald was transfixed. "How many strings does that thing have?"

"Twenty-three."

"Twenty-three! How do you play that many?"

Neeti laughed. "You only play six of them. The others are sympathetic. You don't touch them. The vibration from the main strings sets them off. That's what makes the beautiful harmony. Listen." Neeti plucked a series of notes and Gerald watched fascinated as a set of strings underneath vibrated with perfect resonance.

"To make music," Neeti said, "truly beautiful music, you need the main strings to be played with confidence and the sympathetic strings to support them. Without both working together, it's a mess."

Gerald nodded. He glanced across to the tents and saw that Sam, Ruby, and Alisha were stretching their backs following a night on the ground.

Neeti played on. "Gerald Wilkins?" she said.

"Yes?"

"Your song is not yet sung."

Gerald looked back to his friends. He realized there was work to do.

He went back to the tents.

"Where have you been?" Sam asked.

"Getting a music lesson."

"Huh?"

"Never mind. Look, I've got to find this emerald casket. No matter what's inside it, I can't let Green get it first. You can say no if you want, but I'd like you all to help me."

Sam and Ruby didn't hesitate.

"I'm in."

"Me too."

Alisha looked at Gerald with uncertainty in her eyes.

"You want me as well?" she asked.

"Yes. Especially you."

"Why especially me?"

"Because if you've been lying to us, you know exactly where the casket is. If you're not lying, you're a friend. And at the moment I need all the friends I can get."

Sam nodded across to the fire, where Hoskins and Kali were preparing breakfast. "What about the fam?" he asked. "Are they friends too?"

Gerald exhaled. "I still don't know about Hoskins. If

my great-aunt didn't fully trust him, I'm not sure I should either. But at the moment I don't think I've got much choice."

Over breakfast it was decided that Kali would take Gerald, Sam, Ruby, and Alisha to Mamallapuram.

"What about the two gorillas who jumped us in Agra?" Sam said. "We could use a little muscle."

Hoskins grunted. "Those gorillas are my sons, pea brain. And thanks to you lot one has a broken jaw, and the other can barely see. They were only just capable of raiding the train. You lot will have to do it without them."

"What are we going to do if we come across the thin man?" Sam said. "Or Green? They'll be armed for sure. What have we got?"

"Kali's got a gun," said Gerald.

Kali shook her head. "Our only gun is somewhere back at the Agra fort, where this Gupta dropped it."

Alisha bristled. "I was in the process of being kidnapped, if you recall."

"You only have one gun?" Gerald said. "I thought this was the deadliest cult in India."

"It used to be," Hoskins said. "In the early days. There were a lot of treasure hunters that had to be discouraged— and none too subtly. We've been trading on reputation ever since." He turned to Kali. "You can train this lot how to use the slings."

An hour later a makeshift target range had been set up near the campsite. It consisted of a line of sharpened stakes driven into the ground. Each one had a pumpkin shoved on top at head height.

Kali stood about fifteen paces away. The others grouped behind her. She held the same type of sling that Gerald had seen her use in the alleyway in the Delhi market. She swung the rocks at the end of the rope.

"It's quite easy," she said. "Hold it by one end, swing it above your head, and release. It's all in the wrist. Aim for the throat—the rope winds up the neck and the rocks hit the bad guy on the side of the head. Simple."

Sam had grabbed some charcoal from the fire and drawn faces on each of the pumpkins. Gerald chose the one that looked the most like Mr. Fry. Their first few throws were wild but soon Ruby and Sam were hitting the stakes every time. But they couldn't master the wrist flick to get the sling to wind up and smack the rocks into the pumpkins. Gerald was hopeless; all his shots flew well over the top and ended up yards away. As for Alisha, after one throw that didn't cover half the distance to the target, she gave up.

Kali narrowed her eyes and strode up to the line. The others fell back as she whipped a sling above her head and launched it. The rocks fizzed through the air, spreading out into a triangle of twirling mayhem. A rope caught one of the stakes and wound up the pole in a blur. The rocks hit the side of the pumpkin with such force it exploded in a slurry of seeds and orange gore.

There was a stunned silence as the remains of the pumpkin showered down onto the dirt. "Like I said," Kali smiled. "Simple."

They trailed back to the campsite to get ready for the journey to Mamallapuram. Alisha took Gerald by the arm and held him back.

"Gerald. After you went to sleep last night, Ruby and Sam filled me in on the history of the fraternity. I swear I knew nothing about it."

"It's okay, Alisha. I believe you. And Ruby seems happy enough now."

"You don't understand—your family isn't the only one with old legends."

"What do you mean?"

"Do you know how my family got the Noor Jehan diamond in the first place? My relatives stole it."

"Stole it?"

"Mr. Hoskins told you about Chandra Gupta? About how he led that Roman assassin to find your ancestor? There was some falling out, an argument. You don't argue with a Gupta king."

"The king had the assassin killed?" Gerald said.

"Yes. And they found the Noor Jehan diamond on his body. Did Hoskins tell you the assassin's name?"

Gerald raised a shoulder. This was all such ancient history. "I don't know . . . Octavius something, was it?"

"His name was Octavius Viridian."

Gerald shrugged again. "So?"

"You know how names can change over the generations—alter a bit here and there. It's probably nothing . . . but . . ." Alisha stopped.

"Yeah?"

"Viridian—it's a shade of green."

Chapter Twenty-one

Gerald spent the hours bouncing across the Indian plains in the back of a beaten-up jeep considering the possibility that Sir Mason Green was descended from a Roman assassin named Viridian. The same assassin who had hunted down and killed Gerald's ancestor. It seemed too ludicrous to even contemplate. Then again, Gerald thought, no more ludicrous than half the stuff he'd had to deal with since the start of his school holidays.

By the third time he'd been tossed from his seat after the jeep dropped into a dry gully, Gerald had come to a conclusion: It didn't matter whether or not Green was prosecuting some centuries-old vendetta against Gerald's family. Gerald had to outsmart him. It was while planning that trick that the jeep hit a half-buried log and sent

Gerald's head crashing into the roof.

"Hey!" he yelled. "Have you ever thought about steering?"

Kali wrestled with the wheel as the jeep continued its jostling path. "Anytime you want to take over, just let me know," she shouted back.

Gerald rubbed the top of his head and wondered whether this car trip might not be more dangerous than anything waiting for them at Mamallapuram.

There was an hour or two of light left by the time the battered jeep and its rattled occupants broached the last sand hill and caught sight of the fishing village. Beyond it the Bay of Bengal stretched to the horizon. Kali parked the jeep in the shelter of some spindly trees. She pointed to what looked like a lighthouse on a barren hilltop overlooking the village.

"Let's check the view from up there," she said.

Monkeys squatting at the base of the hill scattered as Kali led the way over smooth boulders toward the peak. A stiff easterly breeze hit them at the top, carrying with it the tang of salt and rotting seaweed. It did its best to cut through the late afternoon heat. There was a threat of rain in the air.

They perched on a rocky outcrop—warmth radiated from the baked granite. They could see the village in its entirety—a modest collection of low-set stone and concrete buildings laid out in a neat grid that extended to the water. A ribbon of yellow sand was dotted with clusters of fishing boats, pulled up above the high-water mark. To the south, stretching into the long sweep of the bay, was a sandy point. At the end of the point, well away from any other buildings, was an arresting sight.

"Will you look at that," Sam said.

An ancient building, carved from stone the color of underdone toast, stood at the end of the spit. It was topped by two pyramid-shaped spires, one taller than the other, both stacked up like tiered wedding cakes.

"The Shore Temple," Kali said. "People come from all over the world to see it."

Ruby pointed to sand dunes farther south. "And that must be where we'll be going."

Gerald switched his gaze and breathed an amazed, "Far out!"

About half a kilometer to the south of the Shore Temple, behind a haze of salt spray, was an enormous archeological dig. A rock wall around the perimeter of the site stretched into the bay. The thrum of generators and pumps came to them on the breeze.

The rock dam was impressive enough. What it protected was a step up altogether: the lost city of Mamallapuram.

The tsunami had uncovered an ancient wonder. Large sections of the site were still to be excavated, but enough had been dug away to give an indication of a once-magnificent city with streets and lanes, houses and shops, a city square, and a space that might once have been a park. At the center of the site, the focus of the city, were six pyramid-shaped temples. It was a glimpse into history. And the might of nature.

"So what do we do now?" Gerald asked.

Before anyone could answer there was a chirruping from Alisha's bag.

"Finally," she said as she fished out her phone. "Some coverage." She checked through her messages and started jabbing at the keypad with her thumbs.

"There's one from Miss Turner from two days ago, telling us to go ahead and get the train at Agra because she and Mr. Fry have been delayed," she said.

"Delayed?" Sam said. "What were they up to?"

Gerald shuddered. "I don't even want to think about it."

"There's one from my father checking how we're going." Alisha thought for a second, then, "I'll let him know we're spending a few days at the beach."

"Not going to mention the kidnap, the escape, the assault by the thin man, or the train hijack, then?" Sam asked. Alisha gave him a you-must-be-out-of-your-mind look.

Gerald checked his watch. "We've only got about an hour before it gets dark. We may as well go have a look."

Gerald led the trek down, half climbing and half sliding over the boulders. Seconds after jumping the last few feet to the ground he heard a cry from above. He looked up to see Kali in a cleft between two rocks. She was clutching at her leg and swearing profusely.

Sam jumped down beside Gerald. "I think she's twisted her knee."

Gerald clambered back up to find Kali doubled over in pain. "I slipped," she said.

Ruby and Gerald helped her slowly to the ground. She sat and rolled up her right trouser leg. The joint was twice its normal size. "You're going to have to do this without me," she said.

Gerald shook his head in frustration. "This is like some bad Tarzan movie. Are you sure you can't walk?"

Kali went to stand but the moment she put weight on the leg she collapsed back to the dirt. "Get me to the jeep. I'm out of action."

They helped Kali into the backseat so she could stretch out. She reached into her pocket and pulled out a small drawstring bag.

"I took this from your skinny friend. It might come in handy."

Gerald loosened the string and upended the bag over his palm. Out slipped the emerald, a rectangular block of the richest green.

"I thought you trusted me," Gerald said. "How come you kept this a secret?"

"My dad thought it safest if no one knew I had it." Kali shrugged. "You can't choose your relatives, I guess."

Gerald, Ruby, Sam, and Alisha pulled on their backpacks and set off.

They crossed the road that skirted the town. Gerald climbed through a gap in a crumbling brick wall onto the dunes. The sea breeze kicked up a notch, lifting the top layer of sand and whipping it along in gusts. By the time they got close to the water's edge, they were covered in grit.

Gerald wiped a hand across his face and marveled at the feat of engineering that lay before them: an entire city reclaimed from beneath the waves. To their left and right the enormous rock walls extended out from the shoreline into the surf. They stretched hundreds of meters into the water—the spray blown up by the breeze made it hard to tell exactly how far. Long inflatable tubes, like a string of enormous sausages, ran along the tops of the walls, forming a barrier against the waves. Floodlights on tall poles dotted around the perimeter emitted their first glow of the evening. A dozen bulldozers stood in a cluster to the north near a number of portable buildings that must have been offices for the archeologists working on the dig. Access to the ancient city was sealed off by a security fence crowned with rolls of razor wire that ran the length of the site along the beachfront. A pair of wire gates was set into the fence, and three guards sat outside a squat gatehouse. Their rifles rested against a wall while they slouched in plastic chairs, bored.

"Don't think we're getting in that way," Gerald said, looking at the guards. "Let's check it out down here."

They trudged through the sand to the south, kicking their way through a line of dead fish and seaweed at the high-water mark.

"Take a look at the size of those crabs," Sam said. "And the pincers!"

Crabs the size of pudding bowls scuttled over each other as they turned the fish remains into shredded flesh and bone. Sam went to pick one up but the crab spun around and lashed out with a claw.

He whipped his hand back and held up an index finger—blood dripped from a gash at its end. "Those things are sharp!"

Gerald scooped up a coconut from the sand. It had been sheared clean in half. "Might be best to keep clear of these guys," he said.

They reached the southern wall and leaned against the security fence, fingers through the wire mesh.

"What do you think, Gerald?" Ruby asked. "Can we climb it?"

Gerald peered up at the fence on one side and the rock

wall on the other. "Looks a bit dodgy," he said. "I don't like the look of that razor wire. And there's no way to get over those blow-up sausage things."

Alisha sniffed and turned away. "I don't do climbing," she said.

Gerald pointed halfway along the rock wall to where a rusted barge stacked with machinery was anchored in the bay. A spout of sandy water gushed out one side like a busted main.

"Must be where they pump the water out of the city," he said.

"How are we going to get in?" Ruby said. "Those guards are hardly going to let us wander about."

"Leave this to me." Alisha powered across the sand toward the gatehouse, waving at the guards.

"What do you think she'll say?" Gerald asked.

"I'm guessing it will involve money," Ruby said.

Alisha had her bag open. Her hand emerged with a roll of notes. The guards were suddenly very attentive. Alisha left them to share out the cash.

"Okay, we're in," she said. "You're archeology students from Oxford on a study tour."

"University students?" Gerald coughed.

"I told them you're part of an accelerated-learning program." She glanced at Sam. "May be best if you don't say anything."

Gerald slapped Sam on the shoulder before he could speak. "Come on," he said. "Let's go exploring."

The security guards looked at them curiously as they walked through the gates. One gave an uncertain salute. Gerald could sense that Ruby was on the verge of collapsing into giggles.

"Are they still looking at us?" she asked after they'd gone about twenty meters.

Gerald glanced back over his shoulder. "Yep. Act like you're interested in old stuff." He squatted and picked up a rock and pointed at it with exaggerated sweeps of his hand. The guards lost interest and slouched back to the gatehouse.

Gerald, Sam, Ruby, and Alisha stood on the threshold to the lost city of Mamallapuram. A burst of late afternoon sun broke through the cloud cover. Everything around them seemed to be carved from the same honey-colored rock that glowed in the last of the day's light. They had a steep walk down to the city floor. Immediately in front of them was a row of squat buildings. The gaps between them formed tight alleyways that weaved into the city proper, branching off at all angles. The spires of the six temples rose above everything else.

Alisha peered down the closest alleyway. It was barely wide enough to walk through. "Let's give this one a try."

The lane veered to the left but after a short way turned sharply to the right. It zigzagged on.

"Get the feeling we're in a maze?" Ruby said as they trudged deeper into the city.

They finally emerged from the alley into an open space. The archeologists had done an amazing job. Hills of sand were pushed back against the dam walls on either side, exposing the majority of the city to air and sunshine for the first time in a millennium. Traces of seaweed and barnacles clung to some of the buildings.

"We must be way below sea level here," Gerald said. "It's like the bottom of a giant skate bowl." The sea breeze might still have been whipping up whitecaps outside, but on the city floor there was an eerie stillness.

Ruby scanned the tops of the rock walls to their left and right. "Hey, check out those sausage things," she said. "They're moving."

The inflatable battens were rising. A curtain of thick blue plastic unfolded beneath them.

"They must float up with the tide," Gerald said. "And the sheeting underneath holds back the water. Clever."

"Let's hope they don't spring a leak," Sam said. "This is real needle-in-a-haystack stuff. Where do we even start to look for the casket?"

There were buildings with darkened doorways everywhere. Gerald peered up at the six temples standing tall and dominant in the center of the site. Ruby followed his gaze.

"They're like a family, aren't they?" she said. "Like six brothers."

Gerald grunted agreement. Then almost choked. "Or seven sisters!"

Ruby looked at him, confused.

"My great-aunt's letter to my mum," Gerald said. "From the video call on the plane. Mum mentioned that Geraldine said if I had any questions about my family history, I should seek out the seven sisters." He pointed up at the temples. "*These* are the seven sisters."

Sam wrinkled his brow. "But there's only six of them," he said.

"Not if you count the Shore Temple back in town as well. Maybe when the sea swallowed up the city, one sister was left behind. Geraldine must have known about this place, but she never told Mr. Hoskins."

"Just a few trust issues in your family?" Alisha said.

Ruby set off toward the temples. "That's as good a place to start as any," she said. Spray fired over the top of the inflatable barriers and rained down on them. The tide was rising.

They found their way through an arched entry into a courtyard. Six spires rose up before them, the tallest and most ornate in the middle.

"Doesn't it blow your mind, Gerald?" Ruby said. "One of your ancestors once walked around here."

"Yep," he said. "My family is full of surprises. Let's start with the tallest sister."

The base of the middle temple was surrounded by rows of stone cows—perhaps a hundred sculptures—all carved from the same golden rock as the main structure.

"Welcome to the final resting place of the entombed ranchers," Sam said as he picked his way through the herd.

The bottom of the tower was laid out as a square, maybe thirty yards on each side. Gerald climbed a stone stairway to a platform and faced an enormous set of double doors. He leaned his shoulder against one stone portal and shoved hard. It didn't budge a whisker.

"There's another set of doors here." It was Alisha, calling from around the corner.

"Here too," Sam called to Gerald's right.

But it was Ruby's faint voice from the far side of the temple that had them all running. "Found it!" she shouted.

Gerald caught up with Alisha and almost lost his footing on the sandy paving on the final turn. Sam arrived from the other direction and the three of them skidded to a stop to join Ruby. She was pointing at the lintel above a tall doorway—carved into the rock was the familiar triangle of arms with a sun blazing in the center.

Sam slapped his palms onto the stone and pushed. Nothing. "Come on," he said. "Give me a hand."

Four sets of shoulders heaved against the doors but they

may as well have been trying to turn back time.

Sam slumped onto a mound of sand. "That thing's not moving for anyone, at least not without a stick of dynamite."

"Maybe the casket is safe, then?" Alisha said.

Gerald stared at his family seal, still clear after so many centuries buried in the sand. "A door isn't going to stop Mason Green. Or the thin man. We've got to find a way inside."

Ruby had joined Sam on the sand pile and poked around some of the half-buried sculptures scattered there. She found a brush left behind by one of the archeologists and whisked sand away from a statue of an elephant.

"That one's Ganesha," Alisha said. "The god for removing obstacles."

Ruby brushed more sand away to reveal a pot-bellied elephant with four arms. "I know," she said. "We've seen him before." She cleared away the last of the sand at the base of the statue. "What's this?"

Alisha peered over her shoulder.

"That's just his vahana . . . his vehicle. All the gods have an animal to carry them around," she said.

Ruby snickered.

"What's so funny?" Sam asked.

"Guess which animal Ganesha rides about on," Ruby said.

"What?"

"Your favorite—a rat!"

Sam scrunched his eyes shut, as if someone had just scraped their fingernails down the inside of his skull. "Shut up about rats, okay?"

Gerald glanced at Ruby. There was a glint in her eye.

"What's the matter, Sam?" Ruby asked, taking a step toward him. "You're not still frightened of little claws on your skin, are you?"

"Shut up, Ruby!" Sam squirmed deeper into the sand.

His sister loomed over him, her eyes wide and her fingers wriggling in the air. "Ooh, the rats are going to get you. They're crawling under your shirt. Their tails are slithering down your back!"

"Shut *up*!"

Sam rolled back onto the sand pile. His face contorted in disgust, the thought of a rat scurrying down his spine sending him into a roiling fit of revulsion. Ruby couldn't help herself.

"Feel the fur! Feel the claws!"

There was a hollow *clunk*. It came from deep beneath the sand. Sam stopped his squirming and his eyes shot open. Then, as if a hand had reached up from the pit of hell and grabbed him by the collar, he disappeared beneath the surface.

The sand settled flat again, as if Sam had been vacuumed from existence.

Chapter Twenty-two

For a full three seconds, no one moved or uttered a sound. Then Alisha dived into the pile, dropping to her knees and shoveling sand aside. Before Ruby and Gerald could get in to help, she sank to her waist. The sand was like a whirlpool intent on swallowing her whole. A plaintive cry of "Gerald!" escaped her lips, then her head vanished under the sand.

"Come on!" Gerald cried. He and Ruby both leaped into the pit. The sand collapsed clean away.

They landed feetfirst in a mound of fine sand, sinking up to their thighs, and stood there like candles stuffed into a birthday cake. The last of the grit showered onto them.

Gerald wiped his eyes and looked at Ruby. She had a pyramid of sand on her head. He started laughing.

"This is all your fault, you know," he said. "You shouldn't tease him."

Ruby shook her head like a dog at the beach. Sand flew everywhere.

"It's his fault for being such a wuss."

They were in the center of an eight-sided chamber. Sam and Alisha were dusting off by an alcove set into one of the walls. A thin beam of light shone through the narrow opening above.

"I don't think we'll be climbing out that way," Gerald said, gazing at the hole they'd fallen through. He slid down the mound of sand to the stone floor. Ruby followed.

"See, Sam?" she said to her brother. "Maybe when you grow up you can be a plumber—drains unblocked to order."

Sam reached into his backpack, pulled out a headlamp, and flicked on the light. "Gosh, you are so funny," he said. "Don't suppose you thought to bring one of these? Lucky for you, I've got spares." Sam dug out three more lamps. He tossed one to Ruby. "Now why don't you use that amazing brain of yours to find us a way out of here? Shouldn't take you more than a hundred years."

Soon four beams of light darted around the chamber as they poked about searching for an exit. The walls were lined with stone carvings, depicting hundreds of gods and demons in various stages of battle. A deep alcove with more carvings inside was set into the center of each of the eight walls.

Gerald and Sam inspected one cluster of stone figures.

"Look at that one," Sam said, pointing to a line of carvings on the wall. "Does that look like a priest raising someone from the dead?"

"Do you have a thing about zombies?" Gerald asked.

"Nowhere near as big as the thing he has about rats."

"Shut up, Ruby!"

Gerald chuckled and stepped into one of the alcoves. He trained his light onto the back wall. He ran his fingertips across the smooth face of a pig-headed demon. How long ago had the artist put the finishing touches to that? Gerald tilted his head. There was a rumbling sound above, like thunder. In an instant, a massive granite slab crashed down behind him, sealing him in. He spun around and threw himself against it but, just like the doors to the temple, it wasn't going anywhere. He smacked the flat of his hand on the rock and yelled. Nothing. If the others were calling out for him from the other side, he couldn't hear them. He was completely cut off, like the dead from the living.

Gerald tried to swallow the rising panic. He was snared in a space no bigger than two old-fashioned phone booths. The light from his headlamp bounced around the walls as he searched for a way out. He raced from side to side, sliding his hands across the walls of his stone prison. There was no hidden panel, no secret switch to open the trap. He called out again but the dead sound of his voice rang hollow in his ears. Then he noticed a trickle of water on the floor. Gerald dropped to his knees. Water was seeping in through a line of small openings at the base of the far wall. The trickle was building to a flow. Within seconds it was gushing in, splashing over Gerald's boots.

The tiny alcove was filling with water.

Gerald pounded on the walls, screaming for help. A searing pain shot through his foot. Two crabs had slipped into his torture chamber with the torrent of water. One lashed out with a nipper. It sliced the tough fabric of his boot, nicking a toe. Gerald kicked out. The crab threw its claw and swam clear. Gerald stamped into the knee-high water, but more crabs swam in through the openings.

The panic that had been bubbling at the surface now cascaded over. Gerald flailed in all directions, lashing out with arms and legs, churning the water into a frothing cauldron. But the higher the water level rose, the harder it was to have any impact on the crabs. A claw slashed through the leg of his pants, cutting into his thigh. Gerald drove a hand under the surface and grabbed the crab by its back. He ripped it free. The claw stuck in the cloth of his pants. He dashed the crab against the wall. Still, the water level rose. And still the crabs came.

Gerald had to get out of the water. He jammed his

shoulders up against the granite slab and pressed a foot against the opposite wall. With a grunt he pushed back and walked himself up the wall.

With his hands pressed up over his shoulders he was able to lift himself clear of the surface and he stretched out horizontal across the alcove. He inched up as high as he could get. But he knew it couldn't last. He flinched. The tip of a crab claw had sliced a neat line through the seat of his pants.

"This is getting serious," he muttered.

Gerald took a deep breath and summoned every spark of strength left in him—then heaved out with his feet, driving hard from the thighs. Nothing happened. The water kept rising. Gerald felt more nips at his backside. But then there was a give, a slight shift in the rock. He heaved once more, crying out like a teenage tennis player.

Whether it was Gerald's brute strength pumped by adrenaline or the buildup of the water pressure, the back wall crashed open, spilling thousands of gallons and dozens of crabs across a broad stone floor. Gerald dropped to the ground and rolled clear of the flashing nippers that snapped at his back. He came to rest on his hands and knees and sucked in deep breaths.

Somewhere in the background he sensed a change— something different in the atmosphere. The pumps had just switched back on. Must have been a blackout, Gerald thought. He picked himself up and stepped over the last of the crabs as they scuttled across the stones, crunching one under his boot on the way. He swung his headlamp around. He was on the edge of a huge courtyard under a vaulted ceiling. A mezzanine skirted the upper walls. Doorways led to rooms and halls that hadn't seen the light of the sun for a thousand years. He ventured into the courtyard. The sound of his footsteps bounced around, the clear echo somehow emphasizing just how alone Gerald was feeling. He had to get back to his friends.

The light from Gerald's headlamp started to dim. He whacked it on the side. It flared, but he knew that time was short. He started to jog toward the far side of the courtyard. He ran up stone stairs to a wall with three doorways. He poked his head inside the middle one. The straining lamp illuminated a narrow passageway.

"This looks as good as any," he muttered, and wandered in.

He could just make out a lightening of the darkness ahead. Finally he stumbled out of the passage.

"Holy cow," Gerald breathed.

He stood inside the base of the tallest temple in the lost city of Mamallapuram.

Each of the four walls that sloped up to the peak played host to hundreds—maybe thousands—of sculptures. They clung to the surface in an endless diorama of figures locked in an eternal battle of good versus evil, no closer to resolution than when the artists had set the fight in motion more than a thousand years ago. They were painted in the brightest hues of red, green, gold, and blue. Each face was an individual and each one a masterpiece. The sculptures climbed all the way to a jeweled ceiling that glowed in a shaft of radiance from the floodlights outside.

Gerald stepped farther into the heart of the pyramid, overwhelmed by the splendor. He scuffed his boots across the vivid red, white, and blue mosaics of the floor. Light streamed into the space through scores of rectangular slots hidden among the sculptures in the sloping walls. The entire structure was like a gigantic cheese grater. Gerald approached a large statue of Ganesha standing directly beneath the apex. It sat cross-legged on a black granite plinth, its face painted with an impish grin.

Each of three of the statue's arms held an item: a flute, a rope of beads, a lotus blossom. The fourth pointed to its right, to an arched doorway. Gerald took a few paces in that direction when a noise seemed to echo out of the passage. He pulled his sling out of his pack. The rocks were wrapped together in a tight bundle. He gripped them tight and moved silently to the doorway. He stood close to one side and raised his hand.

And waited.

A minute later a head emerged from the passage. Gerald

brought the rocks down hard. But two hands caught his wrist before he could connect. His arm was whipped down and he was flipped onto his back. A boot pressed onto his throat. Gerald looked up to see Alisha standing over him, still holding his arm in a wrist lock.

"Don't tell me," Gerald wheezed. "Benefit of a classical education?"

Alisha grinned and pulled him to his feet.

"How come you didn't pull all this martial-arts stuff on Kali when she grabbed you in the market?" Gerald asked, clutching his right shoulder.

"I'm not so good once someone's got hold of me," Alisha blushed. "I really need a clean shot at them."

Sam and Ruby charged out of the passage and grabbed Gerald in a bear hug. They were all soaked.

"We flipped out when that rock fell down and locked you in," Ruby said. "And then there was a blackout."

"The pumps stopped and water started pouring in from all over the place," Alisha said. "We had to swim through that hole in the ceiling. We thought you'd drowned for sure."

"It was a bit tight," Gerald said. "Let's hope the pumps keep working."

"And you remember those crabs?" Sam said. "Another one nipped me on the finger."

Gerald glanced at his boots, the blood-soaked sock that

showed through a ragged tear, and the slashes in the leg of his pants. He untangled a crab claw still stuck in the cloth. "Really," he said. "How horrible for you."

A curious expression crossed Alisha's face. "Gerald," she said, "what happened to your backside?"

Gerald whipped his hands around to the seat of his pants. It had been sliced to ribbons.

"Thought I felt a draft," he said.

Sam laughed. "Nice knickers, mate. Anyway, when the pumps started up again we climbed back down. The entry to that alcove was open and you weren't there, so we figured you must be okay. We came to a wall with three doors in it, took the one on the left, and ended up here."

Ruby turned a full circle, taking in the magnificence of the temple overhead. "Do you think the casket is hidden in here?"

"It has to be," Gerald said. "I don't know why, but I can just"—he paused, searching for the right word—"sense it."

Then, as if floating across from the spirit world, a voice filled the chamber. "Then you'll be able to find it for me."

Slowly emerging from the shadows came a gun. It inched into view: first the muzzle, then the barrel, and finally the grip in the palm of a steady hand. Then into the light stepped the one man in the world Gerald hoped he would never see again.

Chapter Twenty-three

Sir Mason Green's skin was brown and glowing, as if he'd been lounging by a swimming pool at a luxury resort. The tan served to highlight the silver of his neatly cropped hair and added to the impression of someone with time to burn and not a worry in the world. He wore tailored khakis, like an army officer dressed by an Italian designer, in stark contrast to Gerald and his bedraggled friends.

"Is this where I say, 'So, we meet again'?" Sir Mason said.

Gerald's eyes locked on the pistol. "I thought you were in Egypt," he said.

"Ha! Mr. Wilkins, the first trick for a life on the run is to leave sufficient clues to send the police in precisely the wrong direction. I have never been to Egypt and have no intention of ever going."

"So the map in the Rattigan Club was a fake?" Ruby said.

Green tilted his head in her direction. "More of a diversion than a fake, Miss Valentine," he said. "A red herring in the Green Room! But it worked like a charm. The police went blundering off in the wrong direction whilst I concentrated my efforts on the real destination. And, as ever, Mr. Wilkins, you have led me to just where I need to be."

Gerald scowled at the man holding the gun. "How can that be? A week ago we didn't know we'd be coming to India. How could you know we'd even be invited?"

Green smirked. "My dear boy," he said. "Who do you think invited you?"

The answer smacked Gerald in the forehead.

"It was you!" he said. "You wrote to me, pretending to be Mr. Gupta." Gerald swung around to Alisha. "Your father received a letter from me, didn't he? Saying something like, 'We're coming to India—can we stay awhile?'"

Alisha looked stunned. "That's right. We didn't invite you. We thought you were just coming down for a holiday."

Green laughed. "It's amazing what can be achieved with two well-directed envelopes," he said. "And the cost of postage is so reasonable."

Gerald clenched his fists. He couldn't believe he'd been so easily fooled.

"And so here we all are," Green said. "On the verge of finding the emerald casket and the riches it contains."

Gerald could contain himself no longer. "You are a *billionaire!*" he yelled. "What more could you possibly want?"

The old man regarded Gerald evenly. "There is always more, Gerald. Always more."

Gerald racked his brain for a way to escape. He had to play for time.

"Tell me about Octavius Viridian," Gerald said.

A slight narrowing of the eyes betrayed Green's surprise at hearing the name.

"You've been doing some research, Gerald," he said. His expression relaxed. "Yes, I am descended from Octavius, which is neither interesting nor important. What matters is the report that Octavius sent back to the emperor while he was hunting down your ancestor. Forgive an old man his indulgences, but one of the benefits of wealth is the ability to buy things. Mr. Gupta has his gems; I find historic documents far more interesting. It was Octavius's report and a tsunami that led me to this town."

"Why follow in some assassin's footsteps?" Gerald asked. "Surely you're better than that."

"Gerald, your problem is you have too high a regard for the motives of others. People are base creatures at heart. Set your expectations low. You'll never be disappointed."

Gerald was desperate to keep the conversation going.

"That's just being cynical," he said.

"Cynical? Realistic? It's all the same, wouldn't you agree?" Green took a deep breath. "Why, Gerald. We haven't spoken like this since the last time we enjoyed each other's company. In the burial chamber under Beaconsfield."

He paused and eyed Gerald curiously.

"I never got a chance to ask you," the old man continued. "When I placed the golden staff upon your forehead, what did you see?"

Gerald flinched. How could Green know that he'd had a vision? What *was* that golden rod?

"I don't know what you're talking about," Gerald said.

"Is that right? Tell me, Gerald, how have you been sleeping lately? All sweet dreams?"

"You were there!" Gerald yelled. "Inside my head!"

He rushed at the old man, grabbing at his shirt. But Green stepped aside and Gerald went sprawling across the floor. Green pointed the gun at the boy's head. "I enjoyed our little nighttime chats, Gerald. It is amazing what one can achieve with the right equipment. And that golden rod has some truly amazing qualities. Which is why I intend to find the remaining two caskets. But you've already guessed that."

Ruby rushed to Gerald, helping him up from the ground. "I should have believed you about the dreams," she said.

"Indeed you should have, Miss Valentine," Green said. "It was only through the occasional niggle in Gerald's head that I could corral him toward Mamallapuram. You see, thanks to his ancestry, Gerald knows a great deal about the caskets—he just doesn't realize it. He needs the occasional jolt to shake the knowledge free."

Green called back toward the shadows. "Bring him out!"

Gerald was horrified as the thin man appeared at the far edge of the temple. In front of him he pushed a man who was clearly terrified. The man collapsed as he crossed the mosaic floor. The thin man lifted him up and threw him forward as if he were a sack of rice. He fell at Gerald's feet, a sobbing mess.

Gerald gasped. It was the fortune-teller from the market in Delhi. The one who had slipped him the card bearing his family seal. The one who had run away.

Gerald dropped to his knees and held the man. The fortune-teller shivered like a frightened child.

"Are you all right?" Gerald knew it was an absurd question.

Green loomed over them. "Find the location of the emerald casket," he commanded. The fortune-teller didn't move. At a nod from Green, the thin man lurched forward. He had a knuckle-duster on his raised fist. The man recoiled, whimpering like a whipped dog.

"No," he cried. "I will find it." He swiveled in Gerald's

arms. "Give me your hand," he whispered. "Everything will be all right."

Gerald was too shocked to resist. He let the man take his right hand. A tingling shot up his forearm.

"The tenth gate is opening," the man said. He scraped a rough thumb over the skin between Gerald's eyebrows. "The way is almost clear." He closed his eyes and a rattling wheeze broke from his chest. Gerald feared it might be the man's last breath. Then the fortune-teller leaned forward until his mouth was millimeters from Gerald's ear. "You are the progeny," he whispered. "You must survive."

The man tore himself from Gerald's grasp. "I have the location of the casket," he said.

Green dragged the man up by the shoulder. "Show me," he demanded. The man limped toward a door in the far wall.

Gerald was still on his knees. "Progeny?"

"Thank you for your assistance, Mr. Wilkins," Green called over his shoulder. "You are no longer required." He cast a glance at the thin man. "Make it look like an accident." Green didn't look back as he left.

A smile spread across the thin man's fire-ravaged face.

He circled around them. Gerald could see Sam eyeing the knuckle-duster with alarm.

"It will look like an accident," the thin man sneered. "But that doesn't mean I can't have my fun."

He took a step toward Sam. But before he could take another, a whizzing sound cut the air. Alisha was standing with her feet apart and eyes ablaze, whirling a bandit sling above her head. "This will take your head off!" she cried. "Move away!"

The thin man swung around to face Alisha. His hand slipped inside his black jacket and reappeared holding a thin-bladed knife. It didn't take Gerald, Sam, and Ruby long to weigh up the situation. In seconds they too whirled slings above their heads. The thin man retreated a step, slashing the air with his dagger.

Without a word, he spun around and ran for a door in the far wall. They watched as a heavy stone portal fell shut behind him.

"Nice thinking," Gerald said to Alisha. He saw her knees were shaking.

"Yeah," Sam said. "Lucky he doesn't know how rubbish you are at throwing."

Ruby took Gerald by both hands. "Are you okay?" she asked.

Gerald nodded. But he was distracted. The gnawing sense that the casket was nearby would not leave him. He wandered across the twisting pattern of the red, white, and blue floor tiles.

"It's here," he said.

"How can you tell?" Ruby asked.

Gerald gave her a look that said he had no idea. "It's buried here. Somewhere under these tiles."

Sam gazed at the huge expanse of the temple floor. The twisting crisscrossed mosaic added to the impression of an impossible task. "Unless you've got access to a bulldozer, I suggest we just get out of here."

The sound of rushing water suddenly filled the temple. Gerald's eyes darted around him. What had the thin man done?

Then the water arrived.

Great cascades poured in from all sides. Gerald grabbed Ruby.

"The thin man's switched off the pumps. Come on!" he yelled, and raced toward the closest doorway. But it was like running into a raging surf. Water surged across the floor, sweeping them from their feet and sending them tumbling. Gerald was flung onto his back and he lost hold of Ruby's hand. A torrent of water crashed over him, rolling him along the tiles. He held his breath and closed his eyes tight. His feet flew up over his head as he was spun around in a watery corkscrew. The water wasn't stopping—the temple was filling up. His lungs screamed for air and his eyes shot open. He had to find which way was up. He had to breathe.

Gerald kicked hard. His hands swept through the water in a desperate effort to find the surface. But it was like trying to swim in a washing machine. Just as Gerald thought his lungs would collapse, he burst to the surface. He gulped in a lungful of air and fought to keep his head up.

He saw the bobbing heads of Sam and Alisha and swam toward them. The water lapped higher and higher up the temple walls, swallowing lines of statues as it went. The rectangular slots that let in light from the outside slammed closed—shutters set below the openings floated up with the rising water. The higher the level rose, the darker the temple became. The cheese grater was sealing itself off.

Gerald reached Sam, and their first words were the same: "Where's Ruby?"

"She's not a very good swimmer," Sam said, his chin barely above the surface.

"There!" Alisha pointed. Gerald turned his head and saw her clinging to the statues on a wall. But the rising water kept buffeting her away. She was struggling.

Gerald plowed toward her. Shutters continued to snap closed, casting the temple insides in an eerie pink glow. Ruby's hands slapped at the surface and her head lolled as water splashed into her mouth. Gerald was only feet away when she disappeared under the surface.

He duck-dived. In the ghostly silence that embraced him, he saw Ruby suspended like an out-of-favor marionette. Her limbs were splayed awkwardly and her hair wafted up like floating silk. Her eyes were closed and tiny bubbles escaped from her lips. Gerald kicked as hard as he could, surging down. He wrapped an arm around Ruby's chest and strove for the top. They breached together. Sam and Alisha took hold of her. Ruby coughed and water spewed from her mouth. And she breathed.

Gerald fell back, spent. The water was rising faster the higher up the temple they floated. The interior had darkened to a blood red, lit solely now by the beams shining through the jeweled ceiling.

Gerald's strength was flagging. His backpack and his boots were dragging him down. They had to come off. He shrugged his pack clear and it fell away. Then he filled his lungs and again ducked beneath the water. His fingers fought with the sodden, tangled laces and he finally wrestled one boot off. He dropped it and watched as it sank in a graceful arc, laces trailing.

Then he saw it. He was so shocked he almost forgot he was under water. He dashed for the top and took a breath, then dived again. Under the red light that now suffused the temple, the pattern in the floor mosaic changed. The white fell away and the red disappeared altogether, leaving the dark blue tiles dominant. And there, near the statue of Ganesha far below, an emblem in the blue pattern emerged as plain as day: a triangle of three forearms with a blazing sun at its center.

Gerald surfaced. "I've found it!" he shouted. "I know where the casket is."

He swam to the others. Ruby was floating on her back with Sam supporting her head. They looked exhausted.

"That's great, Gerald," Alisha said. "But we've got other problems."

Gerald looked up. The ceiling was much closer than he expected.

"We might run out of air," Alisha said.

The space was getting tighter as they neared the narrow top of the pyramid. Gerald took over helping Ruby. She looked at him with apologetic eyes. Gerald couldn't think of anything to say. He kept treading water, kept holding her up.

The water level surged as they neared the temple ceiling—the walls pressed them close together. There was no room for Ruby to float on her back. Gerald flipped her in front of him and held her close.

"We're running out of air," Alisha panted.

The water lapped their chins. The top of Gerald's head banged up against the red jewels. He had to kick doubly hard to keep his mouth clear and to keep Ruby afloat. He grasped at the ceiling, desperate for a handhold. The four heads now crammed together with just centimeters of space between the water and the top of the temple.

Then the flood paused, seemed to hold steady.

"Air pocket," Sam gasped. His voice was thin in the confined space. The four of them breathed heavily, pumping their legs. Pins of light sparked inside Gerald's eyes. He was close to passing out.

Sam's fingers darted about the jewel-studded ceiling, searching for any openings. There was a large red gem in the very center—a gem the same size as the Noor Jehan diamond and the emerald that Kali had stolen from the thin man.

Alisha saw it too. She reached for it.

Sam grabbed her wrist, holding her back. "If we pull this out, won't the water rise up?"

"Or we can run out of air and drown," Alisha said. "Your choice."

Gerald's eyes grew wide. His vision went to black and white. He was going under.

His face dipped below the surface, but he held Ruby aloft. His head rolled back. His lungs were flattened and useless. Time suspended. The world was on mute. He gazed up as if in a dream, as if looking through a web of cotton wool. Sam's fingers were on the gem. Alisha pounded on the ceiling. Suddenly a shaft of white light burst into the temple. Sam had the stone in his hand. The water rushed upward. There was a pop as the last of the air shot out the top of the structure. The temple was inundated.

The four bodies hung suspended as if preserved in amber.

Silence.

Then the water dropped. Air flooded in from the hole in the ceiling, filling the gap left by the receding water. And four heads popped above the surface. There was coughing and hacking, spitting and wheezing. And, finally, relief. The water was pouring out of the temple now. Shutters snapped open as the water slid down the walls, past the lines of statues, and the temple was again filled with light. Gerald still held Ruby. He spun her around to face him.

She smiled, her eyes bright again. Gerald grinned back. His feet touched the floor and within seconds the temple was flushed clear. The four of them sank to the tiles and looked at the gem in Sam's hand.

"I bet this opens the third casket," Sam said.

"Has to, doesn't it?" Ruby said.

Gerald gazed up to the temple ceiling. "Marcus hid it up there," he said. "He was a stonemason. He must have helped build this temple. And this is where he hid the emerald casket." Gerald stumbled across to an open space near the Ganesha statue. His pack hung by its strap from the elephant's outstretched hand.

"Here," he said. "Can you see it? Concentrate on the blue tiles."

Sam, Ruby, and Alisha looked to where Gerald was pointing.

"Looks like a bunch of swirls to me," Sam said.

Gerald retrieved his bandit sling from his pack. "That's

the genius of it," he said. "You can only see it under a red light, and even then only from above. Marcus set the ruby up there so one day somebody could find the casket."

"But only if they were trapped inside while the temple was flooding?" Alisha said. "How could he know that the city would one day be lost under the sea?"

"Don't know," Sam said. "Don't care. Let's get the casket."

Gerald tapped the tiles at the center of his family seal— of the crest of the fraternity—with the one boot he still had on. It sounded solid enough . . . but in one place there was a hollow knock.

"It's here," Gerald said. He swung the sling above his head and drove it with all his strength into the floor. The stones disappeared through the mosaic, leaving a crater of broken tiles. Gerald dropped to his knees and tore at the hole in the ground. Ruby joined him, sending ceramic shards in all directions. Their heads met over the center of the hole and they peered down.

"Hello . . ."

Gerald reached both hands in and heaved out a rectangular chest. It was about three feet long and covered in tiny jewels. On top of the lid was a carving of an archer with his bow at full draw. And in the archer's chest was an indentation the same shape and size as the emerald.

"Will you look at that?" Gerald said. He ran his

fingertips across the carved detail of the lid. It was truly magnificent. He pulled out the drawstring pouch from his pocket.

Gerald tipped the emerald into his palm. It felt warm on his skin. He placed it into the recess on the lid; it fitted perfectly. With a deep breath, he gripped the emerald and turned. The archer emblem swiveled and the lid opened. Gerald lifted it off.

The box contained a single golden rod, about a foot and a half long and decorated with elaborate filigree. Ruby reached in and took it out.

"Oh," she said with surprise. "This is heavy."

She held it out in two hands toward Gerald.

He looked at the rod as if it was about to lash out and bite him. "It's the same as the one from Beaconsfield," he said.

"So no zombie curse, then?" Sam asked.

"You sound disappointed," Alisha said. "But look at this." She held up the underside of the casket lid. It was covered in ancient writing.

"Zombies?" Sam asked, a little too eagerly.

Alisha shook her head. "It looks Latin," she said. "Hold on. I know this!"

"You're telling me you can read something carved inside a box fifteen hundred years ago?" Sam said.

"Possibly even older than that," Alisha said. "I can't read

it all but I recognize bits of it. It's Horace. From one of his odes. Number eleven, I think."

"Who's Horace?" Sam said.

Alisha looked at him with pity. "Only one of the greatest Latin poets ever. How does this one go? 'Don't ask what final fate the gods have given to me and you . . . How much better it is to accept whatever shall be . . .' Um, oh yes. *Carpe diem!* Seize the day. 'While we are speaking, envious time has fled. Seize the day. Put as little trust as possible in the future.'"

Sam shrugged. "No worse than Shakespeare."

Ruby still held the scepter out toward Gerald. "Are you going to take it?"

The last thing Gerald wanted was the pain he'd experienced when he touched the golden rod under Beaconsfield. But it was compelling. He felt his arm move. He reached out a hand. He couldn't resist.

The moment the staff touched his palm, his fingers clamped around it. His brain was instantly overwhelmed by the sheer volume of images that seemed to flow out of the rod and into his body. His mind was alight with a time lapse of every moment of his life: a baby in a cot, his parents—so young—beaming down at him, a toddler stumbling along a beach, his first football team, the day he met his mate Ox in grade one at school. Then more recent events: Ruby freeing him from the thin man at the British Museum, the romp through the Rattigan Club, Sam facing down Sir Mason Green at Beaconsfield, Gerald's dash through the markets chasing after Alisha. Then the barrage of visions moved into unfamiliar territory. He was in a cave. He was suspended in midair. Water surrounded him. And all the time a scream of unspeakable pain pierced his ears.

Through the visual bombardment, Gerald could somehow sense his fingers being prized open and finally a punch to the chest sent him backward across the floor.

He shook his head and looked up at the startled faces of Ruby, Sam, and Alisha.

"What happened?" he asked, still stunned by the vision.

The others stared open-mouthed at him. Sam was nursing the knuckles of his right hand. "Gerald," Ruby said finally. "Where did you go?"

Gerald went to stand up but flopped onto the floor. He was still woozy and his eyes weaved in and out of focus. Otherwise he might have moved sooner when he saw the thin man grab Ruby.

Chapter Twenty-four

Gerald must have blacked out for a full minute. He was struggling to take everything in. The thin man had Ruby by the elbow and a dagger at her throat. Sam was by the base of the Ganesha statue holding the golden rod like a baseball bat.

"Let her go or I'll bend this thing in half!" Sam cried.

The thin man betrayed no emotion at all. "And I will slice your sister from ear to ear. She will be dead before she hits the floor."

Sir Mason Green stood with his pistol by his side. "Mr. Valentine, I could shoot you and end this quickly. But I'd rather not damage the artifact you have in your hands. Pass it over and I give you my word as an English gentleman that your sister will not be harmed."

Alisha laughed. "My country has seen too many promises from English gentlemen."

Green flashed Alisha a smile. "Don't be mired in the past, Miss Gupta. There's no future in it."

Then, from behind Green and the thin man, a figure walked into the temple. He moved silently, covering the distance between them in seconds. In his hand was a knife. The blade was at the old man's throat in a blur, and with no struggle or protest, Special Agent Leclerc disarmed Sir Mason Green. Ruby wrestled free from the thin man and ran to her brother.

"How did you get here?" Sam said to Leclerc, the golden scepter still poised on his shoulder.

The Frenchman crossed to him and snapped his fingers. "The relic, if you please, Monsieur Valentine?" Sam looked surprised but handed it to him.

"Thank you," said Leclerc, carefully holding the rod. "A pigeon arrived in Delhi in the early hours of this morning. I believe the message was from you."

"The bird got through!" Gerald said. "Fantastic."

"Yes. The pigeon was an unexpected bonus," Leclerc said. "It let us know that you were still on track. So we could prepare."

Gerald was confused. "What do you mean, prepare?"

"For your arrival here, Gerald," Sir Mason replied. "So you could lead us to the casket, of course. Thank you, Rémy.

I'll take that now." The Frenchman passed the golden rod to Green, whose face glowed with delight. "Two now," he smiled. "One to go."

"What?" Sam said. "You mean Leclerc's not with Interpol?"

"Like a steel trap, isn't he?" Green said, taking his handgun back from Leclerc. "No, Mr. Valentine. Monsieur Leclerc is not with Interpol. I doubt very much if Leclerc is even his name. I have paid him a lot of money to follow you over the past week. He set up a GPS tracker on Miss Gupta's mobile phone so it would automatically send us updates on your location. It was only when the phone failed to get reception on your train journey that I had to"—he glanced at the thin man—"deploy less subtle means. Which, unfortunately, didn't go quite as planned."

Alisha turned to Leclerc. "You saved me from the bandit girl in the market just so we could be free to find the casket?"

"It certainly wasn't due to any concerns about your health," Green replied. "When the pigeon turned up, with map coordinates no less, we knew to expect you soon."

Gerald couldn't believe he'd given away their location.

"Wait a second," he said. "If this guy's not with Interpol, how did the pigeon's owner get in touch with him?"

Green's laugh reverberated around the temple. "Because I am the pigeon's owner, Gerald. The birds belong to me."

"What!"

"Your little fraternity wasn't the only one interested in Constable Lethbridge's notebook. During my police interview with him I inadvertently let slip my interest in a certain charity. I had to make sure that information didn't find its way into the investigation. I couldn't afford to have any police attention on India. So it was vital that I find out what Lethbridge knew and remove him from the investigation."

"You fooled Lethbridge into coming to a fake conference," Ruby said, "knowing he couldn't resist anything to do with pigeons."

"Miss Valentine," Green laughed, "you are looking at the entire membership of the Indian Pigeon Fanciers Association. I had a man play the part of a pigeon owner in Delhi and he supplied the constable with his birds. A handy communications backup."

"And the nice man who sat next to Lethbridge on his flight," Gerald said, "who just happened to be reading about me in the newspaper? That was Leclerc." And then a flash hit him. "And that's when he slipped a fake Interpol report into the stuff Lethbridge was bringing here to give to me."

Green clapped his hands in slow applause. "Well done, Gerald. I had to salt a few clues along the way. But I couldn't be too obvious. You see, it was important you made your way here of your own free will. The fortune-teller was concerned any attempt to kidnap you would seal off your inner thoughts. The tenth gate, Gerald, is the opening to your subconscious. Eyes, ears, nostrils, mouth, and two other openings I'll leave to your imagination make up the nine gates of the body. But the tenth gate opens the way to the most interesting path of all. And the fortune-teller was able to see things there that you could not."

Gerald rubbed his forehead between his eyebrows. "You killed him, didn't you?" he said. "The fortune-teller knew where the casket was hidden—he saw it through me—but then took you somewhere else. And you killed him for deceiving you."

Green shrugged. "People seldom cross me twice."

Gerald shivered at Green's cold-blooded manner. "Look, you've got your, your . . ." He was lost for words, then a phrase popped into his head. ". . . cheap old relic. Let us go."

"Cheap old relic?" Green said. "You really ought to show more respect." He paused. "Come with me, Gerald," he declared at last. "We are on the cusp of something incredible. And you, of all people, should witness it. It's your destiny. Haven't you always felt you were bound for great things? Your great-aunt thought so."

Gerald looked at his friends. Sam, Ruby, and Alisha stood near the Ganesha statue, exhausted. Could he abandon them? Then his eyes flickered to the golden rod in Green's hand. Twice he'd tasted its extraordinary power.

What lay behind its secret? He desperately wanted to know.

"Let them go," Gerald said to Green. "And I'll come with you."

Green's mood switched in an instant. "I wasn't opening a negotiation!" he roared. He threw the handgun to the thin man.

"Kill them all," Green said, as calmly as if ordering a coffee. "No witnesses. The Frenchman included."

Green walked from the temple, the golden rod in his hands, leaving the thin man with his victims.

Gerald rushed to the statue to join his friends.

Leclerc squared up to the thin man and brandished his knife, his face a picture of desperation. "You will not do this!" he hissed.

The thin man smiled and raised the gun.

The two men stood there, each waiting for the other to move first. Gerald nudged Sam and Alisha and nodded toward a door behind them. He took Ruby's hand, interlocking fingers, and they all inched back.

They'd gone perhaps ten paces when Leclerc made his move. He sent the knife spearing through the air. It connected with the thin man's hand at the moment the thin man pulled the trigger. The shot rang around the temple. It may as well have been a starter's pistol—Gerald, Ruby, Sam, and Alisha bolted toward the entry. Gerald flung an urgent look over his shoulder. Leclerc was close behind them, running for his life. The thin man had dropped the gun and was scrambling to retrieve it. They had seconds to make it to the door.

They flung themselves into the corridor as the second shot was fired and sprinted toward an arched opening at the far end. They burst into a broad chamber the size of half a football field. The low ceiling was supported by a grid of close-set pillars, hundreds of them, laid out on either side of a central pathway that glistened in the light. It led to a large statue of a dancing god at the far end. It was the most direct way ahead; dodging through the columns would slow them down.

Leclerc tore into the room behind them, as wild-eyed as a hunted animal. Ruby was about to run onto the path when Leclerc shouldered her aside, sending her sprawling.

"*Imbécile!*" he shouted, and surged onto the glossy surface. He jolted forward in a tumbling arc as he sank to his hips, disappearing into a thick syrup of water and sand. His momentum carried him right into the middle of the trench of sludge. Within seconds he was up to his armpits. He struggled and writhed, but the sand was like treacle.

"Get me out!" he yelled, panic ringing in his voice.

The first of the crabs slid up from the depths, huge nippers slicing the air. Two more appeared, silent disks breaking through the surface. Then a half dozen more.

Gerald had no desire to witness what happened next.

He gathered up Ruby from the floor and dodged through the maze of columns with Sam and Alisha close behind. Leclerc's screams followed them out of the room.

Gerald rushed onward, entries to side chambers and halls a blur as they ran past. The thin man couldn't be far behind.

They pounded into a small room at the end of a corridor and skidded to a stop in front of a blank stone wall.

"Dead end," Gerald muttered.

They went to turn but the sound of footsteps was close.

Ruby pointed to six narrow columns clustered in one corner under a narrow opening in the ceiling. Light shone in from above.

"That's our way," she said. "Sam, help out."

Ruby pulled the bandit sling from her backpack and whipped one of the stones around a column, then another around its neighbor. She climbed onto the rung that they formed.

"Give me two more," she said.

Ruby quickly strung the other slings in place and she clambered up the makeshift ladder and out the opening at the top. The others bundled up after her.

The four of them were back on the platform outside the temple. They stared down through the black hole. "Now where?" Alisha asked.

From the darkness, the wraithlike face of the thin man

glared up like a skeleton in a grave.

"Anywhere but here!" Sam said. They set off down the temple steps, a pistol shot ringing after them.

Sam reached the bottom of the stairs first and led them scampering toward the closest seawall. "Where are the security guards? They must have heard the shots."

Gerald caught up with him as they rounded a street corner. "Green doesn't leave witnesses."

They spilled onto a roadway that ran the length of the southern edge of the site. Above them, the curtain of plastic sheeting hung down ten feet from the floating barriers to the seawall, holding back the incoming tide. The *chug-chug-chug* of the pumps on the barge drifted across from the ocean side.

Gerald pointed to a tight cutting in the rock off to their left. "Quick," Gerald said. "Up to the top of the wall. We can run straight out of here."

There was no debate. Alisha was first to the steps, the metal rungs clanging under her boots, followed by Ruby and Sam. Gerald had a hand on the rail when the paving at his feet exploded, peppering his pants with stone shards. He looked up to see the thin man on a square concrete platform abutting the seawall between them and the shore. His gun was aimed at Gerald.

"Drop down!" Gerald yelled. Sam, Ruby, and Alisha flattened onto the stairs, sheltering into the cover of the rock cutting. But Gerald stood exposed.

The thin man's melted face leered at him.

"Your quest ends here, Mr. Wilkins," he called.

Gerald had nowhere to go. Surely he hadn't come this far to die with an assassin's bullet in his chest. He jerked his head up, and a smile broke across his face.

"Now, Kali!" he cried. "Do it now!"

The thin man wheeled around and his eyes shot up to the top of the seawall. The only thing there was the bulging plastic holding back the sea.

By the time he turned back, Gerald had unleashed the bandit sling. For a split second, the thin man was mesmerized by the rocks hurtling toward him in attack formation. But then the pistol was up, the trigger squeezed. Time slowed. The bullet left the chamber and entered the barrel at the instant the sling soared over the thin man's head. Gerald stared, distraught. One rock, then another sailed harmlessly past their target. The bullet started its journey, the rifling ripping it clockwise down the barrel. The pistol bucked in the thin man's hand.

Could time slow this much? Or was Gerald's mind that quick? Did he notice the sling and the last of the rocks clip the thin man's head? It all happened in a heartbeat. The thin man fell back with the blow. The pistol jolted. The bullet's trajectory shifted high. The thin man teetered on the edge of the platform for a second, his arms turning wide circles as he tried to regain his balance. Then he tumbled back and disappeared.

The air was cut by an anguished scream from inside the concrete bunker. The steady *chug-chug* of the pumps burred—a high-pitched whine of motorized protest rent the air. Something had clogged the machinery.

For the first time in what had seemed an eternity, Gerald breathed. It was time to leave.

Alisha was already on top of the seawall, helping Ruby up behind her. Gerald clambered up the stairs, taking two at a time.

"Nice throw," Sam said, clapping Gerald on the back. Gerald bent at the waist, hands on knees to catch his breath. He glanced up at Sam. Stretching back behind him, the plastic curtain was suspended beneath the long inflated tubes. But just above Sam's shoulder there was something else, something that didn't look right. A jet of water shot out from the blue plastic and sprayed down over the pavement below, a tiny fountain springing into the sunken city. It was as if the wall had sprung a . . .

"Leak!" Gerald cried, pointing at the water jet, which was growing in intensity. "The bullet must have gone through."

Before he could say another word, a panel in the sheeting burst inward. The ocean gushed through the shredded opening with a roar. The four of them stood transfixed by the eruption of seawater. The pressure was immense; a torrent arched across the lane and smashed into a line of outer buildings, blasting the walls to rubble. The city was filling up like a soup bowl.

"We need to get out of here," Gerald said. They hadn't gone five steps when the next panel imploded. The inflated tube at the top detonated with an ear-shattering bang. A chain reaction set in. Tube after tube ruptured under the force of the water pressure. The curtain shredded as tons of water burst into the city.

They ran full tilt along the top of the rock wall toward the shore. Alisha led the charge, the twins hard behind her. Gerald trailed. He still had one bare foot from his near-drowning in the temple and the rocks along the top of the seawall were not designed for smooth running. He stumbled forward, his foot pounding the stones. Behind him the line of inflated tubes were going off like a string of cheap fireworks, the blasts showering his back in sea spray as he barely kept ahead of the advancing mayhem. The plastic dam flayed the air behind him like a blown-out spinnaker as the Bay of Bengal sought to reclaim its stolen treasure. The hot air pushed out by the disintegrating tubes blasted against Gerald's back driving him onward. But the rocks were taking their toll on his foot. No amount of adrenaline could mask the sharp edges cutting into his flesh. But he knew he couldn't slow down. The blasts behind him were getting closer. Ahead, Alisha was almost at the sand, and Ruby and Sam were seconds behind her. They launched off the seawall and scrambled up the dunes to higher ground.

Only fifty yards to go and he'd be with them, safe and laughing at their grand escape.

Just fifty yards.

His foot jagged on a rocky point and he stumbled.

The fates weren't done with him yet.

A sheet of plastic blew out behind him, picked him up in its folds, and flung him cartwheeling into the roiling surf below.

CHAPTER TWENTY-FIVE

Absolute quiet. After the wind and the explosions and the snapping of the tattered plastic, Gerald was taken into the embrace of the ocean. He was rolled and cosseted and tossed for what seemed like forever. Gerald had been dumped in the surf before, countless times. He was used to curling his chin to his chest and letting the waves chew him up and spit him out—his head popping up into the air again, a little battered maybe—but nothing like this. He braced for the usual crunch against the bottom, hoping to take the impact on his shoulders. But it didn't come. An endless whirl of water twisted him over and over, lurching him forward with the promise of breaking the surface only to drag him back down. His chest screamed for air. His eyes popped open. Everything was black. Gerald flailed his arms, trying to find the way up, desperate for air. He had to breathe. He opened his mouth. Water rushed in. He couldn't stop himself; it was a reflex action. His chest expanded as his lungs filled . . .

With air. Warm salt-stained air swept across Gerald's face. His chin was on his chest when he was grabbed under the shoulders and dragged coughing and retching out of the surf. But he was breathing. Sam and Ruby pulled him up the dunes and he dropped onto the gritty blanket like a shipwreck survivor. Sam and Alisha plopped down next to him. Ruby had an arm around his shoulders. A round moon was high in the sky and under its light they watched as the waves spilled over the southern wall. The barge bobbed on the waves, its pumps silent.

"Do you think that's where the thin man ended up?" Sam asked. "Minced in those pumps?"

Alisha screwed up her face. "Don't be foul."

"Either that or he's stuck under a lot of water," Ruby said.

Gerald surveyed the scene of destruction.

"It took the power of a tsunami and a team of archeologists on bulldozers to uncover that city," he said.

"Yep," Sam said. "And about an hour and a half for us to bury it again."

Mr. Fry stood at attention as if there were a broomstick shoved down the back of his shirt and into his underpants.

He was on his best behavior, and Gerald couldn't get enough of it.

"You had a run-in with the police in Agra?" Gerald said. "And they locked you in the cells for two days?"

Fry stared straight ahead. A bead of sweat broke out on his top lip. "That is correct."

Gerald smothered a grin. "That is correct, *what*?"

Fry clenched his jaw. "That is correct, *sir*." He spat out the last word as if it were a rotten walnut.

Gerald snickered. He knew he was being a prat, but for some reason, he found the experience incredibly enjoyable. They were back in the plush surrounds of Mr. Gupta's library in Delhi, and Fry was clearly not enjoying the line of questioning.

"Let me get this straight," Gerald said. "You and Miss Turner went for a moonlight stroll that night at the Taj?"

"Yes."

"And you assumed that Constable Lethbridge would be there to keep an eye on us while you went for your little walk?"

"Yes."

"But turns out Constable Lethbridge also decided that he quite liked Miss Turner and he followed along. Is that the case?"

Fry's eyes burned like a blast furnace. "Yes."

"And you all somehow wound up back on the street.

And then you got into an argument with a local policeman because he caught you . . . doing what, exactly?"

Fry pursed his lips. "You know."

"I don't think I do," Gerald said.

Fry swallowed hard. "Miss Turner and I were observed having a . . . ahem . . . public display of affection."

Gerald couldn't hide his delight. "You were caught having a kiss? The police caught you and when you protested they locked you up for causing a public disturbance?"

Fry lowered his head. "Yes," he mumbled.

"And when Miss Turner complained, she was locked up as well, as was Constable Lethbridge. Yes?"

"Yes." Fry shifted on his feet. "If sir has completed this round of torture, I believe there are bags that need to be packed." He didn't wait for Gerald's response before trudging out of the study.

Ruby, Sam, and Alisha waited until the door closed behind him before dissolving into laughter.

"That wasn't very nice of you, Gerald," Ruby said.

"I know, but he was meant to be looking after us. It would have saved a lot of hassle if they'd been on the job."

"Maybe," Sam said. "But then you wouldn't have had the chance to lock lips with Kali, would you?"

A faraway look washed over Gerald's eyes. They'd only arrived back from Mamallapuram the night before, courtesy of Gerald's black American Express card and a charter jet. The enormity of their adventure was only just starting to sink in.

"At least Inspector Parrott seemed happy with the new leads," Ruby said. "Though I can't imagine they'll catch Green."

"I can't believe he killed the fortune-teller," Alisha said. "That poor man."

"He was trying to warn me," Gerald said. "Right from the time in the market. Green sent him there to do his thing . . . read my mind, or whatever. He said someone was trying to stop me. And to tempt me. That card in my pocket was his way of saying watch out."

"Maybe he ran off because he foresaw his own death," Ruby said.

Gerald stared up at the Noor Jehan diamond in the display case. The fortune-teller's words, "You are the progeny," echoed in his mind.

"They're blaming local bandits for the damage."

"Huh?" Gerald was jolted from his daydream.

"The damage at Mamallapuram," Alisha said. "The site was totally flooded."

"I still feel bad about that," Gerald said.

"Come off it, Gerald," Sam said. "The thin man fired that shot, not you."

"Yes. But he was aiming at me. I phoned Mr. Prisk and

told him to make a donation to the Archaeological Survey of India."

"Mr. Prisk? What did he say when you wanted to spend that kind of money?" Ruby asked.

"I didn't actually speak to him."

"Why not?"

Gerald's grin returned. "He was in an all-day meeting."

"And what about the fraternity?" Ruby asked. "Mr. Hoskins is furious the emerald casket's been found."

Gerald shrugged. "He'll rant and rave and howl at the moon. But it won't change anything. Kali was pretty upset too."

Sam laughed. "She was more upset saying good-bye to you."

The faraway look returned to Gerald's eyes. Ruby leaned over and clipped him across the back of the head.

"Oi!" she said. "Concentrate."

"Do you have to go back to London?" Alisha asked. "It feels like we've hardly done anything." She let out a laugh like a note on a Steinway.

"All I know is I've had enough of Sir Mason Green and his stupid caskets," Gerald said. "Whatever those gold rods are, the only person they seem to affect is me. Most sensible thing to do is keep far away from Green and his antiques collection."

Sam cast Gerald a sideways glance. "So you're going home, then?"

"Yep," Gerald said. "Back to Sydney."

"What about that stuff that Alisha found written on the casket lid? What was it? Horace owed a tenner?"

Alisha closed her eyes. "Horace's ode number eleven, you Philistine."

"Yeah, whichever. What happened to *carpe diem*, Gerald? What happened to seizing the day?"

Gerald stared at the ceiling. Surely going home and forgetting about Mason Green, the caskets, and the thin man was the best thing to do. So what if those golden rods made his head feel like it was about to explode? Simple remedy: Don't touch them. He had more money than was morally acceptable for one person to possess and a lifetime to enjoy it. Wasn't there a rock 'n' roll lifestyle out there, just waiting for him to live it? So what if the fortune-teller had called him the progeny? Mr. Hoskins had laughed at the thought of there being a chosen one.

Gerald kicked at a spot on the rug. "The thing that eats at me is Green has got away with it," he said. "Twice now we've beaten him to the caskets and each time he's walked away with the prize."

Sam grunted. "Yeah," he said. "All we got was a couple of gemstones."

Gerald jolted upright in his seat. "The gemstones," he whispered. Then a look of determination crossed his face.

He darted out of the study, and returned a minute later with his beaten backpack. He upended the contents onto a coffee table. A shower of lolly wrappers and his notebook spilled out, followed by a rolled-up T-shirt that hit the table with a heavy *clunk*.

Gerald grabbed the shirt and unwrapped it. The emerald rolled onto the glass tabletop. Gerald fumbled inside the shirt and pulled out the large red stone that Sam had plucked from the temple roof. He felt its warmth in his palm.

"Ruby," he said.

"Yes?"

"No—*this* is a ruby. The last of the chests must be a ruby casket. And this is the key. Do you know what that means?"

Ruby, Sam, and Alisha looked at each other, confused.

"Green can't open the last casket without it?" Sam said.

"That's true," Gerald said. "But also, we now have the three keys to the three caskets. Together with Mr. Gupta's diamond, this is the first time these three stones have been together since Marcus Antonius and his brothers left Rome."

Gerald's eyes returned to the Noor Jehan diamond. "Alisha," he said, "do you reckon we could borrow your dad's diamond, just for a bit?"

Alisha crossed to the display cabinet while Gerald cleared the junk from his backpack off the coffee table. He laid the gems in a row.

"The three of them do make a nice collection," Ruby said.

Gerald's eyes sharpened. "The three of them . . ." he said.

Then he grabbed Ruby by the shoulders. "Let's try something."

A minute later, Gerald stood in the center of the room. He placed his notebook and pen by his feet, then turned to his three friends. Each of them held a glinting gem in their right hand.

"Are you sure you want to do this, Gerald?" Ruby asked.

"Of course. Got to seize the day, like the man said."

Gerald moved across so Sam was on his left with Alisha to his right and Ruby in front. "On the count of three, okay? One . . . two . . ."

As Gerald called "three," Sam lifted his left arm and took Ruby by the elbow. She raised her hand and grabbed Alisha the same way. Then Alisha closed the last link around Gerald's waist: a triangle of arms, clasped at the elbow—the symbol of the fraternity with Gerald the sun at its center. The three gems started to vibrate in their extended palms. They began to glow and Gerald felt a tingling below his ribs. But it wasn't what he'd expected.

"That's funny," he said. "I thought that—"

Then it hit him—like a surge of white light made physical. A rush of energy coursed through his bones. He was a human lightning rod for every electron in the room. The gems lit up like Chinese lanterns as the power thrust through him. His body convulsed and his head shot back, eyes bursting, his pupils disappearing altogether.

He was blind.

But what he could see!

A filtered cry split his lips and Gerald dropped to the floor. The others were dragged down with him and the triangle around his waist broke. Gerald's eyes were shut but his hands searched in spasms until they found his notebook. Eyelids still sealed, his pen scratched across the page in a blur. He started at the very edges and worked inward in a clockwise whirl. In only a few seconds the page was filled with lines. The book spilled from his fingers, dropping open onto the rug.

Gerald opened his eyes.

Ruby picked up the drawing. It was a seascape in amazing detail. In the center was an island with rocky bluffs soaring above crashing surf. On the cliffs stood a castle, as dark and foreboding as anything from a Grimm fairytale.

"It's there," Gerald breathed. "The third casket is there."

Sam looked at his friend, bewildered. "How can you be sure?"

Gerald returned the stare. "Because I just saw it there."

An uneasy silence fell across them. Alisha picked up the three gems and placed them on her father's desk.

"You still going home?" Sam asked.

Gerald didn't reply. The door to the library opened, and Mr. Fry and Miss Turner walked in, each taking care not to acknowledge the other's presence.

"The car is ready," Fry said.

Miss Turner turned to Alisha. "You have your father's permission to accompany your friends to the airport."

Still Gerald stared at Sam. He finally spoke. "Isn't home the best place?" Gerald said. "The safest place?"

He scooped up his backpack and took the notebook from Ruby. Before he could stuff it inside, Miss Turner spoke.

"Oh, I know that place," she said.

There was a sudden change of temperature in the room.

"Are you sure?" Gerald asked. He held out the notebook. "You know where this is?"

Miss Turner nodded. "It's in France. Off the Normandy coast."

Gerald glanced at the drawing. The castle seemed to radiate from the page. He looked to Sam and then to Ruby. They had come so far.

"Gerald?" Ruby said.

He breathed out. Sir Mason Green had to be stopped.

Then again, home would be so nice.

So comfortable.

So secure.

And way too predictable.

He looked again at Miss Turner.

"France, you say?"

Turn the Page to Start
Reading the Thrilling Conclusion
of The Archer Legacy

The photographers leaned against the crowd-control barriers. There were more than a dozen snappers and each one had two cameras: one at the ready and a spare slung over the shoulder. A couple of the shorter ones had brought along stepladders. They all huddled under rain jackets, slickened by showers that had scudded across London all morning, and waited.

People had started gathering outside the central criminal courts of the Old Bailey soon after dawn. There were newspaper reporters, television crews, and satellite vans.

But mostly there were teenage girls.

Hundreds upon hundreds of teenage girls.

Some clutched flowers. Others held teddy bears. There were scores of hand-painted placards, the colors streaked by the rain. A team of mounted police stood to one side. The horses snorted, stamping their hooves, alert to the tension in the air. More police lined the opposite side of the barriers, facing the crowd as it multiplied by the minute.

Everyone was on edge. There was some distracted chatter among the girls, but most of them were concentrating on the fifty-foot expanse of cobblestones that stood between the steel barriers and a set of wooden doors on the far side of a courtyard.

The wait was getting too much for some. A woman in her forties clutching a copy of *Oi!* magazine prodded her daughter. The woman pointed to a photograph of a blonde girl aged about thirteen or fourteen—fresh faced and aglow with a summer tan. The shot had clearly been taken without the girl's knowledge—her head was half turned and the image was slightly blurred. The caption underneath read: *Is this the boy billionaire's love match? Pals say Ruby Valentine has hardly left Gerald Wilkins's side since returning from a holiday with him in romantic India.*

The woman frowned at the photograph. "Who's she to be putting on airs and graces?" she said. Her daughter wiped the back of her hand across her nose, shrugged, and mumbled something. The woman glared at her, then back at the magazine. She tensed, unsure if she should voice what she was thinking. Then it burst out. "Why can't that be you?" the woman snapped. "Why can't you be Ruby Valentine?"

The girl stared down at her shoes. A dozen other girls nearby did the same thing.

Then a voice from the top of a stepladder called out. A photographer wearing a red vest had a camera to his eye. "Here they come!"

A murmur of excitement swept the courtyard. Bodies surged. Two of the snappers were jolted from their ladders and they tumbled into the crowd below.

A robust woman entered the courtyard through an arched walkway. Dressed in an ensemble that oozed new-season Paris with shoes entirely unsuitable for cobblestones, she waddled toward the wooden doors. She was halfway there when a spindly heel lodged between two stones and stuck fast. She stopped midstride and tugged on her foot. It wouldn't budge. She hitched her skirt above her knees and bent down to grab at her ankle when a volley of cries burst from the photographers.

"Vi! Vi Wilkins! This way, darlin'! Over here!"

Shutters snapped and whirred. The woman's head shot up, a look of horror on her face. She redoubled her efforts to free the trapped heel—pausing to straighten and wave to the cameras—before finally abandoning her shoes and completing the walk in her stockings.

As she disappeared through the doorway, three people emerged from the cloisters: a man dressed in a business suit, and his son and daughter. The boy and girl, both fair-haired and tanned, were clearly twins. The boy nudged his sister and nodded toward the crowd. She looked up and a gasp of recognition shot out from the onlookers.

"Ruby! Over here, sweetheart!" The snappers wound themselves into a frenzy. "Over HERE!"

The girl buried her head in her father's side and they hurried through the doors. A second later, the crowd got what it had been waiting for. A barrage of camera flashes whitewashed the courtyard as a thirteen-year-old boy stepped onto the cobbles. His untidy hair fell over his ears and he looked uncomfortable in a gray suit and tie. He dragged on the arm of his father, who was lagging behind him. The man stopped to collect his wife's shoes.

"Come on, Dad," Gerald Wilkins said. "Let's get inside."

"GERALD!"

The crowd was hyped to explode.

The posters declaring undying love were consigned to the muck on the footpath, trampled beneath a herd of hormonal teenagers reared on a diet of celebrity and gossip magazines. The photographers, who had held their line by the barriers, were pushed aside. Stepladders toppled and lenses smashed underfoot. Screams of "GERALD!"—and just plain screams—filled the courtyard. For a second the boy glanced up. He gave a half-hearted wave. It was enough to ratchet the hysteria to another level. A police horse reared at the shrill cries that burst from the mob. But the moment the boy crossed the threshold and a police constable stepped out to pull the wooden doors shut, disappointment fell over the crowd.

The show was over.

The photographers, reporters, and hyperventilating teens drifted away until all that remained were two girls. They leaned glum-faced against the metal railings amid a mush of crumpled cardboard and flowers.

One nudged the other.

"Come on," she said. "Let's get something to eat."

The other girl nodded. A tear rolled down her cheek. She didn't bother to wipe it away.

A long wooden table ran down the center of the waiting room. A dozen mismatched chairs were arranged around its sides. The stench of furniture polish hung stagnant in the air.

Gerald claimed a spot near the door. Ruby and her brother, Sam, pulled out a chair each and sat on either side of him. Gerald's mother headed straight to the far end of the room, to a battered urn.

She wrenched off the lid and peered inside. "This water's none too hot," she said with a sniff. "And I don't fancy it's been cleaned anytime recently. I can't see why they wouldn't let Mr. Fry come with us—he'd get a decent cup of tea out of this thing." She dropped the lid back into place and wiped her fingers on a paper napkin.

"You can't have a butler with you all the time, dear." Gerald's father squeezed past his wife and pulled down a packet of Archer-brand teabags from a shelf. "You managed well enough without him for most of your life."

Vi looked down at the chair at the head of the table and let out a sharp *ahem*. Ruby and Sam's father rushed across to pull it out.

"Thank you, Mr. Valentine," she said. "Most gentlemanly of you." She squeezed her bottom into place as if taking up residence in Windsor Castle. Then she raised a stockinged foot onto the tabletop and put her shoes back on. "The point is, Eddie," Vi said to her husband, "we have a butler now, and it seems a shameful waste not to be able to use him. Especially in frightful circumstances such as these."

Eddie ignored his wife and dangled two teabags into a pot. "Cuppa for you?" he asked Mr. Valentine. "Milk? Sugar?"

"I just hope it doesn't take all day," Vi declared, drumming her fingers on the table. "I have several important appointments this afternoon. And there's Walter to consider."

Eddie placed a mug in front of his wife. "I'm sure the hairdresser won't mind if you're late. And as for Walter—"

Vi held up her index finger in warning.

"Don't you dare," she said. "I have had enough of your negative energy. You are having a serious impact on my emotional scaffolding. You know how important Walter is to my blueprint of enhanced health."

Eddie poured tea into another mug. "Pfft," he muttered. "Blueprint of wasted wealth, more like."

At the other end of the table Gerald sucked in a deep breath. His parents had only returned from their holiday the week before and already he was wishing they'd leave for their next one.

Ruby leaned across and whispered, "Who's Walter?"

"Please—don't ask about Walter," Gerald said. He gazed down the length of the room as his mother continued to scold Eddie. "You don't want to know."

Sam reached over, took a ginger-nut biscuit from a plate in front of Gerald, and took a bite. "You've had a fun week, then?" he said.

Gerald cupped his chin in his hands. "You have no idea."

Just then the door to the waiting room opened. A small man dressed in a suit a size too large stepped inside.

"Ah, Mr. Prisk!" Vi boomed, startling the man. "How much longer are we to wait? I don't fancy paying your fees by the hour if it's going to take all day." She turned to Mr. Valentine and gave him a wink. "Lawyers, Mr. Valentine. A pox on them all, I say."

Mr. Prisk fiddled with his cufflinks. "They've just

started," he said. "You'd better come through."

Vi pushed back on her chair and stood up. "About time," she said. "Walter will be anxious if I'm late."

They followed Mr. Prisk along a dimly lit hallway and gathered in a foyer before a large set of double doors. Vi ignored Gerald's protests as she straightened his tie and patted down a tuft of hair.

"Best behavior," she said to him. "Right?"

Gerald made a point of ruffling the back of his head as they went through the doors and into Courtroom Number One of the Old Bailey.

The trial was already underway.

Gerald followed Mr. Prisk's directions and joined the others in the front row of the public gallery. The scene before him was straight from an old courtroom movie. A judge in red robes and a white wig sat at the bench, peering down at the prosecution counsel to one side and the defense counsel to the other. A jury of seven men and five women watched as a barrister in a black gown stood up at the prosecution table.

"The Crown calls the defendant to the stand."

Every eye in the court moved to the dock. A silver-haired man dressed in a navy-blue suit and regimental tie rose to his feet and stepped down from the raised wooden enclosure, then crossed the short distance to the witness box. He turned and fixed a firm gaze to the barrister.

The prosecutor straightened a pile of papers on his desk. "For the record," he said, "please state your full name."

The man in the witness box stared out at the court, as if searching for a friend in a crowd. His eyes passed across the jury, journeyed beyond the table of lawyers, cleared the packed press gallery, and came to rest on the face of Gerald Wilkins. Then the man smiled.

"My name," he said in a voice of clear authority, "is Sir Mason Hercules Green."